Culture, Nature and Literature

Culture, Nature and Literature

Usha Bande

RAWAT PUBLICATIONS

Jaipur • New Delhi • Bangalore • Hyderabad • Guwahati

ISBN 978-81-316-0554-7

Published by
Prem Rawat for **Rawat Publications**
Satyam Apts, Sector 3, Jawahar Nagar, Jaipur 302 004 (India)
Phone: 0141 265 1748 / 7006 Fax: 0141 265 1748
E-mail: info@rawatbooks.com
Website: www.rawatbooks.com

New Delhi Office
4858/24, Ansari Road, Daryaganj, New Delhi 110 002
Phone: 011 2326 3290

Also at *Bangalore, Hyderabad* and *Guwahati*

Typeset by Rawat Computers, Jaipur
Printed at Chaman Enterprises, New Delhi

Contents

Preface 7

1 Introduction 9

2 Of Parrots and Mynahs: Reconstructing Gender through Folklore 15

3 Re-mapping Culture through Literature: Narratives as Vehicles of Culture 29

4 Tagore's Chitra and Folklore's Hidimba: Power of the Feminine 39

5 Humour as Resistance: The Female Voice in Folklore 55

6 The Con(Textual) Contours: A Study of Four Short Stories 63

7 The Primordial and the Modern: "Snake" and "Night of the Scorpion" 76

8 Gauri – Myth and Reality 84

9 Culture, Literature and Human Rights: A View from Indian Fiction 95

10 Can We Exonerate Balram Halwai? 114

11 The Collapse of "Cultural Maps": Terrorism in Asian Literature 126

12 Re-visiting Ithaca and Re-casting Manali: Quest Motifs in *Journey to Ithaca* and "Scholar and Gypsy" 139

13 Milk and Honey: Mother-Love in Anita Desai 151

14 Flight from Responsibility or Search for Freedom: A Study of Withdrawal in Fiction 158

15 Cactus Country: An Assessment 166

16 Gender, Education and Development: Issues in Life and Literature 171

17 Human Values and Dr Radhakrishnan's Concepts of Education 182

18 Rethinking Indian Culture with Dr Radhakrishnan 186

19 Gandhian Ideals and Nehruvian Vision: Notes on the Idea of India in Bollywood Cinema 198

20 "The Contact Zone": Translation and Transmission of Folklore 204

Index 215

Preface

This book is a collection of papers written for and read during various seminars and conferences I participated in over the years. That explains the variety of topics/themes of these papers – from culture to ecology, from mythology to feminism and from terrorism to human rights. Since these were not published, I thought of putting them together for younger scholars. But, this exercise was not an easy one. Many a time I felt I could have written a fresh, new paper faster and with more ease than correcting and adding to the old ones. Yet, feedbacks, the change in my own perspective over the years, and experience gained after discussion with scholar-friends of the standing of Professor Jasbir Jain and others made the task compelling, irresistible and enjoyable.

I take this opportunity to thank all those who were present during the seminars, commented on the papers and gave me feedback to think, correct and present them in a finished form.

Usha Bande

1 Introduction

The essays presented here represent a variety of critical positions and constitute a re-examination of some of the central issues in Indian literature. The defining feature of Indian writing is the quest to specify a space of cultural identity outside the hegemony. Thus, the need to preserve and project a distinct cultural identity has always been accompanied by the simultaneous incorporation or rejection of a colonizing alterity. Majority of the papers contained in the volume, therefore, attempt to look at and understand culture from various angles. The purpose here is two-fold: to make available to researchers some new strands to critically view Indian writing and to analyse specific issues concentrating on textual and historical evidence. Many of the papers are linked by an interest in gender issues, although few address feminism directly. A few more offer a commentary on aspects of life across postmodern landscape but do not address postmodern theory as such. Those that have their origin in colonial and postcolonial situations do not dwell on the positive or negative attributes of that period. The book deals with culture, literature and nature to examine the central sites of their representation. The works explored here are not homogenous in that they belong to different sections of contemporary Indian society but this pluralism is indicative of the basic nature of literary criticism.

Four essays work out literature-folklore interface. The first "Of Parrots and Mynahs" concentrates on the problematics of gender through a study of three small folktales. Usually, views on women, both popular and academic, are stereotypical. Labels such as docile, gentle and nurturing connote social realities but they have become universal that they do not call attention to the conditions that give rise to them. As Jasbir Jain points out, the images of women projected in history and myth render them as secondary and reinforce inequalities. "Yet it needs to be recognized that there is an innate split even in the projected conventional images. The rebelliousness is present in attitudes and stances which women have adopted in mythology as well as in history. Women have risen above these limitations in various ways – by sustaining an oral tradition, and deconstructing patriarchal structures through individual questioning" (2002: 21). The tales are narrated in brief and then an attempt has been made to see the existence of subtle modes of resistance to the social and cultural hegemony present in the tales, investigating how women writers in re-telling the tales focus on the various cultural constructs like women's silence, their relegation to the private domestic space and their resistance to hegemony. The situation in which women find themselves creates conflict between the desire for creativity and the cultural notion of femininity that hampers articulation. With the help of bird metaphor, the tales/their writers reconstruct the definition of female agency.

The second paper dealing with folklore takes up two tribal women from the Mahabharata – Chitrangada and Hidimba. Both show enormous power of the feminine and feminist assertion though their depiction is not identical. Tagore's Chitra is a romantic figure. Tagore invests her with delicacy, maturity and self-assuredness. Hidimba is a vibrant presence in the oral tradition of Himachal Pradesh. Hidimba and Chitra are mythic figures placed in contemporary realities and illustrate women's authority and agency. Both display such attributes as one would like to find in a modern Indian woman.

Women and a sense of humour are probably contradictory terms; so do many critics aver. Women have social constraints and inhibitions that do not allow them to cross the line. In literary works humour is generated by satire, humorous dialogues or comic irony. In written literature a writer has to generate humour through the use of language but on the stage voice inflection and bodily movements can whet it and make it effective. Oral literature, particularly performances of women, like the 'Gidda' from the Punjab, or other folk forms, has a rich treasure of humour of everyday life. The essay "Humour as Resistance: The Female Voice in Folklore" looks at some folk songs, tales and dances that women use to diffuse tension and generate laughter. It is an effective means to resist the social structure playfully, thus making a space for themselves.

The last of the four papers studies folk narratives from Maharashtra and Himachal Pradesh as translation and transmission to show the basic solidarity of Indian culture. Translation and transmission of folklore is not only a linguistic process; it is also a challenge to the negotiation of a complex cultural conception and to its popularity.

Some of the papers take a comparative stance. In "Re-mapping Culture through Literature", three narratives have been studied in postcolonial light. Gita Mehta and Arun Joshi, by reverting to the traditional narrative strategies, work out an indigenous framework to reclaim cultural identity in the postcolonial settings. The discussion focuses on the cultural consciousness of the authors which shapes their texts. In the novels studied here, the Ganga, the Narmada and the Himalayas are the bearers of the culture, witness to a historical reality and repository of ancient wisdom. While Arun Joshi hints at the self-destructive trends of power politics, Gita Mehta weighs the mysticism of *Vanprastha* in the scale of modern rationality.

Northrop Frye considers myth as literary archetype. For him archetype means a symbol which connects one poem with another and thereby helps to unify and integrate our literary experience. The paper "The Primordial and the Modern" studies D.H. Lawrence's "Snake" and Nissim Ezekiel's "Night of the Scorpion" as celebration of the primordial over modern. The poems deal with the non-human life as juxtaposed with the human and present commentaries on the civilized responses to the two situations in which man ultimately appears puny in the face of the elements. The poems depict four phases of the development of the mind of man through ages: the primordial, the magic or superstitions, myths, and contemporary education. Of these, the poets reject the last three phases and return to the primordial. It is their march from experience back to innocence.

Yet another view of Indianness with focus on the culture is provided in "The Con(Textual) Contours: A Study of Four Short Stories". It is difficult to limit the definition of Indianness within set parameters because it is an all-inclusive term engulfing our entire culture, traditional conception of human life, spiritual conditions, value system and ideas and ideals that have moved us since time immemorial. Add to these the present-day influences of consumerism, feminism and globalization. Textual analysis of four stories suggests that Indian writers in English successfully interact with the culture, tradition and the prevalent situations by portraying the Indian situation, giving the readers a peep inside, and an insider's view of the social and psychological reality.

Two papers, "Can We Exonerate Balram Halwai?" and "The Collapse of 'Cultural Maps'" examine socio-cultural angle of the political problem of the times. *The White Tiger* can be read as a pointed revelation of the trap of intriguing politicians and the lure of easy money. It is the world of a hardened criminal for whom nothing is sacred. Despite satire and presentation of the ruthlessness of power and survival strategies of the disadvantaged, the question remains: Can we really exonerate Balram of his crime?

Terrorism has become a lived reality all over the world. The paper, "The Collapse of 'Cultural Maps'" focuses on terrorism in three Asian countries – Afghanistan (*A Thousand Splendid Suns*), India (*The Inheritance of Loss*) and Sri Lanka ("SMS", a short story). Terrorism, the stories reveal, cannot be measured in terms of violence; it is a monster of loss – loss of peace, of humanity, sense of security and ultimately a shattering of faith which upholds human beings.

Literature has often taken up the cases of the downtrodden and drawn the attention of the readers to human rights issue even before the UN Declaration of Universal Human Rights came into being. One of the significant postmodern trends is subversion of the given myths. Writers like Mulk Raj Anand in *Untouchable*, Shashi Deshpande in *The Binding Vine* and Sanjay Bahadur in *The Sound of Water* give voice to the subaltern to expose the society's attitude towards poverty, discrimination and power politics. These portraits of the oppressed enable us to view them as humans with their individuality, human rights and human dignity.

There are two papers on Anita Desai. One studies the problem of the western instant nirvana seekers and the other the significance of mother-love in Desai's novels. The nirvana seekers come to India to be disillusioned and disenchanted because the journey to nirvana does not have a mapped route. What is significant and satisfying is the experience of the journey which can ultimately become the journey of self-discovery. "Milk and Honey" gives a kaleidoscopic view of the characters affected by mothers and mother-figures – some positively, some negatively. Anita Desai seems to believe that mothers are central to one's life, for the psychological and physiological growth of a person. The novelist demystifies motherhood, shows the lop-sided development of the protagonists as directly linked to the absence of the mother. She does not glorify the mother and though she allows the mother her human weaknesses, she is covertly critical of her erroneous ways.

A clearly feminist stance appears in Mulk Raj Anand's *Gauri.* He subverts the Sita myth and reconstructs Gauri as an epitome of strength – the Kali figure. Gauri embodies Anand's faith in the strength of women to achieve self-realization. She exemplifies his design of starting a new life afresh in spite of failures, to discover new freedoms in order to invest meaning in human life.

Another paper "Flight from Responsibility or Search for Freedom" deals with quest motif in women's fiction. Traditionally, questing is a male domain but in Anita Desai's *Where Shall We Go This Summer?* and in Kate Chopin's *The Awakening*, the heroines transgress their limits, choose to leave the security of their homes and embark on a journey into the self. While Edna Pontellier walks into the sea, Sita adopts a more reconciling attitude. After introspection and retrospection, she decides to return to the security of her home. Both Sita and Edna make attempts to affirm their freedom and reject choicelessness.

"Cactus Country" is an assessment of Manohar Malgonkar's novel that celebrates the army code of conduct. Set during the liberation of Bangladesh the novel is written from the point of view of Aslam Chisti, a Pakistani army officer. "Gender, Education and Development" looks back at the time when women's education was a hotly debated issue. The paper focuses on life and literature in the early 20th century to see how the question of women's education and social realities created a criss-cross pattern and the role literature played in bringing changes in social thinking. Dr Radhakrishnan's contribution to Indian culture and value system has been taken up in two essays. Pandit Nehru's vision of a shared history and multi-culturalism was duly propounded by early Hindi cinema. The paper "Gandhian Ideals and Nehruvian Vision" discusses some of the films that carried forward the great Indian dream of national integration, secularism and rural reconstruction. This is a thematic study of films with social message.

Thus, the essays in this volume examine a whole range of experiences and concerns that go into the making of literature. The work, it is hoped, will give rise to further debate offering fresh insights into historical and critical perspectives on Indian writings taking into account some of the major changes in literary and cultural criticism, especially those brought about by the use of contemporary critical theory.

Reference

Jain, Jasbir. *Writing Women Across Cultures*. Jaipur: Rawat Publications, 2002.

2 Of Parrots and Mynahs

Reconstructing Gender through Folklore

This paper addresses the problematic of gender through a study of three small folktales from Himachal Pradesh, Punjab and Maharashtra (three provinces/states of India). It first recounts the tales and then attempts to see the existence of subtle modes of resistance to the social and cultural hegemony present in the folktales, investigating how women writers in retelling the tales focus on the various cultural constructs like women's silence, their relegation to the private domestic space and the situation of "double-bind" that creates conflict between the desire for creativity and the cultural notion of femininity that hampers articulation. The "Parrots and Mynahs" of the title do not necessarily allude to the legendary "Tota-Mynah" tales; these could well be crows and sparrows or robins and peacocks as some of the stories discussed here may illustrate. The stories by themselves are potent enough to provide a space from which to look at and identify the gendered perspective; when subverted, they show how "revisionist mythmaking", to use Adrienne Rich's famous term, can reconstruct the definition of female agency (1980: 35). At the outset, I would like to raise and answer two questions: first, what could be the efficacy of the simple social edict of the folktales when applied to examine the feminist discourse, which is primarily an academic exercise; and second, how the transpositioning of the bird analogy can concretize the gender issue.

To answer the second point first, women writers find the bird metaphor aptly suitable to convey their sense of beauty, the urge to fly all the way to heaven, the constant fear of being caged and be unheard and silenced. Ellen Moers in her *Literary Women* discusses how writers from Christina Rossetti to the Bronte sisters, from George Eliot to Virginia Woolf have been using the bird analogy to explore women's agonizing search for the "wings of liberty", for articulating their selfhood, and for exercising an independence of will.[1] Likewise, Susan Glaspell's play *Trifles* is scripted round the central theme of a bird, a canary killed by wringing her neck. Mrs Wright, the protagonist is also like the canary trapped in the lonely house, whose song is muted and "self" is annihilated by her husband's strict diktat. Nora in Ibsen's *The Doll's House* is also described as a bird. Nearer home, Anita Desai uses the peacock analogy in *Cry, the Peacock* to highlight Maya's obsessive fear of death. Suniti Namjoshi rewrites popular fables from the revisionist mythmaking technique in her *Feminist Fables*. Shashi Deshpande's short story "Why a Robin?" beautifully portrays the conflict of a mother who is anxious not to lose her daughter's faith in her ability; read culturally, it reveals the irony of our postcolonial education system that is still cut off from the soil: Why not write a composition on a Peacock rather than a Robin, a bird not indigenous to us, wonders the mother. The folktales about the birds, discussed here, provide not only the cultural base but also appropriate metaphor for women's silencing.

Going back to the first question raised above, we find that folktales scrutinized from feminist angle show a progression among the postcolonial female writers from modernism to postmodernism. By rewriting the folktales into their literature the women writers are providing a body of literature that helps women see themselves as a community to resist the oppressive structure. To claim that these folktales are primarily about women and that they are strategically motivated to provide representation to women would be a gross oversimplification and misinterpretation. These are not predominantly about women; they are, rather commentaries on the authenticity and moral worth of a tradition. But by shifting the emphasis and re-visioning the tales the writers create a discourse that privileges women to refute their image as mute victims of a repressive tradition as also critique the male-authored gender ideologies that perpetuate the dominant discourse. In some cases, the women writers enclose the folktale within the metastory and follow the traditional Indian pattern of framing a text within a text to contextualize the sub-story. This is what A.K. Ramanujan calls the tendency of the Indian culture to "think in terms of … the context-sensitive … rules."[2] The stories of the mynah, the koel and the sparrow show how the creative use of our tradition can have a direct bearing on important socio-cultural issues. As Madhu Kishwar asserts, our traditions have great potential to fight anti-woman stance of the culture; the need is to identify them, recognize their strength and put them to creative use (1999: 49).[3]

The first story is from Himachal Pradesh but it seems that its various versions are also popular in other parts of India and in some countries of Asia. The title of the Hindi version, "Malik Ki Bhasha" eloquently expresses its connotation.

> A mynah once flies into a farmer's house. As she hops around, her tiny crest, deep colours and cheerful voice charm the children who befriend her. Soon the bird learns their language. She is, however, a minute observer and has the uncanny ability to understand and remember the day's events and the skill to recount them. One day their neighbour's goat strays into the farmer's garden. The farmer catches it and the family feasts on its meat. They smoke the remaining meat and hide it in the basement. In the evening the shepherd comes to inquire if they had seen his goat. The farmer pleads innocence and says, "Friend, I couldn't possibly hide such a big and active animal. If it were here, you could see it." The mynah feels uncomfortable at this falsehood. She blurts out the truth. The farmer is put to great shame and humiliation. In rage, he drives away the mynah.
>
> Puzzled by the entire episode, not understanding her offense, the mynah sits brooding on a tree when a parrot notices her. The mynah tells him her tale of woe. The parrot volunteers to go and see if human beings could be so vile. He arrives at the farmer's house and soon becomes a member of the family. He charms the family not only by his attractive red beak and green feathers but also by his talent of repeating the exact words of the farmer without the unpleasant knack of understanding the deeds of the

> master. After some time the parrot goes back to report his findings to the mynah. "The farmer is not a bad man after all. He loves me and I am quite comfortable there," says the parrot. "Just wait and see. It is only the beginning. He will hate you too, after a while," the mynah retorts. "No chance," boasts the parrot. "I am not a fool like you. I only say what the master teaches me to say. Wisdom lies in repeating the master's language, not in reciting his secrets, you silly," says the parrot as he flies away.

The story obviously questions the authenticity of articulating experience through repetition and the use of master's language to evaluate woman's knowledge, existence and values. This impedes all chances of self-development because language is actually a way of subscribing to a given value system. The clash between experience and language forces women into silence. The silence of women and the forced use of the master's language is the subject of much of feminist writing, particularly of the French feminists like Julia Kristeva and Luce Irigaray to which we shall return after the second story.

The second story is by Dalip Kaur Tiwana and the English title is "The Innocent".[4] It provides the transvaluation of a popular folktale by transforming the language.

> A koel lives in a happy country that is peaceful, beautiful and without problems. The writer describes it graphically:
> "Snow clad mountains all around.
> Cool. Quiet, pure breeze.
> Verdure.
> Calm.
> Bliss.
> That was the land of the koel" (71).
>
> Travelling long distance, a crow comes to visit the koel but he feels desperate and lonely in that peaceful land as he is not accustomed to such beauty and serenity. "Your country is very lonely, very sad, very still," the crow says. The koel reacts. "Not at all. The river speaks and runs, Clouds come, ask riddle and go away. Trees and plants talk to each other. Birds carry message to one another" (71). After inviting the koel to his land, the crow goes

away. The koel decides to return the courtesy and visits the crow's country. It is crowded, hot, noisy and full of chaos. "People were dashing here to there and there to here, like mad. Overloaded buses were crawling like ants" (72). This is Delhi, says the author. The koel compares it to her country and feels nostalgic. The city and its ways bewilder her: a gardener snatches a mango from a child's hand and leaves him crying, marriage means swearing before God to live together, "even if they don't feel like"; in this country a man is awarded medal for killing two hundred enemy people because the enemy is grabbing the country's portion of the land. The koel cannot subscribe to the logic of fighting for land. For her all land belongs to God. Bewildered by the value system she scarcely comprehends, she has many queries. The crow who does not appreciate her questions and criticism asks her to shut up. But the koel keeps on commenting. Her voice makes her visible. At that moment a stone comes whirring, hits her and she drops down dead. Craning his neck, the crow laments, "Didn't I ask you to shut up!" (75)

While the first tale focuses upon the issue of using master's language, the second one takes up the problem of women's voicelessness. By implication both the folktales interrogate the representation of women in life and literature. Feminists agree that women are under-represented, not because of any malicious plotting but because of various factors like lack of education, burden of domestic obligations, familial and social restrictive norms. Once woman gets the authorial power to tell the truth and represent herself, the immediate patriarchal reaction is to disown and discard her. Mary Jacobson points out how women writers become "exceptionally articulate victims of a patriarchally engendered plot" (1981: 522). Toril Moi views the literary establishment as antagonistic to women writers and asks, "How did women manage to write at all given the relentless patriarchal indoctrination which surrounded them from the moment they are born" (1981: 64). The problem of literary production, of speaking out the truth, is associated as much with women's voicelessness as to the question of what Julia Kristeva calls the "semiotic" – a play of forces that can detect inside language. A woman writer has to work within the dominant order, and if she tends to work outside that order she is either dead or branded mad. This is because by subverting the male-dominated form, she generates an ideological conflict that attacks the symbolic order and threatens hegemonic power.

In telling the truth, the mynah has in fact attempted to break the dominance of the male inscription, and displace authority. The obvious result is the disappearance of the female (the mynah) from the text and the installation of the male (the parrot) as a more acceptable substitute. In the fate of the mynah the stratified meaning of the story serves to implicate the society as a whole. This kind of reading of the folktale raises some pertinent questions regarding the narrative voice in general. The incorporation of another's speech in another's language makes it difficult to locate any identifiable narrational voice in a discourse. Moreover, since males and females move in a context of sexual inequality, there is a strong differentiated behavioural expectation. As Nancy Henley et al. point out, "Language has been used in the past, and is still used, to dehumanize a people into submission; it both reflects and shapes the culture in which it is embedded" (1990: 395).[5]

The first step into silencing a woman is her elimination. The koel gets a severer punishment in Dalip Kaur Tiwana's story. Tiwana has reappropriated a fable to recontextualize woman's story, to deconstruct the stereotype image of woman and to give her the power to articulate, not only as a female but also as a writer. The crow's oft-repeated advice and command to the koel is not to criticize the dominant order (the crow's country) and not to be visible. The moment the koel becomes too articulate, she loses her life. The portrayal of the incident is both powerful and meaningful:

> "Naught your country is," the koel said looking at the gardener who was shooing away the birds.
> "Don't say anything against my country. Otherwise I'll leave you. I haven't married you yet. So you can't claim any alimony."
> The koel laughed aloud.
> "Shut up. If the gardener hears, he will sling a stone *at you.*" [*mark the words "at you" not at the crow* (emphasis added)].
> "Are people, who talk like this, put to death in your country?"
> Hardly had the koel completed the query a stone whirred through the leaves and struck her dead (75).

Obviously, women are not supposed to question or criticize the dominant discourse; they are not expected to know more than what is laid down for them; the best possible course for them is to remain "invisible". In *The Thousand Faces of Night,* Githa Hariharan draws attention to the practical and ethical obstacle in women's act of questioning. If they get their voice and exercise their right to speak, to ask the potent "why", they pay a heavy price. This is what the old retainer Mayamma tells the protagonist Devi, "So be careful, Devi ... when next you ask a question" (1992: viii). Mayamma has learnt this wisdom at a cost. When she dared to ask "why" she got a good thrashing from her mother-in-law. Gayatri Spivak's question, "Can a subaltern speak?" and her answer that a woman being doubly subaltern cannot, holds good in this case.

A potent "why" and an equally powerful urge to recount the truth (as in the first tale) come from the women writers. Writing itself is an act of resistance, of empowerment. But for women, writing usually creates conflicts and the tensions. As a result of the deeply ingrained cultural pre-suppositions, a woman writer has to deal with the realization that while men write out of their experience which is almost genderless, women have to counter the pre-empted notion that the "feminine" life and experiences are trivial and hence irrelevant. They are deemed unfit to tackle the fundamental issues of humanity. Women writers are constrained by a "double-bind" – a situation in which they have to struggle to cross their private, muted boundaries and yet to remain within the prescribed space of domesticity. Conflict is generated by the demands of attachment versus autonomy, the desire for creativity and active participation in social and cultural life, on the one hand and the restrictive roles assigned to them by the culture. Many of Shashi Deshpande's heroines are trapped in the situation of "double bind" – creative writers, journalists, and finally a musician, all seem locked in the image imposed by the cultural code. It is Savitri Bai Indorekar, the great musician in Deshpande's *Small Remedies* who breaks the rule but at a massive psychic cost. Helene Cixous admits that it is difficult for women to speak but all the same they must muster up courage to articulate. "Every woman has known the torture of beginning to speak aloud, heart beating as if to break, occasionally falling into loss of language; ground and language slipping out from under her, because for woman speaking – even just opening her mouth – in public is something rash, a transgression". The mynah in the first story and the koel in the second, suffer for opening their mouth. Despite the threat, Cixous wants women to write and be heard, that is the best bet against her relegation to silence (1999: 75–88).

Feminist critics have discerned that women's writing is characterized by silences and diffidence because of their distrust of the borrowed language, with the result that they are unable to assert themselves as the voice of truth. In *Articulate Silences,* Chinese-American critic King-Kok Cheung observes that the reticence to articulate and skepticism about language and textual authority "has led women writers to embrace open-endedness and multiplicity in their fiction"; instead of subscribing to any one "master narrative"; they exemplify what Dale Blau Dupleissis calls "both/and vision" (1993: 4–5) Mikhail Bakhtin terms this as "double-voiced discourse" which reveals the speaker's orientation towards another's discourse in which the code is made up of a "dominant" and a "muted" story.

Reading closely, we notice how the "double-voiced discourse" operates within the framework of Tiwana's "The Innocent". In the act of retelling the folktale, the author uses two speakers at the same time and expresses simultaneously two different intentions: the direct intention of the characters that are speaking and the indirect and hence refracted intention of the author. In the land of the crow (the male), the koel feels nostalgic for her homeland. She wants to reconnect and reclaim her sense of identity and is pulled by two worlds – on the one hand there are the powerful memories of the past without which she would be rootless, on the other, she has to face the consequences of her choice in coming to the crow's land. This "double consciousness" leaves her frustrated. The term "double consciousness" was first used by African-American scholar William Du Bois to describe the experiences of African-Americans who are caught in the clash of two cultures – Negro and American (1903: 45). Using this analogy for the koel (and by implication for the female) we find that she is also trapped between two cultures – one of peace, the other of aggression and competition.

Let me digress for a while and go back to 1905 when Rokeya Begum, an early activist during India's freedom struggle and a writer from East Bengal (now Bangladesh) wrote a charming satirical piece "Sultana's Dream". In this story, the protagonist dreams of her visit to an all-woman land where fearlessness, peace and non-violence reign because men are not out on the streets; they are in their *Mardanas* (as opposed to the *Zenana* in the protagonist's country) and they live in Purdah. The same kind of a country is probably the koel's. This does not, however, suggest that women live in a different culture (they are part of the mainstream culture) but women live in "ambivalent affiliation" with the patriarchy as Gilbert and Gubar assert, which is a complex relationship. Moreover, transplantation from natal home to the husband's home also produces conflicts and tensions generated by uprootedness. The koel's tirades against the crow's country are also motivated by her subordinate status in his land where she is not allowed to vent her feelings. The double standards of the patriarchal value system operate within the story. The koel is threatened of dire consequences if she tries to be critical whereas the crow, while in the koel's country, feels free to criticize her land. Interestingly, the koel does not get angry nor does she warn him, instead she gives only justifications when the crow calls her country boring.

The third story is a children's folktale popular all over Maharashtra and part of Karnataka where it is told with local variations.[6] In Marathi, it is called "Kau-Chieu chi Goshta" – the story of a crow and a sparrow. Women writers find this tale valuable and crucial to understanding woman's situation in life. In the usual folktale pattern it starts with a direct statement:

> *"There was a crow"*
> and ...
> *"There was a sparrow".*
> The crow has a house of mud and the sparrow has a beautiful house of wax. Once it rained in torrents. The crow's house is washed away, the sparrow's house stands firm and strong. The crow comes to the sparrow and knocks on the door, "Sparrow sister, sparrow sister, open the door." The sparrow takes her own time to open the door as she is busy in her multiple household chores. She responds, "wait awhile, crow dada (brother), I am

bathing my little ones." Then at the subsequent knocks, she tells him that she is feeding them, putting them to bed and so on. Finally she opens the door and lets him in. The sparrow has a store of all niceties stacked in her home – sacks full of rice and dal and sugar and coconut copra. She offers the crow to choose his perch. He opts to spend the night on the bag of coconut copra. The crow is cunning and has evil designs. Throughout the night he eats the delicious copra, dirties the floor with night soil and before the sparrow could see the mess, he slyly flies away.

Many Marathi knowing women writers have questioned the story and have also subverted it. In the story, the sparrow has a beautiful home of her own. But the socio-cultural reality belies this fact. Shashi Deshpande's heroines reject the myth of a woman having a home of her own. Her heroine Saru (*The Dark Holds No Terrors*) wonders how this misleading and deceptive statement could have crept in the tale. This brings to mind Naseera Sharma's story "Mera Ghar Kahan" (Where is my Home). The title itself eloquently expresses homelessness. One of the writers to have exploded the *Kau-Chiu* myth is Gauri Deshpande.[7]

A bilingual writer – writing in Marathi and English with equal ease – Gauri Deshpande raises several interesting questions with her usual wit and intriguing undercurrent of sarcasm. Reversing the entire scenario, Gauri writes a new story. She titles it "Kavlya-Chimni chi Goshta" and within the folktale framework weaves another story of a man and a woman. The crow of the folktale is a woman in her story (she-crow, obviously) and the sparrow is a man. In the tale, the crow's home is ugly and shaky, made of dung, but in real life a woman's home (if she has one) is supposed to be dilapidated and ugly because she does not have the pillars of strength, self-assertion, self-confidence and self-identity to support it. Again, the man does not go to a woman's home, it is the woman who has to make his home as her's. In Gauri Deshpande's version of the tale, the hero (sparrow) goes to the woman, exploits her physically and financially, drains her out and when fed up, comes back to his own sparrow (wife). The jilted woman, finding herself in difficulty, asks for help but the man and his sparrow hide themselves in their comfortable home, and refusing to open the door, shut her out callously. After a while, the man, satiated with his sparrow, locates the woman who by now has become self-supporting, and asks her "would you come to my home?" The author does not give us the woman's reaction; she leaves her story open-ended.

This revisionist technique used to read a popular folktale deconstructs the accepted myth and by retelling the story, it acts upon its language and gives it a new tinge. Revisionist mythmaking is not simply a retelling of an old story but it involves scrutinizing, revising and recreating to impart it new connotation. Adrienne Rich in her much-quoted call for women's revision of literary texts exhorts women to look back; to re-focus on the past to show how women were trapped in the patriarchal constructs. Rich defines revision as an "act of looking back, of seeing with fresh eyes, of entering an old text from a new critical direction" (1980: 35). For Adrienne Rich it is an "act of survival" whereas for Alicia Ostricker it is "instructions for survival". Revision is a method whereby a writer chooses a culturally accepted tale or heroic figure and appropriates it for altered ends that makes cultural change possible. More significantly revision leads to breaking the silence and transforming language itself. It can be termed a process of recovery and reformation. The old myths are spirited away from their oppressive contexts and rejuvenated by reinterpretation, re-reading and re-writing.

The three folktales discussed here follow different modes – the first story is recounted as it is told in the oral tradition, but it contains within itself a directive to the subaltern to use master's language; the second tale is retold by the author from her perspective with necessary changes and it conveys woman's voicelessness; the third is reformulated as revisionist mythmaking and it erodes the myths associated with cultural presuppositions. As Kumkum Sangari observes in one of her recent articles, "... a history of female agency and the difficulty of 'owning' a voice is a part of the new problematic. It calls for a reconstruction of the complexity and historically changing definition of female agency – as it is attributed to women and as it is enacted by women – alongside transitions in notions of female selfhood and individuation" (2002: 36). These folktales and the women writers who re-write them are trying to break with the canon with an advantage as the entire exercise provides a space from which to look at the shift and to challenge the patristic canon in literature.

A feminist reading is meant to see how the old texts can yield new meaning. In the process, one does not claim any definitiveness or structural completeness for different readings, but only the texts' usefulness in decoding woman's silence and understanding woman-as-author.

Notes

1. See Mary Eagleton ed. *Feminist Literature: A Reader.* Oxford: Basil Blackwell, 1986. 209–10, for Moers' discussion on the bird metaphor in literature.
2. A.K. Ramanujan focuses on the context-free and the context-sensitive grammatical rules in his article "Is There an Indian way of Thinking? An Informal Essay" in Mckim Marriott ed. *India Through Hindu Category.* New Delhi: Sage Publication, 1990: 41–58. From grammatical rules he shifts to culture and then to literature and shows how cultural tendencies can be categorized as context-free and context-sensitive. In Indian culture and literature the preferred formulation is the context-sensitive rule. "No Indian text comes without a context, a frame, till the 19th century." And "Texts may be historically dateless, anonymous; but their contexts, uses, efficacies, are explicit" (48).
3. Madhu Kishwar and Ruth Vanitha focus upon the real life problems of women in their study *In Search of Answers,* New Delhi: Manohar, 1999. According to them women have enormous burden on them of varied nature – housework, child-rearing, violence and so on. In addition, the pervasive popular cultural ideal of womanhood also becomes a death trap for them. But these and various such problems cannot be countered with Western feminist paradigms. The activists who are fighting for women's cause, writers, social workers and women at the grassroots must draw from India's own cultural sources. "Our cultural traditions have tremendous potential within them to combat reactionary and anti-women ideas, if we can identify their points of strength and use them creatively. The rejection of the harmful is then made much easier than attempts to overthrow traditions totally or to attack them arrogantly from outside, as most of us Westernised modernists tend to do ..." (49).

4. Dalip Kaur Tiwana's story is titled "Masoom" in Punjabi and has been translated into English by Manjeet Kaur Bhatia.
5. See Nancy M. Henley, Mykol Hamilton and Barrie Thorne, "Womanspeak and Manspeak: Sex Differences and Sexism in Communication, Verbal and Nonverbal," in Sheila Ruth ed. *Issues in Feminism*. London: Mayfield Publishing Company, 1990, 394–406. Discussing women's silences and the expectations of the society with regard to their verbal and nonverbal communication, the authors posit that language is not only a medium for communication; in real ways it reflects and creates culture.
6. A.K. Ramanujan tells the Kannada version of the story of the Sparrow and the Crow but his discussion takes into consideration its implication for childhood training. See "Telling Tales" *Indian Horizons*. 41.4 (1992): 55–79.
7. Gauri Deshpande (1942–2003). Gauri Deshpande, a bilingual writer writing in Marathi and English with equal ease passed away on March 1, 2003 after a brief illness. Gauri dealt with women's issues but she saw women as individuals, with identity of their own holding on fiercely to their independence. In her stories the male characters are often kindly and accommodating but the action takes place in the inner and the outer worlds the female inhabit and in her recent writings one sees the resolution to reach the goal and the triumph of arrival.

References

Bakhtin, Mikhail. "Discourse in the Novel." *The Dialogic Imagination*. Ed. Michael Holquist. Austin: University of Texas Press, 1981, 259–422.

Cheung, King-Kok. *Articulate Silences*. Ithaca, NY: Cornell University Press, 1993.

Cixous, Helene. "Sorties: Out and Out: Attacks/Ways Out/Forays." *The Feminist Reader*. Eds. Catherine Belsey and Jane Moore. Houndsmill: Macmillan Press, 1997, 91–103.

Deshpande, Gauri. "Kavlya-Chimni chi Goshta." *Ahe Hey Asa Ahe*. Mumbai: Mauj Prakashan, 1986, 1–4.

Du Bois, William E.B. *The Soul of Black Folk*. New York: New American Library, 1903.

Hariharan, Githa. *The Thousand Faces of Night*. New Delhi: Viking, 1992.

Henley, Nancy M. Mykol Hamilton and Barrie Throne. "Womanspeak and Manspeak: Sex Differences and Sexism in Communication, Verbal and Nonverbal." *Issues in Feminism: An Introduction to Woman's Studies*. Ed. Sheila Ruth. London: Mayfield Publishing Company, 1990.

Jacobson, Mary. "Review of *The Madwoman in the Attic: The Woman Writer and the Nineteenth-Century Literary Imagination,"* by Sandra M. Gilbert and Susan Gubar. *Signs*. 16 (1981): 522.

Kishwar, Madhu and Ruth Vanitha. *In Search of Answers: Indian Women's Voices from Manushi.* New Delhi: Manohar, 1999.

Moers, Ellen. *Literary Women*. London: The Women's Press, 1978.

Moi, Toril. *Sexual/Textual Politics: Feminist Literary Theory*. London: Methuen, 1985.

Ramanujan, A.K. "Is there an Indian Way of Thinking? An Informal Essay." *India Through Hindu Categories*. Ed. Mckim Marriott. New Delhi: Sage Publications, 1990.

Ramanujan, A.K. "Telling Tales." *Indian Horizons.* 41.4 (1992): 55–79.

Rich, Adrienne. *On Lies, Secrets, and Silences: Selected Prose, 1961–1978*. London: Virago, 1980.

Sangari, Kumkum. "Feminist Criticism and Indian Literary History." *Language, Discourse, Writing.* 2. January–March 2002: 33–49.

Tiwana, Dalip Kaur. "The Innocent." *Indian Literature*. 139. September–October 1990: 71–75.

3 Re-mapping Culture through Literature

Narratives as Vehicles of Culture

> The schoolmaster is abroad, and I trust more to him, armed with his primer, than I do the soldier in full military array, for upholding and extending the liberties of his country.
>
> —Lord Brougham (a speech in the House of Commons, January 29, 1929)

Cultural implication of the colonial experience is one of the significant aspects of literature studies in the postcolonial period. The main preoccupation of the literature of the erstwhile-colonized countries has been to resist the imperial myths and fallacies by writing back to the centre. The effort is to preserve one's self-image and establish an indigenous identity. As Franz Fanon opines, colonialism not only enslaves a people politically, it devalues their pre-colonial history and invades their culture. The victims of this historical process suffer loss of identity and undergo psychological conflicts. In the postcolonial era, therefore, the urgent need of the society is to re-possess its past and take control of its own reality by "charting the cultural territory", to use Edward Said's words. In literature this is termed as *reinscription* (252–259). What Said asserts in his *Culture and Imperialism* is that while identity is crucial to the postcolonial, just to define it, as "a different identity" (57) is not enough. The important thing is to be able to see and show others that even the subaltern has had a history capable of development, as part of the process of growth and maturity. That is where re-writing or reinscription assumes significance. While some Indian critics see postcolonial theory of literature as "ideologically an emancipatory concept" given to a "rigorous scrutiny on the continuities and ruptures in the de-colonized societies" (Mukherjee, 1996: 3), some others question its efficacy and efficiency for the Indian situation. These critics feel that though the postcolonial literature tends to write back to the centre it does not solve the question of marginality. Postcolonialism, Jasbir Jain asserts, is a "question of attitude which goes beyond the attempt to confront colonialism to become an attempt to transcend it, to step outside the influence and the framework, to reclaim an autonomous and free identity" (Jain, 1999: 35).

In this paper an attempt has been made to study three Indian English novels to see how the authors reclaim their identity by re-mapping their cultural territory and how by reverting to the traditional narrative strategies they work out an indigenous framework. The novels selected for discussion are Arun Joshi's *The City and the River* (1990) and *The Last Labyrinth* (1981), and Gita Mehta's *A River Sutra* (1993). The discussion will focus on the narratives, analysing the cultural consciousness of the authors, which shapes their texts. In these stories, the Ganga, the Narmada and the Himalayas are the bearers of the culture, witness to a historical reality and the repository of ancient wisdom. The novels show the authors' cultural efforts to restore the community and repossess the culture. Both Joshi and Mehta uphold the cultural dynamism of traditional thought and hold a mirror to the destructive trends in power politics and consumerism-oriented greed. The fictional narratives, by re-creating an indigenous culture, displace the historical discourse and help us read into the text the mythological, archetypal, metaphysical and religious perception in the native literature.

Arun Joshi's *The Last Labyrinth* was published in 1981. A Sahitya Akademi award winning work, this novel recounts the story of a modern Indian torn between the inner and the outer forces, the instinctive cultural leaning of the inner self and the rational, scientific yet consumer orientation of a Westernized Indian. The shares of Aftab's Company that Som Bhaskar desperately wants to grab are in the possession of Krishna in a temple on the Himalayas. Som's greed makes him undertake the difficult journey up the mountain, through the formidable crags and valleys, the glaciers and the frozen lakes; he dreads it, it is nightmarish but he is fascinated by it, all the same. As the author describes the mission one realizes that the Himalayas and Lord Krishna assume significance as cultural symbols. Som broods with a kind of cultural pride and admits unabashedly, "No, there is nothing simple about Krishna. Had it been so, He would not have survived ten thousand years. He would have died long ago with the gods of the Pharaohs, the Sumerians, Incas. Krishna was about as simple as the labyrinth of Aftab's Haveli" (173). Som's journey through the Himalayas is reminiscent of the last climb of the Pandavas commonly known as *Swarga-rohan*; only, Som lacks attitudinal change; he tosses between an urge for self-understanding and the inability to forget his recent past and consequently his journey becomes one of nightmares, unfulfilled desires and failure. For a brief while, Som gets a kind of illumination, a short spell of peak experience that could have transformed him into a self-realized man, but as he admits, "This little flame of mine ... yielded nothing beyond an ounce of tranquility" (209). Throughout the climb we are not allowed to forget that it is the Himalayas the protagonist is climbing up on. Symbolically, his companions are Doctor K. and a friend called Vasudeva. K. could be read as an abbreviation for Krishna while Vasudeva is one of the many names of Lord Krishna. Thus the journey assumes obvious cultural overtones. The author juxtaposes the puniness of man with the vastness of the unfathomable. The entire fabric of the narrative is dominated by the author's efforts to re-claim the culture and the inability to revert to the past.

In his last novel *The City and the River,* published in 1990. Arun Joshi deals with the existential angst of the entire culture. It is a muffled portrayal of post-independence India, a kind of allegorical picture, where intrigues, nepotism, ostracism and violence are rampant. The regime of the Grand Master in a particular city is full of fawning sycophants, self-seeking ruling classes and the helpless, hapless masses. The scenario, in fact, draws parallel between the Emergency in India and the oppressive regime of the Grand Master. The city becomes the victim of the greed of the purblind rulers and is destroyed by the angry river. The "City" is unnamed and so is the "River" but both gain multi-dimensional meanings when read in the national and cultural context. The narrative pattern of story within a story told by an old, wise teacher to his keen disciple follows the typical Indian narrational technique of *katha.* In the Indian narrative tradition a *sutradhar* or the main narrator recounts a story with the help of which the story (or the novel in the present case) advances. Often the framed stories are variations of some broad human behaviour. *Panchtantra, Kadambari, Katha Sarit Sagar*, and even epics like the Mahabharata and the Ramayana, and a whole lot of our traditional narratives follow the pattern of "framed narrative".

In *The City and the River,* the Great Yogeshwara tells the story to the Nameless-One. After giving enlightenment to his disciple in the "Prologue" the teacher, the Guru, starts thus: "That is good. I shall tell you now a tale and in my telling, perhaps, you will know who you are. Listen, this is how it goes"(11). The story starts with the chapter entitled "The Grand Master's Dream" and ends with the city's doom. Then follows the "Epilogue". Again, the teacher-pupil duo appears. The novel ends but not the cycle of comings and goings. The Nameless-One has been entrusted with the task of purifying the city "of egoism, selfishness, stupidity" (263). The cyclical movement is thus inevitable: "On the ruins of that city ... a new city has risen. It is ruled by another Grand Master," it has the same people – Professor, Bhumiputra, the boatmen and so on. Of course, the men have "other names but the forces they embody remain unchanged" (262). The Great Yogeshwara wants his disciple to try and "prevent this endless repetition, this periodic disintegration" (262). The circular movement communicates human continuity. The Indian concept of life-death-reincarnation implies the cycle from creation to the end and again a new beginning. The reappearance of the Nameless-One signifies a period of future hope for humanity.

The third novel we propose to discuss is Gita Mehta's *A River Sutra.* A retired Administrative Officer decides to renounce the world and stay in a secluded spot. He reaches the Narmada Guest House and during the course of his stay learns much about life through interaction with Tariq Mia and the others who frequent the guesthouse. Gita Mehta also adopts the traditional Indian narrational technique. The several threads of narrative run parallel with the main story and are held together by the frame narrator. Each tale, narrated from the point of view of some specific narrator, be it the diary of Nitin Bose or the first person tale of the courtesan/monk, is discussed by the frame-narrator. The analysis and the comments bear upon the limits of human understanding. The novelist seems to have consciously evoked the Guru-Shishya (teacher-pupil) dialogue on the pattern of the Upanishadic framework. In the beginning of the novel the bureaucrat-narrator says: "Do you know what the word Upanishad means? It means to sit beside and listen. Here I am, sitting eager to listen" (13). While Joshi's novel *The City and the River* is in third person, Gita Mehta shifts between the device of first person and third person narrative strategy, according to the exigency of the story. In Joshi's novel, the Great Yogeshwara tells one long tale of human greed and shameful actions and lets the "river" take its revenge. In *A River Sutra* there are six isolated stories all joined by common threads: at the human level by Tariq Mia and/or the bureaucrat-narrator, at the archetypal level by river Narmada, and at the metaphysical level by the bonds of human love which lead to divine love. The movement of this novel is linear, meandering like the river but going forward. The Narmada has a life of its own – the pilgrims on its banks, the dancing waters eager to join the sea, the aquatic life inside the river, and the whirling eddies. The river is a living force with a personality of its own. It is a delightful river. Joshi's river, on the other hand, can be angry, incomprehensible, and vindictive. Within these structural patterns, though alike to an extent but different still, the two novelists weave stories deeply rooted in the culture. Both join the contemporary India with the ageless, immortal India; the present with the past, the modern with the traditional, the mythic with the rational.

The nameless river in Joshi's novel is the archetypal symbol of the great mother. It is interesting to note that the novel does not have any memorable female presence except the "River". True, the "headman" of the boat people is a woman but she is not a feminine figure, she is an abstract concept. There is Shailaja, but she fails to be a palpable presence. Only the river is the moving loving, protecting force to whom the boat people owe allegiance. For them the river "is a symbol of the living mother. Of God himself"(22). The rational, modern and consumer mind of the Grand Master is not ready to accept this superstition. He tells the Astrologer, " it is these things that keep our people down" (22), because to him what is the river but a stream of water. That the boatmen should have allegiance to the river than to their Ruler is beyond his comprehension. "They prefer a stream of water, no doubt beautiful, no doubt sacred, but nonetheless a stream, to me, the scion of a family that gives all to this city" (22). The boatmen consider themselves children of the river, their archetypal mother, the harbinger of peace and plenty. This tussle is a pointer towards the conflict going on in contemporary India – fast moving towards Western rational approach yet tied down to the unconscious, to the old beliefs. Joshi carries the question to the end of the novel when it assumes philosophical proportion and becomes a treatise on the question of man's allegiance " to God or to man" (262).

The answer to this question can be found in *A River Sutra* when the Naga Baba alias Professor Shankar asserts towards the end, dismissing the divinity of river Narmada, "If anything is sacred about the river, it is the individual experiences of the human beings who have lived here" (267). Suddenly then, a reader returns to the epigram from the "Love Songs of Chandidas":

> Listen, O brother,
> Man is the greatest truth.
> Nothing beyond.

The novel, we realize, affirms human dignity. Narmada becomes a palpable symbol of love, life, and death. Born of Shiva's penance, the river is the "Delightful One" "forever holy, forever inexhaustible". To Professor Shankar, it is an "immortal river", while for Nitin Bose and the tribals it has curative value. Narmada grants salvation to those who die in its water. Suicide is not a sin if committed in Narmada. And, the river sustains love and teaches the lover not to be moved by the puny human passions but to see love as sublime. This is corroborated by the story of the musician who exhorts his daughter to "meditate on the waters of Narmada, the symbol of Shiva's penance," until she has cured herself of her attachment to what has passed in her life. He says "I must understand that I am the bride of music, not of a musician ..." (226). The tale of Naga Baba's love for the child he rescues from the brothel and gives a clean life, is humanistic/philanthropic, while the music teacher's attachment to the blind boy is love at the level of Guru-Shishya tradition. The aesthetic framework moves round love, attachment-detachment, renunciation and involvement. Apart from these, there are rich motifs of divine love – the reference to Kama, allusion to Uma's penance to get Shiva's love, the stories about Veena and the seven notes of music uphold the divinity of love. Gita Mehta quotes profusely from the great Sufi poet Rumi's love lyrics strengthening the images of love as a purifying emotion, above the narrow worldly barriers. In Joshi's *The Last Labyrinth* Gargi exhorts Som time and again to consider his love for Anuradha on the spiritual plain. Could Som get over the physicality of his passion for Anuradha he would have been saved the torture of schizophrenia after Anuradha's disappearance. Som comes to realize the pure quality of love during his trip to the Himalayas but unfortunately for him, he is unable to assimilate the lesson.

In *The City and the River*, Arun Joshi presents predominantly modern India scourged by self-seeking, shortsighted, lusty and power-hungry ruling classes. In *The Last Labyrinth*, he focuses on the greed and lust of an individual character. But in his scheme, there exists a greater, perennial India with its eternal wisdom. The clash of tradition and modernity, rationality and instinct will always be there. What is required is purification. This, however, is hard to achieve. The City is symbolic of the contemporary society. It is the inert battleground of power play. Som seeks the power of money and passionate love in Benaras while the Rulers of the unnamed City want unquestioned political power. The River is a primordial force to which all turn for help. In her anger, she becomes destructive though she is not life denying. On her bosom the Nameless-One is born to continue creation, life and its eternal quest. Taken as an Indian archetype, the river appears to be Ganga. In *The Last Labyrinth* also, it is Ganga at Benaras on whose waters Som is ferried to Gargi's place.

Gita Mehta's Narmada too is a microcosm of India. She is the organizing principle of the novel. The six loosely knit tales give the novel multiplicity but the river vouchsafes its unity. "The resulting figure," as a critic observes, " is one of unitary pluralism." The Narmada Guest House is, indeed, mini-India and it reflects the culture of India. There is the river with its mythology, religion, superstitions, spirituality and archaeology, representing traditional, primitive and modern India. People who converge around the area come from different walks of life and belong to different religious groups. The Narmada joins the north and the south. Its legends are as much known to the tribals in Assam as to the tribals of the Vano village. The pre-Aryan and the Aryan cultures prevail. It is thus a secular river. If the traditional wisdom chants: "O Narmada defend me from the serpent's poison," the rational mind interprets it as the "serpent of desire;" if it stings, the result would be schizophrenic state, symbolized by Nitin Bose in the novel and Som Bhaskar in Joshi's work.

The three novels do not advocate detachment in the sense of running away from life, from action. Naga Baba enters the battle-field of life, "Kurukshetra", after ten years of ascetic wandering. Tariq Mia makes himself socially useful by teaching his students. He is content with his life. The music teacher was attached to his blind pupil; this led him to grief and suicide. The significant thing is to maintain balance. Non-attachment is difficult, as the ugly daughter of the musician says, "It is an impossible penance, to express desire in my music when I am dead inside" (226). But, it is worth trying as Naga Baba alias Professor Shankar shows.

The novels under discussion are the authors' cultural efforts at the restoration of community and repossession of culture. The city in *The Last Labyrinth* is Benaras, the cultural city of India; it is not the colonial city of which Sunil Khilnani speaks in *The Idea of India*. The significance of Indian cities is given in a *shloka*, which refers to seven cities as *mokshadayini*. The *Shloka* runs thus:

Ayodhya, Mathuramaya, Kashi, Kanchi, Avantika,
Puri, Dwarawatishchaiva saptehta mokshdayika

Now, coming to the rivers, to the Indian mind, rivers are not only the geographical features; they are the very sum and substance of our existence. We have mythologized our rivers, given them a form and a life of their own. They are timeless, ageless and immutable on whose banks life has continued for ages and ages. They sustain and purify, give us joy, and in anger, they can even destroy, only to create again. Thus, hope is sustained; culture springs up around them and philosophy, religion, mythology, archaeology take roots. One cannot forget Lord Krishna's frolicking in and around the Yamuna so lovingly described in the literature of India; one is reminded of the Saryu of the Ramayana, Kalidas's Kshipra, the place of Godavari and Kaveri in the psyche of the South, the power of the Brahmaputra (the only male) and the love and awe attached to the five rivers of the Punjab. As for the Himalayas, it is a part of the unconscious of the race. In the *Gita*, Lord Krishna calls himself Himalayas among the mountains.

Discussing the process of de-colonization, Edward Said remarks: "After the period of 'primary resistance', literally fighting against outside intrusion, there comes a period on secondary, that is, ideological resistance," when efforts are made to reconstitute a community and restore its dignity and unity. By this process the subaltern occupies his place self-consciously so as to gain his rightful place. Said gives examples from literature to make his point. Ngugi induces life in the river Honia in *The River Between* and Tayb Salih re-maps the power of the Nile in *Season of Migration*. When compared to Conrad's river in the *Heart of Darkness*, the above two rivers – Honia and Nile – appear living entities. Only an insider who has imbibed the culture with his/her mother's milk can think of nationalism in terms of cultural practices.

Both Gita Mehta and Arun Joshi suggest a rethinking of Indian culture and tradition. Joshi hints at the self-destructive trends of the power politics and warns contemporary India. He advocates purity of thought and action through the story of the city and the river, and through Som's dissipation. Gita Mehta weighs the mysticism of *Vanaprastha* in the scale of modern rationality and finds that the dynamism of Indian thought has always advocated detachment with action, and animism with humanism. The self-contained and inter-connected characters and tales reconcile the rich diversity of doctrines in the flow of Narmada – the symbol of our cultural multi-plicity and unity. The Narmada guesthouse is symbolic of this world where people come, stay awhile and depart. This oriental view reminds us of Omar Khayyam's *Rubayyat* likening this world to a "Caravan Sarai". The bureaucrat manager of the guesthouse represents the modern seeker – confused and unable to decide what to choose: this world or *Vanaprastha*. He is knowledgeable but his knowledge is pre-eminently in the shape of information, not wisdom. As Tariq Mia often says teasingly, one has yet to learn a lot about the world before one seeks renunciation.

References

Fanon, Franz. *The Wretched of the Earth.* New York: Mentor Books, 1969.

Jain, Jasbir. "Interpreting the Past: Culture and History in Sahgal's Works," in *Writing in a Post-Colonial Space.* Ed. Surya Nath Pandey. New Delhi: Atlantic, 1999.

Joshi, Arun. *The Last Labyrinth.* New Delhi: Orient Paperbacks, 1981.

——. *The City and the River.* New Delhi: Vision Books, 1990.

Khilnani, Sunil. *The Idea of India.* London: Hamish Hamilton, 1997.

Mehta, Gita. *A River Sutra.* New Delhi: Penguin, 1993.

Mukherjee, Meenakshi. "Interrogating Post-Colonialism," in *Interrogating Post-Colonialism: Theory, Text and Context.* Eds. Harish Trivedi and Meenakshi Mukherjee. Shimla: Indian Institute of Advanced Study, 1997.

Said, Edward. *Imperialism and Culture.* London: Vintage, 1994.

4 Tagore's Chitra and Folklore's Hidimba

Power of the Feminine

Somehow, Chitrangada and Hidimba stand out as epitomes of feminine power and feminist assertion in the Mahabharata as well as in literature. The role assigned to them in the Epic (Mahabharata) and in folk and mainstream literatures focuses on their strength, independence of spirit and intelligence. Rabindranath Tagore's lyrical drama *Chitrangada* is based on the Mahabharata story of the warrior-princess whose quest for love has both feminine and feminist overtones. Similarly, Hidimba, from the present Kullu area of Himachal Pradesh, is a folklore figure who has become a part of folk psyche and has achieved divinity. These two women are not identical; though contemporary, they belong to distant parts of the land, with different value systems and social set-ups but both are strong and both represent an era that illustrates women's authority and agency. It is interesting to explore how Rabindranath Tagore makes changes in the Mahabharata story to give his heroine the attributes he would like modern Indian women to possess and how the folklore of Himachal Pradesh elevates Hidimba from the daemonic to the human and then to the divine.

My effort is to problematize Tagore's views of feminine power, not in absolute terms in its masculine connotation but in its vigour which gives woman her sense of identity and personal worth. When Tagore lets his Chitrangada declare, "Ami Chitrangada" I am Chitrangada, we see her as a self-assured, mature woman, conscious of her selfhood as a woman. Though this declaration comes towards the end of the play, it gives us sufficient ground to pick up our discussion from this point. In order to contextualize the Hidimba story one needs to turn to the folk practices in Kullu-Manali area, the temple lore of Hidimba Mata in Manali and the reverence with which the erstwhile royal family hold the goddess. Significantly, Hidimba remains vibrant in the oral tradition but as folklore scholars assert, oral literature represents an appropriate expression of religious, mythological, historical and cultural milieu of the rural folk and offers a continuum to the culture. Chitra and Hidimba both are mythic figures placed in contemporary realities but since myths appeal "to emotion rather than to reason" (Shaw, 1976: 10) they can stand perennial questioning and re-working of the Mahabharata myths.

Chitrangada of Mahabharata becomes a fascinating and picturesque figure in Tagore's hands. The writer's art has created a woman who is only remotely recognizable as from the epic. Tagore's Chitrangada is both traditional and modern. He probes her heart, places her in the psycho-social reality of the culture and then constructing a psychological matrix, he assigns her a role that one can identify with role-distancing rather than role-playing.

Let us first recast the two women from the Himalayan region as portrayed in the Mahabharata. Hidimba was the sister of the tyrant Hidimb, the Rakshasa ruler of the western Himalaya area which is Kullu-Manali in the present state of Himachal Pradesh. While the Pandavas were roaming in that area the ruler Hidimb was angry at the intruders and sent his sister to ambush the Pandavas and eliminate them. That the ruler should send a female – his sister – to locate the enemy portends well for the esteem with which female power was recognized. Hidimba saw Bhim, lost her heart to him and approaching him directly, expressed desire to marry him. Initially, Bhim repulsed her advances. In the meanwhile when his sister did not return for long, Hidimb went out in search of her; saw the Pandavas and attacked Bhim. Hidimba was aware of her brother's daemonic powers. She could not let her lover be defeated and killed. She used her esoteric powers to help Bhim. Hidimb was killed and Bhim ultimately agreed to marry her. Ghatotkach was born to them who played an important role in the Mahabharata from Pandavas' side. Hidimba took over the reign of Hidimb's kingdom. She was an accomplished ruler and after Bhim's departure, she reared her child efficiently and with care.

The Chitrangada episode in the Mahabharata is short. Chitrangada was the daughter of Chitravahana, the ruler of Manipur, during the Mahabharat era, was called Mekhele. Since the king did not have a male heir, he brought up his daughter like a son. Once during his wanderings in Manipur Arjuna saw Chitrangada. Enamoured of her he wished to marry her. Chitravahana agreed to the proposal on the condition that the son born to Chitrangada would be the ruler of Manipur. Arjuna lived in Manipur for three months and departed. Babhruvahana, also called Vabruvahana, was born to them whom Chitrangada brought up as a Pandava prince, inducting in him higher values and bravery of his father Arjuna.

Now, the questions before us are: how does Tagore look at the Chitrangada episode? How does folklore of Himachal Pradesh treat Hidimba? Tagore's Chitrangada is different and so is folklore's Hidimba. In the folk psyche, Hidimba is not the young princess; she is an old woman, they call her the "grandmother". The erstwhile princely family give her a place of reverence and during Dashehra festival, she is the supervising presence. Folklore has it that an ancestor of the present ruling dynasty came to the hills from the Mayapuri (near Haridwar). While wandering in the unknown mountainous region, feeling lost and tired, he was about to give up when he met an old woman carrying a bundle on her head. She looked fatigued. The young stranger offered to help her. The old woman was happy and before leaving, she revealed herself as the goddess and blessed him with success in establishing his kingdom. The young man defeated the local chieftains and became the ruler of Kullu area. In our interview with Shri Mahendra Singh of Kullu, he revealed that the royal family holds Devi Hidimba as family member. "She is the grandmother of our family. She is one of us. We celebrate the festival (Dushehra) together. If she were the deity, she would be a far off figure but since she is family, she is the loved one" (Bande and Chatterjee, 2011: 91). According to another folk tale, Hidimba is called "Hudka", she is married to Bhim, gives birth to a son and after Bhim's departure feeling sad and concerned for him she goes to Kurukshetra. Unfortunately, when Draupadi comes to touch her feet the holy ash that Draupadi has in her fist falls inadvertently on Hukda's feet and she is accidentally burnt to death. Draupadi is repentant, she accepts Hudka's son as her own (Kashyap, 1999: 128–133). Though different versions of the story come down to us because of the nature of orality, it cannot be denied that Hidimba or Hudka or Hirma are the different names of Hidimba and she is deified in the region.

As for Tagore's Chitra, the princess, the dance-drama *Chitrangada* projects her in all her feminine beauty and grace. The Tagore story is briefly thus: one day Chitra goes hunting in male attire, she encounters Arjuna, addresses him perfunctorily and pokes him with an arrow as would a boy, "With a careless tone,/To move away I asked him; but he/Neither moved nor looked at me./Thus provoked with anger impatient/Poked him I, straight with the tip of my arrow" (Tagore, Preface: 3). Arjuna looks bemused at her considering her a boy. When Chitra comes to know that the man whom she addressed so authoritatively is none else than Arjuna, she loses her heart to him. Next day she comes dressed as a woman and expresses her desire to marry him. Arjuna is not impressed by the plain woman. He tells her that he is under vow of celibacy. Thus rejected, Chitra invokes Madana (the god of love) and Vasanta (the god of spring and eternal youth) to help her and give her dazzling beauty for one day. But Madana and Vasanta grant her the boon of beauty for one year. Arjuna is smitten by her beauty; they stay together for some time but Chitrangada is not happy. What pinches her is the fact that Arjuna loves her borrowed beauty, not her real being. She reveals herself as Chitrangada in the end.

Leaving aside the twists and turns that folklore and Tagore give to the original tales, at the basic structure the two Mahabharata stories are strikingly similar – Hidimba is from the western Himalayan region whereas Chitrangada is from the eastern Himalayas. Both are princesses and tribals – Hidimba is from Rakshasa clan and Chitra from Maite of Manipur. Hidimba uses her esoteric powers to win over Bhim; Chitra uses divine intervention to get Arjuna. Both women rule over their respective kingdoms ably and rear their sons as single parents – a concept much debated in feminism today. But whereas Hidimba acquires the status of the patron goddess of Kullu-Manali area and is a significant presence in the psyche of the people, Chitrangada is not a folklore figure. It is poet's art that has made her immortal. The Hidimba Devi temple in Manali finds mention with due reverence in the travel writings of Europeans like A.P.H. Harcourt, Penelope Chetwode, Christina Noble, and others. The Dungri Hill where the Hidimba temple and a tiny shrine nearby dedicated to Ghatotkach are located is the tourist attraction of Manali. Thus, Hidimba lives as an embodiment of oral/folk tradition. *Chitrangada,* the dance drama is read and watched by hundreds of lovers of literature. So Chitra becomes a living presence in the mind of those who witness the show or read the play.

The point of departure in the representation of *Chitrangada* is Tagore's handling of the theme. His Chitra has little resemblance to the Chitrangada of the epic. Many a critic rues the fact that she is not Chitrangada at all, except for her name. In his preface to the first edition of the dance-drama Tagore admits that he has based his play on the Mahabharata episode but has modelled her to suit his thematic concerns. A careful reading of the preface shows two parallel ideas on which Tagore foregrounds the presentation of his protagonist – first, the balancing of the physical and spiritual aspects of love and second, the power of a woman's physical charm as against her inner strength. At some crucial point these aspects converge when Chitrangada stands forth as man's mental and spiritual equal, strengthening Tagore's concept of womanhood.

The preface also details how he chanced upon the theme. He was travelling from Shantiniketan to Kolkata on a beautiful spring day in the month of Chaitra. Along the railway track he spotted some blooming flowers. That led him to think of the short-lived nature of beauty. At that moment he was reminded of the tiny mango fruit forming out of the flowers on the mango tree in the courtyard. The fruit is the inner core of the flower and has strength to endure even when the flowers wither. Similarly, if a beautiful young woman has virtue and inner strength of character she can hold her lover through all the vicissitudes of life. There would be no satiation, no fatigue and no ennui in such a love. "Then and there, I was desirous of expressing the concept in the form of a drama and simultaneously I remembered the tale of Chitrangada in the Mahabharata." He further adds that this "tale was concealed in my mind in a different form for a long time. At last, I got the happy opportunity of writing it down in a quiet village in Orissa, called Padua".[1]

Tagore wrote *Chitrangada* in 1892. Its English translation was published in 1914. The late 19th century saw a period of Bengal renaissance with its movements like the Brahmo Samaj, women's education and other social changes ushering in rapid socio-cultural transformations. By and large, Tagore's views about women were bold and radical and he put them forth in his writings with unflinching frankness – expressing women's emotive love, extra-marital affairs, and frank articulation of their desire. In that, his representation of women is pre-eminently feminist, especially in his dance-dramas, though he is not a feminist by label. He was naturally sensitized over the plight of women and wanted to establish the individuality of women so as to ensure dignity, self-respect and sexual independence to them. In his novels and short stories he experimented with women's emancipation and sexual freedom and expressed his views on the gender question. In his dance-dramas Tagore's depiction of women is bold and experimental; the portrayals are ideologically oriented but the feminist inclinations are obvious.

In the *Mahabharata*, Arjun is "smitten" by Chitrangada's charm. But Tagore wanted to place a woman at the centre of his discourse; to give her the agency so as show her strength and by focusing on her ability to understand the temporary nature of beauty as against the depth of character to express his philosophy of life. By juxtaposing asceticism and sensuality in the play, he points the way to evolve a balance between the two. As K.R. Sriniwas Iyengar points out, Tagore, a unified man, a whole man was aware of the inter-connectedness of everything in the universe and was "an example to his country and a missionary to the West, who still points the way to final harmonizing of our differences and therefore toward our mutual strength" (Iyengar, 1965: 10). In Chitrangada, he rejects both – ascetic denial of life as well as the sensual denial of spirit. In doing so, Tagore's art weaves an altogether different picture – a girl of his time on the road to the 20th century India. Chitra becomes that metaphor, a metaphor for the esoteric in woman that underlines her power – power to hold, to let go and yet to bind. Arjuna becomes a ready prey. He looks pale as against her brilliance and Tagore brings forth the ultimate woman – delicately feminine and fiercely feminist, a female who recognizes her strength, takes on the responsibility for the "self" to emerge as the "female hero".

The concept of the "female hero" is discussed by feminist psychologists like Marcia Westkott and others of the Stone Center, Wellesley College. Westkott opines that when a woman gains consciousness of herself as an acting subject capable of exercising her own choice and ceases to depend on external validation, she overcomes her defensive reactions and the desire to hide. The desire to hide is the result of the accumulated fears which personality theorist Karen Horney calls "the intricate mixture of facts and fantasy" (Westkott, 1986: 20) that she is being mistreated because she is weak; this victim syndrome blocks her strength to exercise her choice and to confront actual abuse. Once she is able to deconstruct the dependent character structure that sustains this fantasy, she demystifies the past, acquires self-knowledge that she does not have to be extraordinary to be worthwhile. Even otherwise, myths and legends portray women as strong and able.

This is exactly what Chitrangada intrinsically understands. Her speech towards the end of the drama bears the above characteristics when she says:

> I am Chitrangada, the daughter of a king
> Not goddess to be worshipped and put up on a pedestal;
> Not one to be ignored, subjugated, and treated with indifference.
>
> If you deign to keep me by your side during good times and bad
> If you let me be a part of your endeavours,
> Then only you'll know me for
> Who I am.

"Who I am?" is not Chitra's question; it is probably her most intense self-assertion. Who is Chitrangada? Not the princess, not even the beautiful damsel, nor the ugly girl, but a woman who does not want to be forced into the ideals of womanhood. She does not want to be a paragon of virtues to be looked up to. She rejects being an object of desire or an insignificant being to be neglected. She is the representative of womanhood that would have men to treat them as human beings, to be accepted and recognized. She confesses without inhibitions, "Your child I am bearing" and assures Arjuna that if it be a boy, she will train him in heroic trends and at last, "when I send him to salute his father's feet as Arjuna the second, then my dearest, would you perceive my descent." The avowal to bring up her unborn son as a single parent is significant here. It is indicative of power. Culturally and historically, power is men's prerogative. But when Chitrangada exercises her personal power, she seems to derive it out of an implicit acceptance of her identity. Discussing social power, sociologists often argue that power rests with men; as regards women's power it is often unassigned or personal and born out of an individual's right to make decision about particular aspect of social life. In Chitrangada's case, there is legitimacy to her actions, not because she is a mythic figure but because of Rabindranath Tagore's poetic imagination and psychological insights into the inner workings of the feminine mind. Chitra is, as a critic says, "Tagore's another attempt to justify the role of woman, not only as a beautiful agent of nature but also as an interpreter of truth" (Jha, 2004: 137).

When Chitrangada asserts her identity, Arjuna is left spell-bound by the "bare simplicity of the truth". Tagore states in his preface to *Chitrangada* that he wanted to reconcile the dichotomy between beauty and character, sensuous love and its sublime form, "I do not know why suddenly and simultaneously I had also begun to think that if a beautiful young lady believed that she had conquered the heart of her beloved by virtue of the phenomenal emanation of youth, then she could accuse her youth and beauty of sharing in the principal part of her good fortune she acquired and show such contempt for her beauty as he would show for the co-wife of her beloved. This beauty is her outward possession as if got from Spring, the king of the seasons. It is a means of fulfilling bodily needs through a temporary spreading of fascination. If she had real strength of character within herself, then her gift to her beloved out of that fascination-free force would be a very valuable achievement for him and that would really help to a successful going on of the lives of the couple. That gift is the manifestation of the soul's real nature and even the last phase of life has neither fatigue not satiety and so, its brightness is not spoiled by a constant deposit of dusty layers of what is known as habit." The play ends with Arjuna's words, "Today blessed I am, my love."[2] Do we see here Arjuna overwhelmed? The statement is short and ambiguous, "Today blessed I am." What intentions do these words contain? Will he desert her in disdain? Or has he accepted her in totality? The open ending leaves much to speculate. It seems Tagore is not interested in revealing further. Nor is Chitrangada worried over the outcome of her revelation. She tells him the truth with a careless grace which seems to say, "here I am, what I am. Take it or leave it." She has made her choice. She has chosen the exact moment when to divulge the truth and she has offered her true self to his view – she is Chitrangada "feminine in affection and manly in valour".

Prior to this denouement, Arjuna was curious to know the real Chitrangada, the princess, because he heard stories of her valour. He was imagining Chitrangada "on horseback, holding the bridle in her left hand and bow and arrow in her right," not knowing that his unnamed beloved is the real Chitrangada. He wanted to meet that woman who is "Lakshmi and goddess Jagdatri" – one the feminine giver, the other the fearless fighter. Ultimately, Tagore shows that Chitra is not the lovelorn playmate of the great warrior-hero but she is his soul-mate, "A companion in happiness and sorrow". Tagore's concept of love accepts the demands of the body but this love also knows that there is real fulfilment and peace beyond the body's desire.

In the beginning of the play Chitrangada is so enamoured of the handsome Arjuna that she is desperate to earn his love. Her first encounter is significant for her as it makes her aware of her true identity – she is not a boy but a woman with a woman's heart in the boyish garb. "What I long forgot flashed into my mind," she says, "the moment/At that face I looked and that figure/Completely self-composed I saw, I knew that a woman I was" (4). Her only wish at this moment is to grab his attention but considering her as a boy, Arjuna looks at her in bemused silence. Next day, she discards the manly attire, dons a red dress and bangles and other befitting embellishment for a girl and tries to woo him. But Arjuna is not impressed; he rejects her. The second revelation comes to her that she is not beautiful. She is too spirited to let go the rejection as a bad dream. She seeks help from Madana, the god of love and Vasanta, the god of "Eternal Youth" to make her beautiful just for a day. She regrets that Arjuna feigned celibacy to reject her. "Abstinence of a man!" "Shame be on me, Shake even that I couldn't." She is accursed as she could not shake a Kshatriya's vow when a woman's beauty can unsettle even the sages. Let us admire her boldness when she frankly shares her intimate, amorous thought with Madana and Vasanta. They give her the boon for one year and happily she woos Arjuna afresh. Now it is Arjuna who is completely under her spell. Even this is not what she would have visualized. She chides him, "Go, go back: Go back hero; worship not a thing unreal, at its subtle feet sacrifice not your courage, valour and greatness" (20). She cannot tolerate that a great hero like him should fall a prey to something unreal. "How much do you know me? For whom do you forget yourself! For whom do you in a moment's impulse break your vow and make Arjuna Un-Arjuna?" But these are love's little games. Both come together and have a period of unsullied bliss.

Slowly, as the year draws to an end, Chitrangada becomes restless. She realizes that it is her "borrowed beauty" that has enamoured Arjuna. She feels guilty despite the physical pleasure of being with him. Things change for Arjuna as well. Rabindranath has astutely projected the male psyche. First, Arjuna loses all sense of judgement and wants to possess the beautiful damsel but within a year of their first encounter he seems tired of inactivity. So far he has been content to be in the young beauty's pleasurable company. But he realizes that he does not know anything about her. Now, he wishes to know more about his beloved's background – her home, her name, her kith and kin. She enjoys his discomfiture and teases him that she is like a drop of dew and has neither name nor a home. Arjuna is satiated with the kind of idle life he is leading and he thinks of his hunting trips with his brothers; next he feels inquisitive about princess Chitrangada. The forest Rover has described her as "parent in love, the queen mother in affection and the prince in valour". This feminine and feminist aspect of the princess now becomes the point of curiosity for Arjuna. The more he wants to know about her, the more his beloved (Chitrangada) discards his query with a careless, "what more would you like to hear about her?" She paints her as "ugly and uncouth", whose firm and strong arms can pierce a target with efficiency but "can't tie a hero with such a soft serpent noose". Here Arjuna is inquisitive like a child. He has learnt that princess Chitra is "feminine in affection/And manly in valour". Well, is Arjuna fed up with the feminine charm of his beloved, i.e., the beautiful Chitra? Is he looking for strength which he has pawned? Or is it just the curiosity of a questor? These and many such questions create as much conflict in the readers' mind as in Arjuna's.

Let us now look at Chitrangada's mental conflict. Chitra is young, and is in love. Her hero first ignores her taken in by her boyish dress and later rejects her not impressed by her plain looks. It hurts. Particularly painful is the fact that Arjuna may have thought of her as a shaky and embarrassed woman, wanting in self-control; a woman like any other ordinary woman. And surely, she not ordinary. Chitra is no fool. What she shares with Madana and Vasanta amply illustrates that she is constantly undergoing self-analysis. "I am not the kind of woman who with silent patience suffers constant pangs in night-long tears" and hides them in the morning. She is not like the thousand others. She is more than that. When read with Chitrangada's last summing up of herself these analytical remarks compare well with the feminist bent of mind. She knows she can "open the door of his heart and make a place there forever". But she has no time and she cannot wait. With borrowed beauty she wins him over, is in ecstasy intoxicated by the first flush of love.

Chitra has taken full advantage of her "borrowed" beauty, has asserted her sexuality unabashed and offered her body passionately. This portrayal of idyllic romance is commensurate with Tagore's idea of emotive love. But why does Tagore, after letting his Chitrangada enjoy voluptuous sensuality, shifts his focus to ethical values and from thence to spirituality? As a woman from mythology, Chitra has no inhibitions that bog down women in contemporary society. Jasbir Jain recognizes this fact – not about Tagore but in general – when she writes, "Interestingly enough, myths unconsciously project women as strong characters. Gods and men are presented open to temptation and in need of protection and support. They succumb to their circumstances, while women rooted in nature display the ability to stand alone and by themselves. When men fall the blame is thrown on others; when women fall they have only themselves to blame! They are called upon to develop their own resources" (Jain, 2002: 19).

In her intense relationship with Arjuna, Chitrangada recognizes two factors that perturb her – first, she has taken recourse to falsehood; and second, Arjuna loves her "borrowed beauty" and not her real self. The proud Chitrangada who had told Madana that she is not the one to shed tear like any other woman is now overwhelmed by her sense of guilt and lack. Arjuna does not love Chitra, he loves her shadow; Chitra is not fulfilled, it is her rival that is satisfied. She laments that her beauty is the "witch", the "co-wife" always ready to usurp her rightful place. "This false beauty will fall off soon like petals of a flower over-bloomed." A realization of her self-worth dawns on her as she admits, "superior I am to this disguise." She resolves to reveal herself to Arjuna. If he departs in disgust, she would not mind; if she were to die of heart-break, she would welcome it. Either way she is prepared to face the consequences than living in deceit.

Twice does she change her disguise – once discarding her male attire and then abandoning her "unreal beauty"; the first instance she discovers her woman's heart, and in the second, she becomes her actual self. Of these which Chitrangada is real? The one who wandered in the jungle as a man unaware of her female body? Or the ugly one who disdains her looks? Or the beautiful one who allures Arjuna? The question is not whether Chitrangada is beautiful or not; the issue is the conflict, the tension to re-define her real self, her womanhood that makes Chitrangada really desirable. The one donning man's dress is the saviour Chitra; the beautiful one is the thirsty Chitra; but the one who reveals herself in all inner beauty of womanhood is the real Chitra – Arjuna's equal in companionship, the mother of his valiant son, and feminine in affection but manly in valour. It is this Chitra that Arjuna is fascinated with at the end.

Tagore brings his protagonist to the centre of his discourse with a wholly new sensibility. One of the significant aspects of Chitrangada's character is her determination to get what she wants, to go to any length to fulfil her desire; yet she is not deceptive, nor is she gullible. She exercises her power and agency in her choices in life and as a self-assured, mature woman conscious of her selfhood and female desire she takes full responsibility of her actions and their results. Her journey is a spiritual journey through desire to discover her own self and her spiritual growth.

When we read the three changes Chitrangada undergoes, in the context of feminism, we are reminded of the three segments that Ellen Showalter has given – feminine, feminist and female. Feminist psychologists also envision these three categories. Feminism is the period of imitation, of submission; feminist is that of anger and the search for new paradigms and the female stage is the one of recognition of strength as a woman. Chitrangada as the boyish entity is in the stage of imitation followed by her surrender to Arjuna; she is feminist in her anger against her disguise and the female self when she recognizes her female power.

Chitra made choices – she has chosen her husband, she has openly invoked Vasanta for beauty, she has used her charm to the full, she has realized its temporary appeal and finally she has chosen the time to reveal the truth.

Reading a text based on mythological episodes require some probing into the portrayal of women in the original. In her paper entitled, "Mahabharata through the Eyes of Women" Kavita Sharma opines that in the great epic the central issue that stands out is their sexually defined roles. The structure of the society is patriarchal and women's sexuality is regulated by patriarchal norms. But the paradox of the situation is that "Although women gain status through husbands and sons, they create a remarkable space for themselves within the limits set for them, almost subverting patriarchal order" (Sharma, 2002: 112). This can be substantiated by the examples of Chitra and Hidimba – independent, self-confident and bold. These are their female qualities but they do not lack feminine appeal – attractiveness, motherly feelings and submission. Another paradox emerges here: it is through their sons that they gain name – Vabruvahana/Babhruvahana and Ghatotkach. Each assures her husband/lover that in his absence, she will rear the son as a true Pandava. Ghatotkach is as brave, burly and brawny as both his parents – Hidimba and Bhim; Vabruvahana/Babhruvahana is as brave and expert a soldier as his father and mother – Arjuna and Chitra. The women perform their motherly roles meticulously and show the spirit of sacrifice when they send their sons to fight.

Interestingly, what is the role or attitude of the fathers? We do not know about Bhim's feeling during Ghatotkach's fight but

Arjuna, when confronted with his son Vabruvahana/Babhruvahana challenges him to fight with him (Arjuna) as a king and not supplicate as a father. The story stretches to the point when Arjuna is killed in his fight with his son, revived by Ulupi, Arjuna's wife and Chitra's co-wife.[3] But these facts are not narrated in the texts/lore we are discussing. Some critics like Rollo and Thompson object to Chitra's presentation by Tagore on the ground that she seems to be existing only for man's pleasure – nurturing his child, rearing him like his family, not hers, and preparing the boy to render service to the father (quoted in Sen Gupta, 150).

Critics were not comfortable with Tagore's representation of Chitrangada. Even though new concepts were emerging and the society's ideas about women were changing, the open romance as depicted by Tagore was jarring for the socio-cultural rules of propriety. Lines like "drink-drink from these lips" and many others were unacceptable. Moreover, the absence of parents and society in the play was also criticized. There are only four characters – Arjuna, Chitra, Vasanta and Madana. The Rover appears briefly in the middle of the play. But he is an important link because he tells Arjuna about their princess Chitrangada who is "parent in love,/The queen mother in affection and the prince in valour". This becomes the turning point in the play.

The representation of Chitra and Hidimba needs to be seen from another angle too. Feminism, we agree by now, does not mean breaking social norms but it stands for creating a social structure where women are free and able to take decision and make choices. The social settings in which the two heroines move are conducive to freedom. They roam about freely in the jungle, are fearless, have choices and the society seems to have accepted these norm. Their feminine body does not become a hindrance rather it is a site of pleasure, love and fruitful fulfilment. Both history and myth signify the past but they have their importance. As Jasbir Jain posits, "deconstructing the past can help us retrieve our lost bearings and identities. It provides a sense of continuity and imparts a sense of tradition. The past is important on another count, its influence has been internalized by generations of people; it needs to be reviewed as a process of self-renewal" (2002: 15). The Mahabharata stories of Chitrangada and Hidimba and their folk and literary versions can help us evaluate our stand on feminism – the frank expression of the urge of the body, single parenthood, acceptance of girl child/woman as a ruler and the ability of the female to know where to draw the line. On close reading the stories reveal a beautiful balance of the female and feminine. In a *New York Times* article the writer puts it beautifully, "Chitra, however is a surprise. We did not look for an oriental even though a seer, to write a book (especially twenty-five years ago when this was written) that might serve as evangel to the most advanced among modern Occidental women – yet this is just what Rabindranath Tagore has done. By "advanced", be it understood, we are not referring to that group of biological freaks to whom the term is sometimes applied, but to the sane and sincere women who are endeavoring – whether by advocating political equality with men or by opposing it is a detail – to secure the highest good for their sex" (March 22, 1914).

It may be mentioned before we end this paper that Tagore endowed his Chitra with a fiery beauty, accomplishment and intellect. She is just irresistible. It was this woman of inner strength that Pandit Jawaharlal Nehru was fond of. He saw in Chitrangada a symbol around which a new gender construction could be built. In a beautifully written article on this aspect, Reba Som points out that Tagore projected an integrated image of woman's sexuality and her identity as man's comrade in the sphere outside home. The central theme of Chitrangada's philosophy is that she may not accept being ignored, nor being placed on a pedestal. She visualizes being his companion in life sharing equal responsibilities. Nehru saw this as an indication of gender equality breaking all mental blocks and attitudinal prejudices (Som, 2009: 34–54).

Notes

1. See "Tagore's Preface to Chitrangada" in *A Complete Translation of Tagore's Chitrangada*. Trans. Birendra Nath Roy. Calcutta: Sribhumi Publishing Co., 1957 (edition). Tagore elaborately states how he chanced to think of the theme and how his is not the story of Chitrangada but of sublime love beyond its physical aspects.
2. In the Birendra Nath Roy's translation that I am using for this paper the final words are, "Today blessed am I, my love." But some other translations have different versions like, "Beloved, my life is full."

3. Ulupi was the daughter of the Naga king Kauravya who was infatuated with Arjuna while he was in Manipur. With her esoteric powers she induced Arjuna to marry her. Arjuna-Chitrangada's son Vabruvahana (also Babruvahana) held the Ashwamedh horse, fought with Arjuna at his behest and killed him. As Arjuna lay slain, it was Ulupi who was called. With her supernatural powers she restored him to life.

References

Bande, Usha and Him Chatterjee. *Forts and Palaces of Himachal Pradesh*. Jaipur: Literary Circle, 2011.

Iyengar, K.R.S. *Rabindranath Tagore: A Critical Introduction*. New Delhi: Sterling Publishers, 1965.

Jain, Jasbir. *Writing Women Across Cultures*. Jaipur: Rawat Publications, 2002.

Jha, Gauri Shankar. "Feminine Sway in Tagore's Plays." Ed. Mohit K. Ray. *Studies in Rabindranath Tagore*. Vol. II. New Delhi: Atlantic Publishers, 2004.

Kashyap, Padamchandra. *Aitihasik Yevam Pauranik Kathyen*. New Delhi: Himalaya Pustak Bhandar, 1999.

Sen Gupta, S.C. *The Great Sentinel: A Study of Rabindranath Tagore*. Calcutta: A. Mukherjee & Co. (year not mentioned).

Sharma, Kavita. "Mahabharata Through the Eyes of Women." Eds. Malashri Lal and Sukrita Paul Kumar. *Women's Studies in India: Contours of Change*. Shimla: IIAS, 2002, 104–123.

Shaw, Harry. *Concise Dictionary of Literary Terms*. New York: McGraw Hill, 1976.

Som, Reba. "Chitrangada Not Sita: Jawaharlal Nehru's Model for Gender Equation." Eds. Malashri Lal and Namaita Gokhale. *In Search of Sita*. New Delhi: Penguin, 2009, 34–54.

Tagore, Rabindranath. *Chitrangada*. Trans. *A Complete Translation of Tagore's Chitrangada*. Birendra Nath Roy. Calcutta: Sribhum Publishing Co., 1957.

The New York Times, "Tagore's Ideal Woman." March 22, 1914.

Westkott, Marcia. *The Feminist Legacy of Karen Horney*. New Haven: Yale University Press, 1986.

5 Humour as Resistance

The Female Voice in Folklore

> A keen sense of humour helps us to overlook the unbecoming, understand the unconventional, tolerate the unpleasant, overcome the unexpected, and outlast the unbearable.
>
> —Billy Graham

In his book *Humour and Laughter* Mahadev Apte posits that women do not lack a sense of humour, nor is men's sense of humour superior, only the prevalent social norms and cultural values prevent them from utilizing their talents to the full. Women lack courage because of the constraints of social acceptability:

> First, women's humour reflects the existing inequality between the sexes, not so much in its substance as in the constraints imposed on its occurrence, on the techniques used, on the social settings in which it occurs, and on the kind of audience that appreciates it. Second, these constraints generally, but not necessarily universally, stem from the prevalent cultural values that emphasize male superiority and dominance together with female passivity and create role models for women in keeping with such values and attitudes. (Apte, 1985: 69)

In literary works humour is generated by using satire, humorous dialect, comic irony, hyperbole and understatement (meiosis). In written literature, a writer is always at a disadvantage when it comes to expressing humour because unlike an actor on the stage, he/she cannot and does not have the facility to use voice inflection and bodily movements to cause laughter. But, in oral literature, coming particularly from women and the subalterns, this limitation is got over and one finds rich treasure of humour in folk forms. The popular notion that women are frail and humourless because they are the producers of sentimental literature is challenged by folklore. In the Indian context, women's folk songs, tales, dances and other forms are rich with humour and laughter.

Wit, humour and repartee are the best ways to diffuse anger, enliven the atmosphere and relieve tension. "Laughter," said a wit, "is the best medicine without side effect." Men often allege that women in general lack sense of humour; they have no wit, nor the ability to repartee. To such a contention, I can only give a rejoinder by referring to Lady Astor's repartee. Once when she was speaking in the House of Lords, a heckler, not happy that a woman should have the floor tried to be witty, "By the way, Lady, tell us how many toes a pig has." Taken aback, the lady paused awhile but recovering her wit instantly, she replied, "Why ask me, gentleman? Take off your shoes and count for yourself." One can imagine the discomfiture of the heckler taking his seat amid guffaws of laughter.

In the field of literature, women's writing is generally dubbed as "that sentimental stuff," which may express anger or show aggression but never a streak of light-heartedness that may produce a chuckle or two. It is because, men contend, women can be the subject of humour but never its creator. Nothing can be farther from the truth. One just has to have a look at women's folk songs to understand the subtle sense of humour with which they have learnt over the centuries to resist ill-treatment, subjugation and the dominant discourse.

Folk songs have a vast reservoir of humour generated from everyday observations, the stress and strains of life, its tears and laughter. Women's cloistered in existence so far has its moments of fun and frolic when they gathered for some ceremony and experience sense of freedom for a couple of hours. It is then that their songs and dances gather momentum; the juxtaposition of true-untrue situations and the humorous portrayal of the in-laws spread much mirth and cheer. These songs or tales have evolved over the years, subtle modes of resistance to hegemonic forms of traditional hierarchy. Since speech is equated with agency and power, silencing women and imposing restrictions on their movements to the domestic space has always been a means to dismissing their power. Kamala Visweswaran posits in one of her papers on subaltern speeches that the idea of "speaking subject" is central to the philosophies of humanism because the normative operation of subject position disguises its dependency on relations with others by claiming for itself a "self-authorizing" and autonomous agency. Visweswaran further claims, "Speech as agency, invokes the idea of self-originating presence, so that conversely, lack of speech is seen as absence" (Visweswaran, 1997: 91).

The robust sense of humour can be seen in the Gidda of Punjab. It is a lively, all-woman performance popular in the state. The Gidda verses, called *Bolian,* have been the best way through which girls and women have flung humour at their husbands, in-laws and others. The verses sung with pleasant and vigorous dancing steps bring out the whims and fancies of the mother-in-law, the eccentricities of the father-in-law, the peculiarities of the husband, and as the other girls/women pick up singing, they all enjoy the mental images that are familiar to each in her own peculiar way. These pictures which could not have been much different from what they know or experience are tickling. Each singer has a short tale of woe to tell or it could be an account of a mischief played to avenge a reproach, as in the following couplet:

> Chaulan da pani ni main vede wich doliyan,
> Anda-janda phisla gaya,
> nikal gaya ni meri rondi da hansa,
> nikal gaya ni meri rondi da hansa

(I threw the water of the half-cooked rice in the courtyard near the threshold and saw passers-by slipping and falling. I could not help laughing despite my tears.) Obviously, the girl was unhappy, maybe she was weeping over some bitter words. But she found a way to take revenge. It is crude but the discomfiture of her in-laws' family delights her.

After marriage a girl becomes the "other" for her natal family but the ties cannot be severed. She visualizes all that is good, desirable, and even imperial to belong to her parental family; all that is bad or beggarly describes her in-laws' family. In one of the

Marathi folk songs, the "vaid" who comes with a message from her parents is described as richly clad, showing not only their family status but also the prosperity of her native village. He is wearing gold brocaded dhoti and turban, his shoes are jari studded and he is carrying a silver plated walking stick whereas, the "Vaid" from the in-laws is clad in a dirty dhoti, torn turban and worn out shoes. This is how the newly-wed elevates herself and feels empowered as against the constant taunts of the in-laws regarding her impoverished parents. A similar song in the Kangra region of Himachal Pradesh describes the poorly dressed messenger.

Once the girl departs to her husband's "home", it becomes difficult for her to get permission to visit her parents. But once back to her natal home she shows unwillingness to go back. Her dilly-dallying to accompany the messenger who has come from the in-laws is shown in many a song of women from almost all regions. In one Gidda *Boli* the girl refuses to go back on small pretexts, so flimsy and hilarious are her arguments that the entire group cannot help billowing in laughter. Similarly, in a Marathi song the girl sings: "Tell them I don't want your gifts, tell them I refuse to come; Brother, unleash our ferocious and hairy dog on the fellow." This rebellious spirit produces fun and the girls singing in chorus enjoy the imaginary plight of the messenger chased by the dog. But they all are aware of the reality that one can hardly say "no" when summoned back. Thus, by substituting imaginary pleasure for the protean reality, the song helps to dissolve tension in laughter.

The abode of the in-laws is an unpleasant place and a girl from Kangra tells her mother:

> Chhalian di roti ni amma,
> Khane jo dende,
> Hathi dende fafru da saag,
> Ammaji main naiyyu basna.

(They give her coarse bread and a vegetable made of wild grass to eat, so she does not wish to go.) The whims and fancies of the mother-in-law and her cruelty also become a butt of ridicule. One Gidda *Boli* says:

Saas meri ne dibbi bheji,
Dibbi de vich naag,
Naag peya jag
Naag tan main bach gayi,
Es Gabru de bhag

(My mother-in-law sent me a box containing a serpent. Unsuspecting, when I opened the lid the serpent awoke. But I am saved because of the good fortune of my husband.)

In one Kangri song the woman refers to her *saas* as a ball of fire and her sister-in-law as the flash of lightning. A Marathi song satirizes her miserly in-laws who ask her to get half-a-paisa worth of oil. The woman does not want to make such a beggarly purchase, because she comes from a wealthy family; she is loaded with the heavy jewelry given by her parents. But she cannot say no, she buys half-a-paise worth of oil and recounts satirically what all she did with the oil: the entire family has a good oil bath; somehow the remaining oil gets spilled; it starts flowing towards the village boundary; a camel coming that way is drowned in that flow and an elephant has to swim across it. It is interesting to hear the song which sings thus:

Urlele tel jhkoon thevla,
Landoricha paya lagla
Veshi paryant oghal gela
Unta ala vahun gela
Hatti ala, pohun gela

In the alien atmosphere of her new home, the only succour can be the husband. But if the husband is a dumb wit or mismatched, the girl's life becomes miserable. Making fun of the situation a Gidda *Boli* runs thus:

Saas meri ne Kainta gadaya,
mainu kendi pa kude,
Ranzha mera loon ghotna,
pava keede chaa kude

In sum, the song satirizes mismatch when a beautiful girl is married to an ungainly husband. The mother-in-law to placate her gets a fine piece of jewelry and asks her to wear it but the woman asks her friends as to what enthusiasm she has to decorate herself tied as she is to a dwarf. In a Marathi song the woman sings of her moron husband. She has no incentive to cook dainties because her husband cannot understand worth of the delicacies she cooks.

To say that women always take negative points to excite humour at the cost of their husband's household or cash in on the deformity or defect of the people around them would be erroneous. Humour can be generated on simple everyday incidents. Let us take, for example, this charming *Boli* which recounts how the husband comes home with a pumpkin and the woman tells her friends, he brought a pumpkin (probably, not a favourite vegetable) but she prepared it with so much dexterity that the husband came twirling his mustache.

A Marathi folktale brings home the truth that a jawain (son-in-law) should not overstay in his in-laws' home. The story runs thus: a young son-in-law decides to visit his in-laws and bring back his wife from her parents' home. As he is about to leave, his mother tells him, "Do not stay till the edge" (Kathale lageto rahu nako). He does not understand the enigmatic words. He enjoys their extraordinary hospitality and stays on, never wishing to leave the place. Slowly, the in-laws get fed up but they cannot be openly hostile. One day, the mother-in-law prepares a dish which he likes immensely. At night, he goes to the kitchen to eat more of it. Utensils fall down and make a crash. People come rushing. Fearful of being detected, the son-in-law hides in the enclosure of sheep and his clothes are covered with their wool. At night thieves come to steal sheep. They find a fat sheep and carry it in their sack. On reaching an isolated spot they quarrel over the share of the loot. From the gunny bag the man blurts out, "My share, my share!" Taking him to be a ghost the thieves run away, and somehow the distraught young Jawain reaches home. This story of the discomfiture of the son-in-law is told with great relish and is enjoyed by all – old women, young women and children as it frames the son-in-law who overstays his welcome.

Some of the songs represent women's oral traditions that have helped them compose their own mythologies and be empowered. One of the most eloquent examples of women's humour can be seen in the *Tota-Maina Kissa* in which the female never lags behind in leg pulling. She is more than a match for the parrot's (that is man's) wit and sarcasm. Women's songs and tales may not carry the authoritative versions of the traditional male canonical writing but they consistently compose ironic and subversive commentaries on their life. These folk songs are some of the ways women have derived to mock convention and the dominant discourse of patriarchy. Their narrative potency lies in their ability to satirize the surroundings without hurting directly. Humour thus becomes an effective tool of resistance.

The cliche that women are humourless and that they to not have a sense of the comic is usually countered by the feminists with tongue-in-cheek rejoinders. Some contend that had women not had sense of the comic they would not have put up with men; others retaliate that the things that tickle men to laughter are often bizarre and absurd enough not to humour women. Humour denotes a capacity for laughter and not exploitation of language to attack and caricature another human being or her status. Language and culture both being patriarchal structures are male prerogatives and the society/culture does not expect women to use the tool of humour, for the sense of the comic borders on the un-lady-like use of language which may be corroding to the existing sense of the feminine. In an elaborate paper on women's verbal and non-verbal communication, Nancy M. Henley et al. opine that males and females "move in a context of sexual inequality and strongly differentiated behavioural expectations. Because interaction with others always involve communication of some sort, verbal and nonverbal, it is through communication that much of our pattern of sexist interaction is learned and perpetuated" (1990: 394–395). Since body language communicates power and status, in domestic performances of folk practices or story telling or dances and songs occupying more space and attention is women's domain of showing more control and dominance. When Dorothy Parker points out that for humour "there must be courage," she has a point: women do not show humour because they are not strong and self-reliant. Men laugh at their cost because women are unable to laugh at themselves (Parker quoted in Walker, 1981: 5–22).

Marathi saint poet Bahinabai's mother-in-law was a highly witty woman. Through her jokes and wisecracks she would tell even the bitterest truths to teach or castigate others. In one of her verses Bahinabai writes:

> "Naava thevi awaghyala! Kari sarvanchi nakkal!
> Hasvata, hasvata, shikvi re akkal"

(She criticizes everybody, she mimics everybody, she makes us laugh but with her wit and humour she teaches a lot of sense.)

This is exactly what women's humour does – put sense in others, show them their weak points and resist the social structure to make space for themselves.

Laughter is a social phenomenon and is controlled by the hegemony but Frances Gray believes that laughter, like nuclear energy, has no opinion – positive or negative, about *status quo* but it has power and potential as a force for change. This force exists in direct relationship to the intensity and commitment with which it is used by the forces of change or stasis. Women have always contrived to create laughter, in public and in private, but since it has been read in the light of masculine theories or its existence has been denied so long, it is necessary now to reckon it as a force and provide a theory of female laughter (Gray, 1994: 33).

References

Apte, Mahadev L. *Humour and Laughter: An Anthropological Approach*. New York: Cornell University Press, 1985.

Gray, Frances. *Women and Laughter*. London: Macmillan, 1994.

Henley, Nancy M., Mykol Hamilton and Barrie Throne. "Womanspeak and Manspeak: Sex Differences and Sexism in Communication, Verbal and Nonverbal." *Issues in Feminism: An Introduction to Women's Studies*. Ed. Sheila Ruth. London: Mayfield, 1990.

Visweswaran, Kamala. "Small Speeches, Subaltern Gender: Nationalist Ideology and Its Historiography." *Subaltern Studies IX: Writings on South Asian History and Society*. Eds. Shahid Amin and Dipesh Chakrabarty. Delhi: Oxford University Press (1994) 1997, 83–125.

Walker, Nancy. "Wit, Sentimentality and the Image of Women in the Nineteenth Century." *American Studies*, Vol. 22, No. 2 (Fall, 1981), 5–22.

6 The Con(Textual) Contours

A Study of Four Short Stories

> We cannot write like the English. We should not.
>
> —Raja Rao

The above two short sentences from his "Foreword" *Kanthapura* show an undercurrent of pride that Raja Rao displayed in writing as an Indian, like an Indian. Although here he was talking of the use of English for creative writing, the words could well be applied to thematic and other concerns of Indian English writing.

"Indianness", of course, is an all-inclusive term and engulfs our entire culture, our traditional conception of human life, social structure, spiritual conditions, value system and the ideas and ideals that have moved us since time immemorial, forming our character and sensibility. To this, we add the present-day influences of the processes of modernity, industrialization, consumerism, feminism and globalization. The literature produced in modern India, be it in English or in regional languages, cannot but be influenced by these processes. To deny the existence of the current forces would be unrealistic.

Writing about the "Indianness" of Indian literature written in English, K.R. Srinivas Iyengar wrote as far back as the 1960s that what makes Indo-Anglian literature an Indian literature is the quality of its Indianness in choice of themes and the treatment given to the subject matter:

> It stands to reason that what makes Indo-Anglian literature an Indian literature and not just a ramshackle outhouse of English

> literature, is the quality of its Indianness – in choice of subject, in the texture of thought and play of sentiment, in the organization of material and in the creative use of language. To be an Indian in thought and feeling and emotion and experience, yet to court the graces and submit to the discipline of English for expression, is a novel experiment in creative mutation. (Iyengar, 1972: 5)

V.K. Gokak voices almost similar sentiments when he asserts that the Indianness of Indian writing consists in the writers' intense awareness of his entire culture; and C.D. Narasimhaiah feels that as long as the "operative sensibility" is Indian, it is Indian literature, "Indian writing in English is to me primarily part of the literatures of India, in the same way as the literatures written in various regional languages are or ought to be ... so long as the operative sensibility of the writer is essentially Indian it will be Indian literature" (Narasimhaiah, 1969: ix). By "operative sensibility" he means the writer's awareness that the Indian versus Western issue needs to be examined in relation to the sense of cultural orientation. The question of Indianness continued to worry critics half a century after the Independence. Writing in 1998 about the anxieties of writers in maintaining Indianness in their writing in English Meenakshi Mukherjee states that the Indian writers in English are conscious of the tag of Indianness because of the baggage of culture, tradition and ethos that he/she has to carry; which is not so with a regional language writer. It is because "the 'tradition' of Indian writing in English is discontinuous; there is no genealogy that can be traced satisfactorily, however much scholars might attempt to create one" (Mukherjee, 1998: 85). Discussing Raja Rao, Amitav Ghosh, Vikram Seth and others who are not bothered about projecting an Indian identity but whose works are Indian all the same without any proclamation Mukherjee further points out that "these writers have successfully manipulated the fabulist narratives and postmodernist mode with local legends and popular fables as mythicising contemporary reality" (89) and have never been defensive about their choice of language.

"Indianness" of Indian literature can be mapped on three levels: the creative use of the English language; the technique of story-telling adopted by the author; and the cultural milieu within which the author sets his story and builds his characters. These aspects have unlimited possibilities and can be debated for hours no end. I am, therefore, limiting the purview of this article to textual analysis of four short stories, viz., Dina Mehta's "Absolution", Jhumpa Lahiri's "The Treatment of Bibi Halder", Bhabani Bhattacharya's "The Faltering Pendulum", and Khushwant Singh's "Karma".[1]

The author is aware that these stories are not "recent" in the strict sense of the word, but be it granted that they are fairly recent in that all are written in the 20th century India. Further, the choice of the stories has not been made at random, but with a specific design in mind: the author interested in exploring how the cultural consciousness of the story writers to build up their themes and sketch out their characters, the actions and reactions of their characters, and the response they generate to a given situation. Moreover, the range covered, though not all-inclusive, is broad enough to give us a glimpse of some major social fields – the changes wrought in by modern forces and modern Indian woman's resistance; the social set up which disregards a woman's needs and violates her individuality; the loneliness and suffering brought about by social taboos; and the fate of a marginalized man. Stories from Hindi and other Indian languages where necessary to establish a point or two would also be referred to.

Critics have often called Dina Mehta's "Absolution" as the modern "Sitayana" as against the traditional *Ramayana*. It is the story of a young, docile and submissive wife who, after suffering long from her husband's infidelity, pays him back in his own coin. The author has chosen the mythological names Ram and Sita for her characters, probably with an express desire to show that if the modern Ram is not the prototype of his mythological namesake, there is no need for his Sita to be a model of purity. Thus, by subverting the Sita-myth, Dina Mehta recounts the story sometimes with tongue-in-check style and sometimes matter-of-factly, tills the reader smiles with the protagonist at the husband's discomfiture.

Ram, an executive in an office, is an incorrigible womanizer and is proud of his unconventional outlook. Interestingly, after every act of infidelity Ram comes with flowers in the morning, places them in a vase on the dining table as if to say "these are for you" and to condone his infidelity. Significantly and symbolically, he brings carnations (recall the love lyric, "Roses are red, violets are blue, carnations are sweet, and so are you"). The story opens with a party where Ram openly flaunts Evelyn, his chic secretary, a new addition to his list of women. He looks at his wife "with cold, amused eyes" as if to declare, "I am free of all cliché, conventions, formalized gestures." But little does Ram realize that the "permissive order" gives as much freedom to the female as to the male, and that even his "slow, obedient and old-fashioned" wife could partake of the liberty. Dilip, her husband's bachelor colleague, awakens Sita to her miserable lot. Once when Ram leaves for a couple of days on the pretext of going on a tour, Dilip visits Sita, recounts the truth about Ram's whereabouts and makes his intentions clear. After initial (but weak) resistance, Sita decides to suffer humiliation no more and surrenders to Dilip. Next morning she wards off all sense of guilt, anger and remorse from her conscience by consciously enjoying her boldness. The act has not only liberated her but has also transformed her. The story ends on a triumphant note. Ram on his return notices fresh carnations in the vase at its usual place on the dining table. To his query, "who sent you those?" her retort is, "They are not for me. I ordered them for you." Then she adds cheerfully, "Aren't they lovely?" and seals his fate.

It would be preposterous to believe that Dina Mehta, in letting Sita fall from the ideal, has sanctioned adultery. The narrator-protagonist does not jump into the extra-marital experience frivolously. Sita has ages of conditioning behind her. As Dilip says, she is the "docile, chaste and devoted Hindu wife" ... with that age-long tradition of "womanly faithfulness and days of long-suffering patience, all that disarming passivity," forcing her to conform to the stereotype. She finds herself attracted to Dilip, but she scrupulously keeps him at a distance. Only when Ram gives the final humiliating blow to her womanhood by his deceitfulness, does she react sharply, and takes her revenge.

Though marriage enjoins fidelity on both the partners, socially it is incumbent upon the woman to be a model of faithfulness, purity and submissiveness. The first person narration reveals Sita's side of the story. In order to mitigate her hurt Sita endeavours to believe that her husband sends her flowers after every act of infidelity because he feels guilty. The flowers, she says, are an offering "at my shrine in expiation of his guilty deeds" and the offering signifies "asking for absolution". This is Sita's version, but considering Ram's self-centredness, it is doubtful whether he could ever have been burdened with guilt. Rather, he enjoys Sita's distress. Sita too offers him flowers but she makes no plea for "absolution," nor does she appear conscience-stricken. In fact, she does not want to lose the "splendour" of her decision by distorting it as "something graceless". Hers was a conscious step meant to teach her husband a lesson. She acquires a "radiance, a singular warmth" after the night. Sita retaliates with remarkable strength: it is almost like Shakespeare's Caliban saying to his master: "you taught me language, and my profit on't/Is, I know how to curse." Woman, like Caliban, is trained for docility, dependence, and when rejected she may react and use the master's tool to take revenge.

Ironically, in Sita's rebellion, there is less feminist rage than what Elaine Showalter terms, the urge for imitation. She does what Ram is guilty of – adultery. She succumbs to the charms of Dilip. Like Nayantara Sahgal's Sim in *The Day in Shadow,* Sita allows a strong male (rather a male chauvinist) to dominate her. Both Sita and Sim are mute before the tirades of their male friends. Dilip shakes Sita into awareness and Raj is always up against the "self-effacing" Hindu character. Rebellion against husband's extra-marital forays is not new to literature. Savitri in R.K. Narayan's *The Dark Room* shows her resentment by walking out of her home. But there is marked difference between Sita ("Absolution") and Savitri *(The Dark Room).* Savitri does not (and she cannot) think of retaliating in the manner Sita does. Interestingly both the names – Savitri and Sita – symbolize the Indian ideal womanhood but Narayan, a male writer, writing in the 1960s shows the female anger without letting her fall from grace; Dina Mehta subverts the Sita-myth in the postmodern stance, and by giving her heroine more freedom, tries to show the attitudinal changes in the social psyche. However, before reaching at any conclusive understanding of the two situations, we must remember the basic positing of the two protagonist – Savitri is from a small town and is tradition-oriented; Sita is from the modern elite environment of a big town, possibly the mega-city, Bombay (Mumbai).

Moreover, Dina Mehta's Sita need not slam the door on her husband and walk out, nor does she need to be apologetic, ashamed or guilty. She is very much like modern Nora painted by Clare Booth Luce in her play "A Doll's House, 1970," wherein her modern American Nora says, "I'm not bursting with self-confidence, Thaw. I do love you. And I also need ... a man. So I'm not slamming the door. I am closing it .... Very ... gently." Sita makes an explicit assertion of her individuality. Whether right or wrong, her step has made it clear to her man that even passivity has numerous possibilities, and that a woman, though docile, cannot be a doormat.

Jhumpa Lahiri who took the literary world by a storm by winning the Pulitzer Prize for Fiction in 2000 for her *Interpreter of Maladies* has given a realistic portrayal of the female urge for sexual fulfilment in "The Treatment of Bibi Haldar". It is a saddening story of an epileptic young woman who suffers when her craving for marriage is thwarted because of her ailment. Bibi Haldar has everything negative to be a desirable commodity in the marriage-market: no looks so to speak of, no education, no parents, and above all she is epileptic and a simpleton at that. The story opens graphically, "For a greater number of her twenty-nine years, Bibi Haldar suffered from an ailment that baffled family, friends, priests, palmists, spinsters, gem therapists, prophets and fools" (158). Further, the newspaper matrimonial advertisement is of no help in getting her a husband as her crafty cousin worded it rather unsympathetically: *Girl, unstable, height 152 centimeters, seeks husband*. The slyness of her cousin and his wife juxtaposed with the naivety of the unfortunate Bibi Haldar helps in creating the required ambiance of the social set up. Bibi Haldar's cousin and his wife ill-treat her, extract a lot of work from her and finally considering her a burden, they forsake her. Bibi Halder manages to stay alive with her own resources and the kindness of the neighbours. Somehow, she fulfills her desire, begets a son (from whom, nobody knows) and is miraculously cured of her ailment. The story, Jhumpa Lahiri says in an interview, is based on a woman she knew living in her neighbourhood in Calcutta (now Kolkata).

The depiction of the cultural, social and familial milieu is realistic, with helpful and sympathetic neighbours showing enough fellow feeling and pity towards the unfortunate being, juxtaposed with the selfish kin devoid of feelings to evoke the readers' amiable response. The first paragraph graphically portrays the synthesis of superstitious beliefs and modern scientific approach. It also speaks of human desperation at an incurable disease which forces people to try all cures irrespective of religious faith. At subtler level, one can spot violence towards woman in the treatment meted out to Bibi Haldar. Helpless women like Bibi Haldar are victimized not only by their families but also by the society.

Of the nine stories in the collection *Interpreter of Maladies,* four have Indian setting. Out of these, two, "The Treatment of Bibi Halder" and "A Real Darwan" show situational clash and give voice to the subaltern and put forward important points to be considered. Textual evidence bears out that *Interpreter of Maladies* is replete with Indianness and makes a convincing reading. What Chitra Banerjee Divakaruni, accounting for the attraction multicultural themes hold for her readers, remarked can well be mentioned here. Divakaruni opines that most women: India, American, and even immigrant women, feel interested in the fiction written by Indian women because they are curious to know the life and life patterns of the Indian/Asian women. "Many of us articulate in our books the deepest fear and trauma faced by women in India and here – and show them emerge, at least in many cases, as stronger and self-reliant women. Some of our characters are good role models for women readers and women activists" (Bala, 2002: 21).The story under consideration, located in Kolkata, depicts the crisis of human values as also the human bonding that helps Bibi Haldar to survive even after her cousin's desertion. There still exist those values that keep us human, the author seems to suggest. Lahiri's vision of India is limited to her visits to Kolkata which she terms "tunnel vision" of India.

> "My own experience of India was largely that of a tunnel imposed by the single city we ever visited, by the handful of homes we stayed in, by the fact that I was not allowed to explore this city on my own. Still within these narrow confines, I felt that I had seen

enough of life, enough details and drama, to set stories on Indian soil" (Internet interview).

The result was the narration of two touching stories of the helpless women and the callousness of the society.

From the gender issue discussed earlier, we now turn to another angle of the social question depicted in Bhabani Bhattacharya's "The Faltering Pendulum", the story of the suffering of a woman on account of her poverty and the social stigma of barrenness. Together they produce alienating effect on the victim, make her slightly abnormal and account for her utter loneliness. A way out of this quagmire, the rag woman rightly realizes, is to wipe out her stigma and to find some company to release her pent up emotions. At the weekly bazaar she barters for a goat and three pumpkin seeds on which the entire story moves.

With these purchases made at the weekly *haat,* starts the story of the old, desolate and unhappy rag-woman who develops close ties, almost mother-son relationship, with the tiny goat and unburdens her heart. She talks to him and he listens attentively, responding occasionally with a bleat or two. That animals serve as therapists for human beings is a well-established fact. In literature we come across many incidents of men or women sharing their grief or intimate feelings with birds or animals. Iona, the cab driver in Anton Chekov's story "Grief", for example, empties his sorrowful heart to his horse. Nearer home, in K.A. Abbas's "Sparrows", the birds help Rahim regain his lost human touch after his contact with a sparrow family in his loft. The rag-woman, too, achieves her lost balance after finding a mute but understanding companion.

There is a superstitious belief prevalent in India, particularly among the rural folk that a barren woman's accursed touch can dry up fruits, be they of a tree or plant or a human being. Childless women are shunned like a scourge. No wonder then that the rag-woman is a discarded being. Loneliness and the curse of barrenness make her hard. She is keen to wipe away the stigma vicariously; if her pumpkin vines bear fruit, she would feel reassured that she may be unfortunate but she is not vile; that the vines she planted and tended could bear fruits. Consequently, when the vines show no signs of fruit for long, she is given to doubt about herself. Frustrated, she kills the goatling in a fit of temper because the animal had nibbled away some leaves of the vines despite her warning. But there is another angle to her unspoken psychology, should he continue with his wantonness and eat all the leaves, the vine would dry and all her hopes to see the vines bear fruit would be crushed; this might break her from inside. However, on the obverse side of it, the animal seems to have done her a favour. Through the opening in the vine created by the nibbled part, a neighbouring girl child spots two tiny pumpkins. Symbolically, it is the child who in her innocence and daring helps the rag-woman wash off her curse. The vines, springing to fruitful life after their long barren dead-aliveness have a symbolic significance. The story ends on a note of optimism: "A balance was achieved. The faltering pendulum had regained its swing."

That barrenness is a stigma and is considered a curse in the Indian social set-up is depicted in some of the powerful regional language stories. Mallika Amarsheikh's Marathi short story "Khel" (Game) for example, depicts the psyche of a barren woman who kills a little girl she loves from the core of her heart, not for any superstitious reasons but because the woman would not be able to face the girl's parents after she detained the girl long just to have the satisfaction of playing with her. In desperation, the woman, Durga kaki, beats the child's head to a pulp and after gaining consciousness of her inhuman act, she commits suicide. There are dozes of such strong narratives that not only portray the barren woman's psychological anguish but also indict the society for holding erroneous views and beliefs.

Bhattacharya takes pains to reveal the wounded psyche of the rag-woman. She is not unaware of the core of temper inside her, which she calls "the hard nut". She makes efforts to control it but when the children hurt her, she flays at them like an insane person. Later, she feels ashamed of herself and confides in her goat "you saw? … That angry thing rolled again in my belly." She clasps the animal to her heart as if to make amends for having cursed the children. The rag-woman is neither mad nor wicked; only victim of a situation that makes life hard. She finds a release in nature – the animal with its understanding and the vines with their rhythm of growth and life.

In the postcolonial era, many Indian writers have tended to re-write the empire, which is also termed as "writing back the empire," to show the corroding effect of the colonial situation on the psyche of the colonized. As Franz Fanon maintains:

> "Colonialism is not satisfied merely with holding a people in its grip and emptying the native's head of all form and content. By a kind of perverted logic, it turns to the past of the oppressed people, and distorts, disfigures and destroys it. This work of devaluing pre-colonial history takes on a dialectical significance today". (1982: 169)

Khushwant Singh, in his story "Karma" directs his gaze to a marginalized colonial man who remains the proverbial "Trishanku", neither "here", nor "there". The case of Sir Mohan Lal, the "Brown Sahib" is closely linked with the superiority-inferiority syndrome of the colonial situation. Sir Mohan hates all that is Indian, including his uncouth wife and her kith and kin. He, a barrister and Oxford educated at that, considers himself a Sahib. In the Railway waiting room, he acts out like a real Sahib shouting *koi hai* in a typical English manner and ordering a *chhota* peg. His wife, on the other hand, is content to sit on her trunk on the platform in typical native style, eat out of her Tiffin, belch, chew pan, engage in light conversation with the coolie and board the Zenana compartment on the arrival of the train.

Sir Mohan shows no hurry – hurrying and rushing is for the uncultured natives. For a Sahib like him, there is always a room in the first class compartment. So, happily imagining a fruitful journey with some high ranking British co-traveler in his first class compartment, and impressing him with his reading culture (for, Sir Mohan read nothing less than *The Times*), his Balliol tie, Oxford reminiscences and gold cigarette case, he boards a first class compartment only to be thrown out by two British soldiers. Far from being impressed by his British array – the Balliol neckties and oxford accent – they recognize the colour of his skin even in their inebriated state, call him "bloody nigger" and shunt him out unceremoniously. The climax is reached when his wife spits a gob of red pan-juice from the running train and in all likelihood the "dribble" falls on her pseudo-English husband, standing aghast on the platform. Symbolically, this is the fate the marginalized people encounter; they reject their own people and are rejected in turn by the dominant class.

Khushwant Singh has subtly evoked the colonial situation with its division between the ruler and the ruled. Those who lose their cultural identity are the dangling men. The ruling class is the empowered class. Even an ordinary soldier acquires and uses the subconscious power to subjugate the ruled, irrespective of the latter's social status. In the colonial situation, people like Laxmi are no better either. They are the tolerant mortals who have learnt "to live with the idea of subjection." They live in their "lesser world" under the pretext that it was the whole world, forgetting that it was damaged by the colonial forces. V.S. Naipaul in *India: A Wounded Civilization* maintains that in general, the British were felt only through their institutions: the banks, the railways, mission schools. But in the ordinary world of the ordinary people its impact was not pronounced. Considering R.K. Narayan's works Naipaul says, in Narayan's early novels the lesser world of "small men, small scheme, high talk, limited means, appears whole and unviolated" (1977: 19). Though these people appear to have preserved their identity, they are unconcerned and their attitude is damaging because their "inward concentration is fierce, the self-absorption complete". The educated, half-sahib Indians like Sir Mohan are the privileged-unprivileged occupying an unenviable position in colonized India. Sir Mohan though privileged, is made acutely uncomfortable by his subject status.

The author observes his characters from a distance and without indicting them he lets them play their game and enjoys their foibles. He is not angry nor sympathetic; only ironic and comic. Khushwant Singh shows how the power of the master is felt in both cases – Laxmi, the representative of mute native subjects allows herself to be carried away by the British institution – the Railways here; the "alien insider", the pseudo-English Sir Mohan is already brain-washed by the same power – its educational system. The former of the kind, by being "inward" and unconcerned allows the master to play his game; the latter plays the game of the master and suffers. Tolerance of the helpless, the powerless and the unconcerned does not help solve the identity crisis; what the country requires is the total awareness and ambition of the pragmatic.

Indian writing in English successfully interacts with the culture, tradition and the prevalent situations and distinguishes itself by portraying the Indian reality, giving the readers a peep inside, and an insider's view of the social and psychological reality. A creative writer is not a natural scientist, nor is he/she a social scientist in that a creative writer does not deal with lifeless forces or statistical data; he/she has to deal with the human life and human characters with motivations, emotions and responses. The author has to look at them from his vantage point in time and social positioning and in re-creating them he cannot reject or forget his own roots. The creative writer in English cannot obliterate his/her identity as the thematic pattern and the narrative strategy of the stories discussed here reveal. Indian writing in English has established its strength as Indian literature; it is neither derivative nor imitative; it is indigenous in themes and concerns and it has been able to capture the psycho-social matrix of the society. And when there is no "anxiety about Indianness", to use Meenakshi Mukherjee's words, it is irrelevant in which language one writes because their world is very much grounded where he/she is living. The efforts of the writers have been to find an authentic self-image, an indigenous identity that defies domination and helps the writer repossess the past.

Note

1. For the four short stories, see Dina Mehta, *Absolution and Other Stories*, New Delhi: Vikas Publishing House, 1981; Bhabani Bhattacharya, *Steel Hawk and Other Stories*, Delhi: Hind Pocket Books, 1968; Jhumpa Lahiri, *The Interpreter of Maladies*, New Delhi: Harper Collins India, 1999; Khushwant Singh, *Black Jasmine*, Bombay: Jaico Publishing House, 1972.

References

Bala, Suman, ed. *Jhumpa Lahiri: The Master Story Teller: A Critical Response to Interpreter of Maladies*. New Delhi: Khosla Publishing House, 2002.

Fanon, Franz. *The Wretched of the Earth*, trans. by Constance Farrington. Harmondsworth: Penguin, 1982.

Internet interview with Jhumpa Lahiri quoted by Suman Bala.

Iyengar, K.R.S. *Indian Writing in English* (Rev.), Bombay: Asia Publishing House, 1972.

Mukherjee, Meenakshi. "The Anxiety of Indianness: Our Novels in English." *Mapping Cultural Spaces: Postcolonial Indian Literature in English: Essays in Honour of Nissim Ezekiel.* New Delhi: Vision Books, 1998.

Naipaul, V.S. *India: A Wounded Civilization*. New Delhi: Vikas Publishing House, 1977.

Narasimhaiah, C.D. *The Swan and the Eagle*. Shimla: Indian Institute of Advanced Study, 1969.

7 The Primordial and the Modern

"Snake" and "Night of the Scorpion"

D.H. Lawrence's "Snake" is regarded, generally, as a critique on civilization presented in the form of a dialogue between the poet's two selves – his "I" and the other "voices" in him, revealing "the unknowable otherness of the non-human life" (Sagar, 1979: 121). Nissim Ezekiel's "Night of the Scorpion", on the other hand, is seen as an ironic representation of a society in transition – riddled with superstitions but giving in to skeptical rationalism. Thematically, both the poems deal with the non-human life as juxtaposed with the human, and present commentaries on the civilized responses to the two situations in which man ultimately appears puny in the face of the Elements. Structurally, the poems maintain perfect economy of words, starting with simple, direct statements: "A snake came to my water-trough/On a hot, hot day"; and, "I remember the night my mother/was stung by a scorpion." But, what strikes one while reading the poems is the rich archetypal and mythic element running through them, revealing the ancient, deep-rooted tendencies of human mind.

Each of these two poems has merited considerable critical attention focusing on structure, theme, narrative pattern and symbolic significance. For example, Vivian de Sola Pinto finds in "Snake" an "exploration of a life different from that of humanity and a profound criticism of the world of civilization," (n.m: 139) while Keith Sagar reads the message of "live and let live" so that nothing natural is "rejected by the merely rational human consciousness" (1979: 126). Critics of "Night of the Scorpion" see in the poem a "curious mixture of metaphysics, faith and superstition" (Naik, 1984: 35). The "mocking social observation" (Wiseman, 1976: 247) in the face of a crisis makes the poem socially relevant whereas its depiction of the power of Evil and the enigma of suffering gives it metaphysical depth. M.K. Naik explores four attitudes in the poem – traditional Indian, skeptical rationalist, magical, and lastly, maternal, ingrained in the biological instinct of the mother" (35–37).

A close study of the two poems and of the critical material available on each shows two significant facts: first, both these poems have deep archetypal appeal which is yet to be explored; and second, that a comparative analysis will yield rich knowledge of deep human tendencies. I, therefore, propose to explore the archetypal patterns in the poems and try to establish that despite national and cultural distance the poets meet at points which are universal.

Textually, the poems are based on simple episodes – in Ezekiel's "Night of the Scorpion" the persona's mother is stung by a scorpion; in Lawrence's "Snake" the poet encounters a snake. Thus, the two works can be characterized as "poems of situation", beginning with an incident and ending by throwing light on human nature. The snake and the scorpion, the chief protagonists, are the representatives of the non-human world and have been forced to enter into the human premises by the relentless elements of nature. It is the "hot, hot day" of "Sicilian July, with Etna smoking", that has driven the snake out of the burning bowels of the earth. Further, it is the "Ten hours of steady rain" that has compelled the scorpion to crawl out and hide beneath "a sack of rice". Rain and heat are not simply the phenomena of nature, but are symbolic of the primeval forces. M.K. Naik quotes from Somerset Maugham's short story "Rain" that when the rain falls with "cruel persistency", one felt in it "the malignancy of the primitive powers of nature" (1984: 39). The "smoking" Etna and the pouring rain are the omnipotent spirits sending forth their representatives to encroach upon human precincts, thus exemplifying the awful mythical power of the cosmic processes.

Once these non-human forces enter into human territory they become subject to human perception and evoke mixed responses. The scorpion is symbolic of evil. It is to be hunted out and killed.

The snake assumes heroic proportions and is viewed simultaneously with admiration and contempt. The archetypal nature of these responses is etched out clearly. Levy-Bruhl calls it *participation mystique,* which means what happens without also happens within, and vice versa. Obviously, the myths of Evil and suffering, fear and divine visitations are working on the minds of the poets. Northrop Frye defines myth as a "simple and primitive effort of the imagination to identify with the human the non-human world" (1957: 134–140). He further clarifies that myth becomes a structural principle of story-telling when mythology begins to merge with literature. The initial reactions and responses of the poets under consideration are guided by their respective social, cultural and educational patterns and display the *collective unconscious* of their respective cultures. But finally their responses converge to reveal the universal aspect of the *collective unconscious* which is common to the human species as a whole. This discussion will lead toward that universal and unifying aspect of literature.

I

In "Night of the Scorpion" the reactions and responses of the villagers who come to attend upon the poet's mother, are totally guided by their deep-seated traditional Indian value system. The scorpion, with a "flash/of diabolic tail" has stung a human being. An incarnation of Evil, it has left a trail of suffering, to mitigate which the peasants take recourse to different methods. Some chant the "name of God a hundred times/to paralyse the Evil One" because they believe that "with every movement that the scorpion made his poison moved in Mother's blood." Their belief in rebirth manifests itself in their claim that the sins of the previous birth will be "burned away" and the "sum of evil" will be "balanced … against the sum of good". After thus philosophizing the entire episode, they try magic incantation to take out the poison.

The poem, thus, moves within the given socio-cultural pattern. The atmosphere is typically rural and is charged with fear – the fear of a dark unknown force which emerged from the unfathomed dark and vanished unseen in the night. The poet creates an eerie, primitive atmosphere with a few dexterous touches here and there.

One can almost see the villagers swarming in a room stacked with "sacks of rice". They come with lanterns, candles; they buzz; with them enter insects and "the endless rain". As William Walsh points out, "The choric 'they said', 'they said', 'they said' implies something of the ancient, sophisticated ritual of chanting" (1974: 7). But, it is not wholly a primitive society and the poet does not let us forget the fact. Between the metaphysical and mythical views and magic incantation he places the father's skeptic, rationalist attitude. He, "trying every curse and blessing,/power, mixture, herb and hybrid," also uses modern scientific treatment when he pours "a little paraffin" on the toe and burns the poison. Again, amid this rational point of view, the narrator-onlooker watches "the flame feeding on my mother". This imagery once again evokes the Indian fire-god at his work.

As these various rituals are going on, the main actor, the scorpion, is significantly absent from the scene. But the scorpion remains a pervading presence, a spirit, casting "giant scorpion shadows" on the walls; it has left its poison to run in the blood of its victim; and it has inflicted pain which has the capacity to purify the "flesh/of desire" and the "spirit of ambition". It assumes the proportions of a primeval power – it has the potentiality to evoke fear, purify the spirit and inflict pain. It is a "demi-God" almost. All human efforts are directed in its search, and all human intelligence is engaged in nullifying its influence.

The poem, excluding the last three lines, has three distinct stages: the magic incantation, which is pre-historic and primitive; the mythical, which expresses the collective unconscious of the race; and the rational, which is modern. These stages also mark the development of human consciousness. The most primordial one is, however, the instinctive remark of the mother to which we shall turn at a later stage.

II

Lawrence's reaction on spotting the snake at his water-trough is at once of surprise, admiration, awe, contempt and self-berating. First, he sees the snake and decides to wait till he has finished. This is, in fact, the voice of his education and experience urging him to wait, "must stand and wait, for there he was/at the trough before me." His human experience has taught him to be wary of the reptile, and his education has trained him in good manners, to let the first-comer have his turn first. Obviously, he is not aware of the "voice" of his education till it pesters him to kill the snake. Though these voices create in him moments of tension, and ridicule him for his cowardice, he is reluctant to follow them. He is soon led to self-doubt:

> Was it cowardice, that I dared not kill him?
> Was it perversity that I longed to talk to him?
> Was it humility, to feel so honoured?

The voice that urges him to kill the snake is of his deep-seated cultural consciousness. The reluctance to kill him is a part of his individual spontaneous feelings for life. Snake, in Christianity, is symbolic of evil and hence in the collective unconscious of the Christians it is a fearsome creature to be shunned and killed. This unconscious influence is more potent and primordial than the voice of his education. Education equips him to distinguish between poisonous and non-poisonous snakes, but the archetypal fear of the reptile forces him to throw the log in a bid to kill him. The poet, however, has no respite from fear. Another archetypal image, associated with the Ancient Mariner who was punished for killing the albatross, the life-giving bird, surfaces. So, instead of acting conventionally, he allows his spontaneous feelings of love and acceptance find expression. He wishes to atone for a sin. By appeasing "one of the lords/Of life" he hopes to "expiate/a pettiness".

Lawrence's admiration for the snake is three-fold: first, it is factual. On seeing him at his water trough, he watches him closely and enjoys his movements, colour and action. Second, there is a clash of his Christian values, Western education and spontaneous self when the "voices" warn him of the impending danger. He looks at the reptile with awe and contempt. In the third stage, he admires him for his dignity and beauty. The guest becomes almost a demi-god. His action when he "looked around like a god, unseeing into the air/And slowly turned his head," is symbolic of his uncaring attitude toward a puny human being. *His snake* is raised in stature gradually from a creature come to drink water, to a human guest, then to a divinity.

A significant question needs to be answered here. Why is the poet horrified on seeing the snake go toward the fissure? The poet appears to be undergoing radical psychological upheaval as he watches the snake withdraw:

> A sort of horror, a sort of protest against his withdrawing
> Into that horrid black hole,
> Deliberately going into the blackness, and slowly
> drawing himself after,
> Overcame me now his back was turned.

After this turmoil he throws the log in anger and fear. Freudians interpret the poet's violent hysterical reactions as symptomatic of his horror of the sex act. Viewing it archetypally, I feel that his anger denotes his helplessness springing up from the archetypal depths. The snake, as an accursed being, should have been punished for venturing into human precincts. The snake, as a poisonous creature, also deserves to be killed. But, while the poet stands debating, the snake leaves unhurt and unharmed, without bothering for the man standing there.

III

Initially, both "Snake" and "Scorpion" work within the given cultural boundaries of their creators. By the end, however, the poems cross those barriers and assume universal archetypes. After a brief encounter with human beings, and after having created turmoil in their world, the scorpion and the snake enter into the territory unfathomable to man. The scorpion "risks" the rain and slips out; he is not to be found despite the vigil by scores of eyes. The snake goes into the "blackness" of the "horrid hole", and the dark door of the secret earth is closed for man. Mother Earth has given them shelter and they are, thus, linked to the wider forces of the cosmos. What Lawrence writes in one of his letters applies to both, the snake and the scorpion, that they represent "a deep, deep life which has been denied in us, and still is denied" (Brewster and Brewster 1934: 118). Man's inability to understand these primeval forces gives them mythical proportions, as they touch the deeper stratum of his unconsciousness. They become universal symbols, common to all men, having "a communicable power which is potentially unlimited" (Frye, 1957: 118). The snake, the scorpion, the Mother Earth, the water-symbols (rain and the water-trough), the fire-symbols (Etna smoking and the flame feeding on the mother's toe) are archetypal universal symbols which "connect one poem with another and hereby help to unify and integrate our literary experience" (ibid.: 99). The cyclical process of the appearance and disappearance of the snake and the scorpion completes the cyclical process of nature. We shall now see its working in the human world.

Mother's spontaneous remarks on gaining consciousness and Lawrence's admiration of the snake after hitting him reveal those intuitive faculties which are ageless and uncorroded by any civilized response. After having suffered for twenty hours, the mother remarks, "Thank God the scorpion picked on me/And spared my children." This is an instinctive and primordial reaction – maternal love which is timeless. She, thus, becomes the archetype Mother and the poet, who has been an onlooker so far, experiences her as such. This is established by the poet's silent acceptance of the mother's remarks with which the poem ends.

Lawrence raises the snake to the level of a divine visitation, "a king in exile, uncrowned in the underworld/Now due to be crowned again." The conventional feelings for the slimy creature give way to the spontaneous efforts at understanding life through life; through an awareness of man's unique nature and his intimate relationship with life around him. It brings a feeling of "oneness" and of reconciliation with life. The self becomes the centre of totality and embraces both conscious and unconscious mind.

"Night of the Scorpion" and "Snake" depict four phases of the development of the mind of man through ages: the primordial; magic and superstitions; myths; and contemporary education. Of these, the poets experience and reject the last three phases and return to the primordial in the last part of the poems. The movement is from experience to innocence. As in Dante, the movement is through purgatory: the poet's mother in "Night of the Scorpion" and the narrator in "Snake" suffer (intense pain and remorse respectively), to reach the visionary stage. The two poems afford us the unified and integral experience of literature and human nature.

References

Brewster, Earl and Achsah Brewster, eds. *D.H. Lawrence: Reminiscences and Correspondence.* London: Secker, 1934.

Frye, Northrop. *Anatomy of Criticism*. Princeton: Princeton University Press, 1957.

Naik, M.K. "The Tale in the Sting: An Analysis of Ezekiel's 'Night of the Scorpion'." *Dimensions of Indian English Literature*. New Delhi: Sterling, 1984, 35–39.

Pinto, Vivian de Sola. *Crisis in English Poetry 1880–1940*. London: Hutchinson University Library.

Sagar, Keith. *The Art of D.H. Lawrence*. Ghaziabad: Vikas Publishing House, 1979.

Walsh, William. "Two Indian Poets." *The Literary Criterion*, X, No. 3. Winter, 1974.

Wiseman, Christopher. "The Development of Technique in the Poetry of Nissim Ezekiel." *Journal of South Asian Literature: Nissim Ezkeil Issue*, XI, No. 3–4, 1976.

8 Gauri – Myth and Reality[1]

Bafflingly contradictory pictures of woman appear in life and literature in India. On the one hand she has been glorified and deified as the mother-protector, the inspirer and motivating force; on the other, she is viewed as an object of desire and cherished as a weakling, dependent on man for her survival. In between these two polarities lies the reality of a woman's life – the image of a gentle and docile non-entity that Betty Friedan chooses to discuss under the concept of "feminine mystique". Woman's position in India avers Romila Thapar, is a "curious intermeshing of low status, ritual contempt, sophisticated sexual partnership and deification" (Thapar, 1975: 6). Women always try to conform to the myth of feminity, seeking fulfilment in their husbands and children. Man has rarely considered her a human being capable of feelings, desires, and individuality. Basically, it is the portrait of a pure, subdued and suffering woman that holds his fancy. The traditional myths of Sita, Shakti and Mohini extol her respectively, as the chaste, the powerful and the charming force. These myths are now being exploded by the 20th century authors – both male and female – who look at women from the new angle of reality, as humans with self-esteem, rights, dreams, desires, weakness, and strength. In this paper I propose to study Gauri, the heroine of Mulk Raj Anand's novel entitled *Gauri* (1960) in the light of myth and reality.

Gauri, first published in 1960 under the title "The Old Woman and the Cow", incorporates the story of a simple and gentle village girl. It opens with Gauri's marriage to Panchi, a farmer youth who owns an acre and a half of mortgaged land. In her new home Gauri is ill-treated by her mother-in-law, Kesaro. A couple of days later Panchi quarrels with his uncle, Mola Ram, and establishes a separate household. Kesaro does not leave the couple alone even in their new home. Her oblique suggestion that Gauri is not faithful to her husband instigates Panchi and the thought of "her dalliances with others tended to make him homicidal" (48). Later, on learning of her pregnancy, he bullies her, beats her and drives out of home. The girl seeks shelter with her mother. Her mother, Laxmi, sells her, in connivance with another dubious character Amru, to a lecherous Sahukar (Jai Das) in order to save her mortgaged cow. At Hoshiarpur, Gauri has to struggle hard to protect herself from molestation – first, from Seth Jai Das, and later from Dr Batra. Gauri stays under the protection of a benevolent doctor, Colonel Mahendra and learns nursing. When a repentant Panchi goes to Piplan Kalan to patch up and reclaim his wife, he is beaten up by Amru's men. A police case is registered and Laxmi is reprimanded and ordered to restore her to Panchi. Panchi welcomes Gauri's home-coming, but his joy is short-lived. A malicious gossip is circulating in the village and his mind is now poisoned by the villagers. He doubts her and wants proof of her chastity. Humiliated and ill-treated, Gauri realizes that her husband is a weakling, unable to take a stand or apply his mind. She broods, "He pretended to be a lion among the men of the village. But really he is a coward" (263). She leaves him forever and decides to lead an independent life of self-respect.

Anand uses myth for the first time in this novel. Gauri is named after Parvati, the incarnation of Shakti, but she is the prototype of Sita. The Ramayana heroine is destined to wander, abducted, reclaimed and again exiled, so is Gauri. She is turned out by her brutal husband, sold by her greedy mother and callous uncle and doubted by her husband. Both Sita and Gauri are forced by circumstances to stay in strangers' house. The parallelism, however, ends here. Sita is recovered by Rama, society suspects her, whereupon her husband forsakes her. In Sita's case, mother earth opens up to take Sita in her folds and absolve her of the stigma; Gauri is recovered by her mother under duress of the law and restored to Panchi. The society casts aspersions on her, and her husband demands a proof of her purity. In the end, Panchi does not renounce Gauri, it is she who leaves him with a determination to find independent existence. Thus, the author pursues a myth to a point but then reverses it suddenly. In a way it is the "negative use of myth" and the author seems to suggest that it is "intended to indicate that the same ending is no longer possible (or desirable) in our time (Mukherjee, 1971: 133). Gauri is more realistic than Panchi. She knows that she is not Sita for whom a miracle will be wrought. She has a forward-looking vision. If the earth cannot open for her, it can at least give a firm footing to support her. For a moment she wishes that the earth should part and hide her, but then she shakes off the thought as she feels the ground "hard and solid under her feet and showed no sign of opening up, to prove her innocence" (264). She does not follow the mythical figure. Her foremost thought is that of the road ahead.

Apart from the Sita-myth, Gauri combines in herself traces of other figures from Indian mythology. She is the Shakti, Kali and Mohini. In Kali avatar goddess Parvati is the ferocious destroyer. Shakti is the manifestation of strength destroying the evil and preserving the good. Woman as Kali has annihilating power; woman as Shakti incorporates strength. Gauri is Kali when she encounters Kesaro furiously. Kesaro comes to Rafique Chacha's barn with her usual "hate campaign" and passes derogatory remarks on Gauri, it is then that the latter faces Kesaro with vehemence. Panchi is witness to the scene which leaves him wonder-struck. To him, she appears in her rage, "beautiful like a swaying fire" and Panchi is "overwhelmed by the sudden flashing power that had come into the gentle Gauri, turning her into her other incarnation, Kali, the divine destroyer herself" (95). She repels the advances of both Seth Jai Ram Das and Dr Batra with courage as if "from some unplumbed depth there arose in her, however, Kali, the energy of sheer negation" (165) who impels her to protect herself in spite of her weak physical condition. Gauri, with her beauty is the charming Mohini. In mythology, Lord Vishnu, in his incarnation as the infinitely attractive Mohini, entices demon Bhasmasur and burns him to death. In her Monini-image, woman is viewed as the enchantress. In Gauri's case, the myth works with a variation. Her charm tempts men, but it is not intentional on her part. Her immaculate beauty and bubbling youth attract men. Amru, Sahukar Jai Das and Dr Batra, the villains of the piece, are the victims of their own lust and consequently harm themselves in their blindness. But even the noble and upright Col Mahindra's light-hearted remark, to Laxmi, "Take her away or I might marry her myself" (229), indicates that her spell has worked on him too. Before this incident, the peon in Dr Mahindra's bungalow tells Laxmi that Gauri, the "good-looking girl" has broken up the nursing home indicating that her charm naturally entices men.

Within the framework of these traditional myths, there lies the reality of a woman's life. Gauri has to stand the acid tests of an Indian woman's existence and face its harsh actualities. Anand is aware of the low status of women in Indian society. In his essay on the position of women in India, he points out that woman is worshipped as a goddess and whipped as a slave, "pampered as a doll or kept down and oppressed" (Anand and Huthee Singh, 1947: 16). Gauri is a victim of this dichotomy. Panchi dotes on her as his "childling"; he tries to win her over by bringing her mangoes; he desires her in his physical hunger; and then kicks her when it suits his fancy. Gauri accepts it as the matrix of a woman's lot. She is content to play the passive role of a helpless and weak being in order to "win her husband's sympathy" (43).

Traditionally, feminine mystique trains a woman to imbibe the spirit of subservience and to find an ultimate salvation by serving her man to the end of her life. An Indian girl, born and brought up in the village set up, Gauri has imbibed these values and is governed by these ideas. As Simone de Beauvoir points out, "it is difficult to describe feminine myth because it is various and contradictory. It considers woman simultaneous as Virgin Mary and Eve, truth and falsehood, the cause of man's rise as well as his downfall. It haunts the human consciousness without ever appearing before it in a fixed form" (Beauvoir, 1971: 43). Gauri learns to spend her life at the feet of her God, Panchi, even when he kicks her. She takes self-effacement as her destiny. She loves him in spite of his brutality. In the depths of her heart she believes that he is capable of tenderness. She resolves to remove his suspicion and thus encouraged by her inner conviction she goes "through her daily round with a dignified air which kept her from all sentimentality" (101).

Panchi is upper most in Gauri's thoughts even after his unpardonable behaviour. She condones his act by simple fatalism or naïve faith. "Perhaps Devi is angry with me" (115), she broods and forgives and forgets his beastly behaviour. Gauri is so deeply immersed in the traditional lore of feminine myth that she almost worships him and is ready to wait patiently till she conquers him by her devotion. She "was willing to wait like the Hindu wife and go patiently through everything, to get to the source of that antagonism and distrust and hatred which he showed to her" (100). Today, we may not approve of such complacency of women who always succumb to the image of themselves as suffering heroines. They seem to have been "beguiled by sociological romanticism" that "the sanction for their existence lies only in being the vehicles of the human race and patiently accepting the indignities heaped upon them by their Kismet and their men" (Vasudev, 1963; 69). The concrete grip of the "racial subconscious" of the feminine myth is tight on Gauri and she cannot swerve it. She is the facsimile of an Indian woman symbolizing the value of silent suffering, deep faithful love and hard work.

After her marriage she adjusts mutely to the environment of her new home. This new home is not the proverbial "Paradise" of the newly-weds, but a hard, harsh reality of a rural home with an oppressive mother-in-law. Kesaro keeps her in low spirit and dubs her as an evil-influence. Every ill that befalls any character in the novel, all calamities – familial, social and natural – from debts and family quarrels to drought and famine – are ascribed to her unpropitious presence. Gauri quietly endures all this because she is a woman and is supposed to withstand all discrimination. In her wordless suffering she presents the picture of a helpless, timid and weak being "sisking"[2] in the dark corner of the cottage. She craves for Panchi's benevolent touch or look.

So compulsive is the hold of feminine mystique on social psyche that men also like to see women as mute-sufferers and find their doll-like submission endearing. Many men critics of the novel find the pitiable, meek figure of the heroine loveable "Gauri, sulking on her string cot in a dark room, Gauri beaten and abused by her cowardly husband, Gauri putting up a defence for her husband in front of strangers"(Cowasjee, 1977: 157). In order to show Gauri's capacity to change and take things in her hands, the novelist repeated calls her "like a cow, very gentle and very good" (11) in the early part of the novel. But, constantly bullied by Kesaro, mistrusted and insulted by Panchi, the same docile and meek woman changes into an individual of her own will. The transformation is sure though slow.

If the feminine myth enjoins docility and humility upon Gauri, the masculine myth confers an inflated ego upon Panchi. A delinquent and short tempered youth, he is a weak-willed man who is easily influenced by opinions of Kesaro, Damodar, Rajguru, Rakhi and others. His mood vacillates between love and hate, anger and remorse, desire and mistrust. Feeble minded as he is, he cannot evaluate or control a situation, nor can he judge the depth of Gauri's character. He is swayed by gossip, be it Kesaro's ill-intentioned insinuations or society's malicious indictment. When thwarted by the outside world, he comes home and relieves the fury of his frustrated ego on his innocent wife.

In fact, his actions and reactions are childish, though he prefers to call this wife "childling". Panchi's only asset is that he is born as a male in this tradition-bound Indian society. In his black mood of despair he kicks and raves and growls only to show his annoyance, whereas in the dark corner of his cottage he sheds tears of self-pity and is "ashamed to appear in that guise of girlish weakness before his wife"(89). His "oppressive, all pervading anger and unbreakable silence" is at once whimsical, uncomfortable and puny. However, despite his weakness, he dominates over his wife and gets psychological catharsis by subjugating her. For Gauri, there is no such relief. She endures emotional as well as psychological horrors. In short, Panchi "appears to be highly egoistic, full of self-pity and superstitious beliefs"(Riemenschneider, 1978: 102). His psychology is weak and when influenced by Kesaro's insinuations and his own superstitious nature, it plays havoc with him. He feels miserable on learning of Gauri's pregnancy. For many days he p' ınges into "a veritable whirlpool of doubts which bordered on complete panic" (102). His suspicions and cowardice are responsible for all trials and tribulations of Gauri which shuttle her from place to place.

Many Indologists believe that the Hindu character is narcissistic. Psychological studies conducted in the field of our legends and myths point out that Indians dread social criticism; they are very sensitive to their women's purity and even trivial incidents may make a man suspect his wife though he remains blissfully unaware of his own lapses. Panchi's ego-centric tendencies make him distrustful of Gauri. He has a low opinion of women. As he observes, "the wisdom of women is in their ankles, and they are untrustworthy, falling before every shimmer of shiny cloth. No one can ever vouch for their chastity ..." (249). To such observation, Rafique Chacha the benevolent elder of the village, reminds Panchi of his weakness. His angry rejoinder is meaningful, "This is strange talk for a young man whom I have myself known to wink his eyes at more than one woman in this village" (250). It is obvious that while Panchi doubts his wife, he conveniently forgets his own moral behaviour. Gauri's new fangled notions like using soap or towel that she has picked up in the city (Hoshiarpur) are also the cause of Panchi's antagonism. Ridiculously, he considers her a woman of loose character because she uses modern facilities like a towel and a cake of soap.

Men, in general, think that women have no independent awareness and they live through the consciousness of man. That is why "woman could never be a genius, for genius implies the highest degree of consciousness" (Klien, 1946: 62). When Gauri shows considerable awareness, self-confidence and independence of spirit, Panchi cannot tolerate her progressive ideas. He at once ridicules her. Somewhere deep down his unconscious, envy takes roots. Jealousy, coupled with his ego and social criticism enrage him against Gauri.

So far as Gauri is concerned, she has no claim to any genius, nor to any new-fangled ideas of liberation. An uneducated village belle, she would have been happy leading a life millions of her sisters are enduring. Forced to leave the protection of her home, she has to fend for herself. In the course of her struggle to survive alone in a hostile society, she understands the stark reality of a woman's existence – blind traditions and frayed out customs cannot protect her; what she requires is awareness. The "felt experience" reveals to her that it is necessary to "give up the outworn traditions, conventions and dasturs, if they have no relevance under changed circumstances. One must make up every day to a fresh sun … One must seek the first and the last freedom."[3]

Anand believes that old myths need a fresh interpretation or modification. In one of his letters he asserts that he has deliberately turned some ancient myths "upside down, because many of them seem to be irrelevant to anyone who wants felt experience" (quoted in Verghese, 1975: 156). He at times questions the adequacy of myths with reference to modern age, and feels that the revivalists are taking us back to the philosophy which smothered the rationalism of Indian thought and divided India into hierarchies, thus weakening it. He sees the validity of the contemporary myth of growth awareness as against the traditional myth. It is obvious that he follows a new approach to the reality of a woman's life as he lets his Gauri pass through various mythic situations and rejecting them allows her to march towards a more substantial goal of self-sufficiency. As a feminist critic points out, the images of woman as "the Virgin victim – the Bitch goddess, the faithful wife, the beautiful temptress, the seductive destroyer, the devouring momma, the healing Madona …" (Russ, 1973: 4) are of no value to a modern writer who wishes to depict her in the essence of her day-to-day life. Gauri emerges, not as a pitiable suffering heroine but a woman of awareness. Gauri tells Rafique Chacha how time demands us to acquire a new vision of life and how she herself has acquired a consciousness by the exhortations of the "Daktar Sahib". She narrates how the change has come in her. When she first came to the village she was always worried about the criticism of the villagers. "I had no tongue in my mouth … I certainly could not think. Now, how can you fly if you have no wings"(240). Indeed, awareness and a capacity to think, are the "wings" she is referring to.

These "wings" are given to her by Col Mahendra, who awakens her consciousness: she realizes that she is a human being and not a chatel to be disposed off carelessly. Her march towards self-realization begins in Hoshiarpur and takes a concrete shape when Panchi hurts her self-respect. So far it did not occur to her that self-respect or a positive self-esteem is a basic human need. But on her return to little Piplan, Panchi notices a glow on her face and a power in her limbs. It was "a kind of bewitching light, the reflection of the aliveness of her being. She seemed alert and dignified, her movements full of strength." (252). What raises her character to the full height of dignity is the fact that she does not plunge in the darkness of the past, nor does she brood over the present, but takes a quick decision and resolves to make a fresh start.

A critic observes that in Anand's novels "the select few who hurl defiance at religion, authority, society, state, and tradition suffer banishment like Gauri" (Kaushik, 1977: 109). However, Gauri's final act of leaving the house cannot be termed as exile or banishment. It is self-imposed and is as spirited as Nora's act of slamming the door and walking out of the security of her home in Henrik Ibsen's play "The Doll's House" (1879). Nora tells her shocked husband that she is first of all, a human being "just as much as you are – or, at least will try to become one" (Ibsen, 1933: 679). Gauri utters with equal vehemence and defiance, "I shall go and work in Daktar Mahendra's haspatal and have my child there. And I will not come back again" (263). Both Nora and Gauri leave behind them the image of empty gentility and stamp out of their homes, to find an independent life. As Gauri decides to work out her own destiny, she acquires a new animation, her face changes "from the gentle cow's acquiescent visage of the time when she had arrived in Panchi's house, to that of a woman – with a will of her own" (264).

Indeed, Gauri challenges the traditional belief that a woman has only an empirical reality, and that she lacks individuality and an independent will. Gauri acquires self-esteem as she walks on with her head held high. She does not look back to find some supporting prop in the Sita-myths. She does not look down to escape underneath the earth. She thinks of the road ahead and plans her immediate future. She is determined to find justification for her life. She is determined to give her child a distinct personality. She does not worry whether it would be a male or a female; she is keen only to make her baby a perfect individual.

Gauri is, thus, Anand's denunciation of a society which denies human rights to women. Gauri embodies his faith in the strength of women to achieve self-realization and self-actualization. She exemplifies his design of starting life afresh in spite of failures, to discover new freedoms in order to invest meaning in human life. The decayed and out-moded traditions are binding and morbid. They dim the clear vision of a bright tomorrow. Whether it is a man or a woman, the torch-bearer and path-finder is the one who marches ahead with courage, fortitude and determination. Towards the end of the novel, Gauri looks at the sun and is dazed. The sun is a symbol of life and warmth. Here, symbolically, it is her future that dazzles her. She is reminded, with warmth of affection, of the rhythm of life inside her. Gauri's march towards the town is indicative of her journey towards self-esteem and self-fulfilment.

Notes

1. This paper was written for an anthology sometime in early 1980s. The proposed anthology was not published. I am including the article here without making any changes in the text to see how it feels when we re-visit a text and how in retrospection we can see the growth of our ideas. The only change made is numbered 'references' have been substitutes with "works cited".
2. *"sisking"* is Hindi/Punjabi for "sobbing", an example of Anand's experiment with Pidgin English.
3. See Mulk Raj Anand's piece, "Why I Write?" in Indian Writings in English, ed. K.N. Sinha. New Delhi: Heritage, 1979. Gauri becomes his ideal woman to transmit his new notions and progressive ideas about women's emancipation. In many ways Anand's treatment of rural woman is innovative because by the 1960s when the novel was written, women's liberation movement had not gained momentum in India.

References

Anand, Mulk Raj and Krishna Hathee Singh. *The Bride's Book of Beauty*. New York: Alfred A. Knopf, 1971.

Anand, Mulk Raj. *Gauri*. New Delhi: Arnold-Heinemann, 1960.

Beauvoir, Simone de. *The Second Sex*. Trans. and ed. H.M. Parshley. New York: Alfred A. Knopf, 1971.

Cowasjee, Saros. *So Many Freedoms*. New Delhi: Oxford University Press, 1977.

Ibsen, Henrik. *The Doll's House*. Trans. William Archer, *World Drama*, Ed. H. Clark Barrett. New York: Dover, 1933.

Kaushik, R.K. "Red, Brown and Grey – Ideological Commitment in Mulk Raj Anand's Novels." *Indo-English Literature*. Ed. K.K. Sharma. Ghaziabad: Vimal, 1977.

Klien, Violka. *The Feminine Character*. London: Kegan Paul, 1946.

Mukherjee, Meenakshi. *The Twice-Born Fiction*. New Delhi: Arnold-Heinemann, 1971.

Riemenschneider, Dieter. "Alienation in the Novels of Mulk Raj Anand." *Perspectives on Mulk Raj Anand*. Ed. K.K. Sharma. Ghaziabad: Vimal, 1978.

Russ, Joanna. "What can a Heroine Do or Why Women Cannot Write." *Images in Fiction: Feminine Perspective*. Ed. Susan Koppelman Cornillon. Ohio: Popular, 1973.

Thapar, Romila. "Looking Back in History." *Indian Woman*. Ed. Devaki Jain. New Delhi: Publications Division, 1975.

Vasudev, Uma. "Women," *Seminar*, 52 (December, 1963), rpt. in *Conflict in India*. Ed. Ramesh Thapar. Madras: Macmillan, 1978.

Verghese, Paul C., ed. *Essays on Indian Writing in English*. New Delhi: N.V. Publications, 1975.

9 Culture, Literature and Human Rights

A View from Indian Fiction

> Literature should destroy boundaries – be they of nation, caste or religion.
>
> —Cho. Dharman (Tamil Dalit writer)

De-doxification is a new technique of writing and re-writing "the received versions of tradition, culture, patriarchy, politics" (Kirpal, 1996: 20) to subvert and dismantle power structures. When the existing sites of power are substituted with more egalitarian structures and the received myths are turned upside down, they help the writer to redefine the self-image of the hitherto powerless. Political movements and the writings generated thereby have a goal, while literature has none. Its task is to "create life" and make a subtle appeal for change. But when political cause and literature join hands to redefine the marginalized – be they women, dalits or tribals – the result is an initiation of an ideology of social change; of recognition of human rights for all; blurring of boundaries. Writers with humanist sensitivities like Mulk Raj Anand, Karanth, T. Shiv Shankar Pillai and many others have drawn attention to the plight of the downtrodden even before the UN Universal Declaration of Human Rights came into being.

Mulk Raj Anand's *Untouchable* (1935) written in English is the story of Bakha, in which Anand exposes at great length the sense of self-degradation and the loss of human dignity suffered by Bakha and his community. Karanth's Kannada novel *Choma's Drum* (1919) narrates a moving story of a bonded labour who wishes to gain self-recognition by owing a piece of land. Likewise, in T. Shiv Shankar Pillai's Malyalam novel *Scavenger's Son* (1919), Chudalamuthu makes desperate efforts to live like a human being. The attempts of these and many more writers from Hindi, Marathi, Bengali and other language literature to represent the unrepresented class have been laudable. But many critics felt that these writers were from the mainstream and did not have firsthand experience of dalit or tribal life, hence their accounts were not authentic. When Gayatri Spivak asked "Can the subaltern speak?" she gave us a tool to interpret the silence of those at the margins. The novelists of the later part of the 20th century, many of them from the communities they were portraying gave them voice and made the subaltern speak. Various changes at the national and international levels in political situations, cultural and social conditions helped them to break their silence. There was more awareness about human dignity and human rights.

The UN Universal Declaration of Human Rights, 1948, was the first major step in the direction of recognizing the significance of rights of all human beings to a quality of life which can be termed human. Human rights relate to life, liberty, equality, and the dignity of the individual. These are essential ideals for the democratic process and for a healthy and harmonious social life. Since they are inalienable and universally applicable to all human beings without consideration of caste, creed, sex or race, it was believed that women would be entitled to human rights as such without the necessity of a separate covenant to ensure them their rights. But unfortunately, the patriarchal stronghold, and the cultural and traditional attitudes did not allow women the enjoyment of these rights. In 1979, the UN adopted the *Covenant on Elimination of All Forms of Discrimination Against Women, 1979,* popularly known as CEDAW; and spelt out the human rights of women, contextualizing the rights so as to formulate standards that help implementation of the human rights.

Mulk Raj Anand's works, the tea estate novel of Manohar Malgonkar, Kamala Markandaya's works about farmers all written much before the UN declaration seem to have made way for the contemporary works which force us to introspect – how do we eliminate the slums to build plush multi-storeyed complexes on the site (Kamala Markandaya's *Bombay Tiger*); what happens when the miners are trapped (Sanjay Bahadur's *The Sound of Water*); why did Balram Halwai murder his master (Arvind Adiga's *The White Tiger*); and what is Mahasweta Devi's ire against the society vis-à-vis the tribals? These are only a few examples pointing towards human rights violation and an attempt made by literature to rectify the wrong. There can be myriad such examples. The author wishes to study here the thematic patterns in three novels and a short story to show the techniques literature uses to question the implementation of human rights in day to day life – *Untouchable* (1935) by Mulk Raj Anand, which is the story of the travails of a pariah, his sense of self-degradation; and the loss of human dignity; Shashi Deshpande's *The Binding Vine* (1993), the story of violence against women; *The Sound of Water* recounting the horrors faced by trapped miners and the short story "Nandanar Street" about the anger of dalits who force the authorities to take cognizance of their problem by adopting a not-quite-dignified method.

In the era of postmodernism, the question of giving voice to the voiceless is of paramount importance. How these issues are projected artistically in creative writing will be the point of study. The selection of the works has not been made at random but with a purpose – Bakha represents the Dalit, Shashi Deshpande's protagonists are women – one of them is from the working class; in *The Sound of Water*, the question of workers' safety is of paramount importance and in the Tamil short story the community's anger is projected. This is a long march from Bakha's silence. This paper seeks to analyse social change. Today, the oppressed are no longer mute; their resistance is active, even aimed at open defiance of law. The fact that they are vociferous enough to protest shows that they are aware of their rights.

When Mulk Raj Anand started writing in the early decades of the 20th century, he saw in literature great potential to usher in change. Commenting on the representation of the subaltern in historical text and in literature Gayatri Spivak makes a convincing distinction, "A historian confronts a text of counterinsurgency or gendering where the subaltern has been represented. He unravels the text to assign a new subject-position to the subaltern, gendered or otherwise. A teacher of literature confronts a sympathetic text where the gendered subaltern has been represented. She unravels the text to make visible the assignment of subject position" (Spivak, *Subaltern Studies* V, 91). Anand as creator of literature rejects the concept of "art for art's sake" because for him literature is "criticism and as prophecy with intent to effect change" (Berry, 1971: 27). He was clear that if literature was to be the instrument of social transformation, it must be liberated from the clutches of the conservative classes. While drafting the manifesto for the All India Progressive Writers' Association in London in 1936, he expressly mentioned that the aim of literature was to deal with the basic problem of existence – "the problem of hunger and poverty, social backwardness and political subjugation". The first step towards this direction, he said, was to examine the customs and institutions in the light of reason.

In *Untouchable*, Anand has proved his theory and has focused on the problem of untouchability and its psychological implications. The novel was published in 1935 after being rejected by as many as nineteen publishers. It was only after E.M. Forster saw potential in the work and wrote a preface to it that the publishers realized its worth. Forster gives full-throated praise to the work:

> *Untouchable* could only have been written by an Indian and by an Indian who observed from the outside. No European, however sympathetic, could have created the character of Bakha, because he would not have known enough about his troubles. And no untouchable could have written the book, because he would have been involved in indignation and self-pity. Mr Anand stands in the ideal position ... . He has just the right mixture of insight and detachment, and the fact that he has come to fiction through philosophy has given him depth. (Forster, 1935: vi)

Politically, the 1930s was a time when Gandhiji had made the society aware of the problem of untouchability and other social evils. Writing under Gandhian impact, the writers derived their themes from the ideological basis and the national scene. In Raja Rao's *Kanthapura* and R.K. Narayan's *Waiting for the Mahatma*,

Gandhi is the prime mover and as Meenakshi Mukherjee avers, Gandhi's influence on the thought of the time was so strong that "no discussion of Indo-Anglian fiction dealing with the independent movement would be complete without an assessment of the function of Mahatma Gandhi in these works" (Mukherjee, 1971: 60). She further elaborates her statement and points out, "whether Gandhi would be treated as an idea or as a human being, as a symbol or as tangible reality, is ultimately determined by the point of view of the novelist, and Gandhi's presence ... is justified only if it fits into the internal pattern of events" (62).

The novel under discussion, written under the influence of Mahatma Gandhi, is located in the outcastes' colony outside the cantonment town called Nagar. In the early years of the 20th century, the growing nationalist concern for the downtrodden made them aware of their lot and gave them voice but it was not possible for Bakha and his people to break the shackles of tradition. Though they realized their low status, they preferred to stay within the prescribed norms.

Bakha, the protagonist comes from the lowest strata of Indian society. He is a scavenger who cleans the night soil of the upper classes. As a boy of eighteen, when Bakha's father orders him to clean the public latrines, he obeys without any question just because he knows there is no way out. He starts his work early in the morning without even having tea to warm his throat. He comes back home after his work only to find no water and consequently no tea for him. It is his sister who manages to get some water and prepares tea.

The experience outside the home, in the society, is not pleasant either. When he goes to buy Jalebees, the confectioner throws the packet at him to be caught like a ball because he could not touch Bakha and be questioned by the society. That would spoil his day's business. Bakha enjoys the sweets but in his excitement forgets to give the usual call, "Posh, Posh, sweeper coming." He touches Lalla accidentally and gets a sound berating. Slowly, it dawns on him that he and the likes of him are treated inhumanly just because they are untouchables, the scum of the earth. But Bakha cannot do anything about the social system; the society is conditioned that way and so is he.

Bakha's work includes sweeping the temple courtyard but he cannot go near the temple entrance and if he dares to take a step further, he is cursed and scolded by the priest. Bakha tolerates this but is furious when his sister tells him about being molested by the same priest who professes to keep the outcastes away. Helpless and unhappy Bakha goes to listen to a lecture by Hutchinson, the Salvation Army Missionary. In the course of his lecture the missionary places before his audience three possibilities: first, wait for Gandhi's movement to bring in social change, second, wait for the flush system to be installed, and third, to change their faith and become Christians. These may bring in some change in their condition. Bakha dreams of becoming an honourable man some day if these changes materialize but he cannot and does not think of changing his faith.

Anand is not giving here a picture of untouchability as an abstract practice that is detrimental to human growth but he is taking up the human rights issue. What do Bakha and his ilk suffer? Torments – physical, mental and spiritual! The experience is real. The use of the sweeper's consciousness as the medium through which to comprehend a sociological problem is both realistic and convincing. The author achieves focus by keeping the experience limited to one person and revealing the social evil through his consciousness. He places Bakha, his father and others in everyday situations and shows the reader how the operative forces humiliate them. Bakha is a sweeper because he is born into the family of sweepers. He has no choice but to follow his father's profession and he has no choice but to tolerate the stigma.

Bakha is introduced to us in the second paragraph as a "young man of eighteen, strong and able-bodied, the son of Lakha, the Jemadar of all sweepers in the town and the cantonment." Bakha is aware of his surroundings. The drainage system, the latrines, the dirt and the squalor and the detrimental atmosphere in its totality are revealed to us through this young man who is a helpless witness to discrimination. Ample proof of his daily life is provided to the readers when the author shows the society's attitude to him. Bakha hears mutely the curses showered on him daily by the higher caste:

"Keep to the side of the road, you low caste vermin!" He is told in no uncertain words.

"Why don't you call, you swine, and announce your approach! Do you know you have touched me and defiled me, you cock-eyed son of a boe-legged scorpion!" (33–34).

Anand thus dramatizes an important issue through the story of one man's suffering which becomes symbolic of the total social scenario. Bakha's life is worse than that of a cur. He is shooed away from time to time. But then why does Anand avoid Bakha's conversion to Christianity? Probably, it would have been an easy solution to a grave social problem; moreover, it would be an escape. What Bakha is supposed to do is to wait, dream and imagine change.

Human rights envisage equality and freedom, along with full participation in social life. Equality does not mean elimination of discrimination in law or de-jure equality; it involves removing those disadvantages that hamper growth as a human being.

Juxtaposing Bakha's life with the Human Rights, we can discover the wide gap that persists in what the charter envisages and what the downtrodden like Bakha received. The Preamble to the UN Charter recognizes the inherent dignity and the equal and inalienable rights of all members of the human family. It is the foundation of freedom, justice and peace in the world. The second and third paragraphs of the Preamble put it thus:

> Whereas disregard and contempt for human rights have resulted in barbarous acts, which have outraged the conscience of mankind, and the advent of a world in which human beings shall enjoy freedom of speech and belief and freedom from fear and want has been proclaimed as the highest aspiration of the common people.
>
> Whereas it is essential, if man is not to be compelled to have recourse, as a last resort, to rebellion against tyranny and oppression, that human rights should be protected by the rule of law.

There are thirty articles further elaborating that all human beings are born free and equal in dignity and rights. They are endowed with reason and conscience and should act towards one another in a spirit of brotherhood. Everyone is free to enjoy equality and there should be no distinction made on the basis of caste, colour, creed, language, and social status. No one shall be subjected to cruelty or torture. Besides, everyone has the right to participate in the cultural life of the community, to get adequate education, strive for self-development, have freedom of opinion and expression and finally the right to rest and leisure.

How many of these rights does Bakha enjoy? Mulk Raj Anand has taken up an important issue and drawn the attention of the society to an evil that is gnawing at the roots of the social structure. Anand wrote this novel at a time when awareness was coming to the society and when Dr Ambedkar's efforts were directed at the upliftment of the Dalits.

Looking back from our vantage point in time we realize that much has been achieved. The so-called downtrodden have got all the rights and are enjoying life on par with the other higher classes and castes. Moreover, it would not be an exaggeration to say that they have snatched away the share of the deserving candidates only because of their Dalit status. The tables have turned round and the outcastes have no grounds to complain now.

If Mulk Raj Anand chose to focus on the outcaste in his 1935 novel, Sanjay Bahadur, an IAS officer draws attention to the plight of the miners trapped in the mine in *The Sound of Water* (2008). The novel is based on a real-life account of an aged miner who was trapped underground for a week in a flooded coal mine in 2001. The disaster claimed forty lives but what is more harrowing than these deaths is the attitude of the authorities towards safety, the psychological trauma of those trapped and their reactions. These are the people who live at the margins of the consciousness of the educated, urban middle class, whose problems are viewed by the privileged as "just one more disaster" to be read about, viewed in the media and forgotten. But this soul baring account goes beyond that and shows us the "alternate reality" of the situation.

The novel begins with an ominous description of the inside of the mine and the fear of watery grave should the water from the lake enter in, "It is comfortable in the tombdark womb of the earth. Two hundred and fifty feet beneath the arid crust it is quiet and cool, the charcoal broken only by the faint rustle of water slithering down the falkywhite walls and pitchdark ceiling" (Bahadur, 2008: 9). It is Raimoti, the old miner who is trying to hear the dreaded sound of water because it may forebode death by water inside the mine. It is the resounding silence of the coal mine that becomes claustrophobic as page after page the suspense is built. Experience has taught Raimoti that the tunnel in which he is working is close to the lake and as the menacing rumble comes from the wall of the mine, the miners know that the "claw of the Beast" is on them (20). Juxtaposed with this reality of their life is another reality that of the rich who are enjoying their chilled drink under the blue sky, not in the dark dungeon of the mine. In this setting where the high officers are sitting, the sight and sound of water offer a lucrative sight. In life, these managers and sub-managers are close to the top brass bureaucrats and politicians and have no time or inclination to pay attention to the "sub-humanity" working underground. Bibhash Mukherjee, Pandeyji and the whole lot of them are hypocrites, selfish and coward sycophants whose only aim is to please the politicians. The officers, like Atul Karna, coming from the higher echelons and from their air-conditioned offices in Delhi hardly have interest in the miners and their problems. They are more interested to make their tour, enjoy liquor and a sumptuous meal and go back to their office to write fake reports. The politicians who receive these papers soon forget about them.

It is the miners who are left to fend for themselves and tackle the dehumanizing and harrowing conditions: "They watched the strange sight, mesmerized by its ghastliness. Water still rises below them but it is perceptible slower. The hunger of the beast has subsided – at least for the moment; and he has left them in relative peace to gorge himself on his latest prey. Narasingh's head floats on the dark water like a coconut smeared red with vermillion and offered to the gods" (76). When the tragedy strikes, the insensitive system has nothing to offer to the miners by way of solution. On the contrary, the management is relieved that the relatives of the miners were in no mood to strike a hard bargain and create problems. "It was fortunate for the GM sahib that Birsa and Sagan came from distant provinces and lived alone in the mining township. Lakhan and Narasingh were each one of several children of their fathers who had worked in the mines for decades and whose families had seen many deaths. Those old mining families had long learnt to accept the ever-looming shadow of death in the mines. Lakhan had two unmarried sisters and if his death translated into some money that would pay for the girls' dowry, his father would be consoled. Ha had four sons. Arif was more feared than liked by most workers and didn't have many friends ... . Luckily for Pandeyji, there were no melodramatic relatives beating their breasts and wailing. That could have whipped up passions that would have spilled over and caused some bother for him" (152). It is sad to see how human worth is gauged against money. The tragedy is not only death underground but the failure of the system to provide security to the workers, the apathy of the government and the selfish attitude of all including the relatives of the miners. Raimoti's brother and sister-in-law wait, not for their man to come out safe but for the confirmation of his death so that they get the compensation offered by the government. And when the money comes they are seen celebrating: his brother pouring a drink for himself and announcing, "They have confirmed it. Raimoti is officially dead"(153). At such a point one wonders whether it is water inside the mine that is the Beast or these perverse human are! Only Tina, Raimoti's niece grieves over her "kaku's" going forever and the "jubilation, the celebration, the bonhomie in the house" for the man who remained uncared for all his life but who gave them a sumptuous two lakh as compensation.

The novel does not focus on the mining disaster only but also on other natural calamities like failure of monsoon, excess rain, damage to crop and the resultant anger of the village youth who take to arms. "In the end it was just the villagers, their hunger and grief. And mounting anger at their helplessness" (58). The Human Rights Charter, the Millennium Development Goals and the concept of globalization have put before us the importance of environmental rights, right to education, equality, culture, dignity, and safety. But ground realities of the life of the poor are different from the reality on paper. Controlling land, labour and resources of the marginalized is usually legimatized with money power and is justified by the notion that the needs of the culturally and materially superior group must get preference over the culturally inferior group. Such dehumanized notions and conditions show flagrant disregard for human rights.

Prior to the publication of *The Sound of Water* (2008) which takes for its theme the 2001 disaster, a report on the Human Rights Conference held in 1992 reiterated that India is aware of human rights and is taking steps to ensure their implementation, "There has been a growing awareness in the country and abroad about the issues relating to human rights. National and international organizations in this field have been highlighting alleged violations of human rights by various government functionaries. There is a growing feeling that the government is not serious about violations and excess and bringing the guilty persons to book" (1992: 1).

It is disconcerting to see how while human rights, Millennium Development Goals and World Development Report, 2000, enjoin on governments to ensure human dignity, alleviation of poverty and providing the basics of life, the self-serving politicians and corrupt officials render all these clauses futile in real life situation. A Tamil short story "Nandanar Street" deals with this problem in a unique way. Written by a dalit writer, Vizhi Pa. Idayaventhan, it is a story of a locality that is denied even as basic a facility as public lavatory. The thickly populated Nandanar street is home to all sorts of hullabaloo, fighting, murder, molestation, dirt and gut-wrenching stink of human excreta. Nandanar Street has grown over the years and is now spilling into the main area of the town. Its population has increased and the resident here are the poor, "transporting sacks (as porters in wholesale market), or vend guavas and bananas, or work as coolies for the day's wage" (170). The problem of the people of Nandanar Street is not just sanitation, it is eve-teasing and molestation when women go out for morning calls. It is no news when the author writes how petition upon petition is piled in municipal office and how the petitioners are disgruntled by the false promises and show off of the officials, MLAs and others. The leader of their community, Koodaipaakkathaan, who lived in a big house called the "Leader's House" poses as a well-wisher of his people but behind the facade of philanthropy, he is filling in his coffers, neglecting the street and his people. Fed up with bleak prospects of improving the situation, the people come up with a novel resisting strategy. They defecate in the early hours of the morning in front of the office rooms of the municipal officials and in the morning when the office opens, people are moving with their handkerchiefs to their nose. The "leader" dubs the act as "disgraceful", but, for the Nandanar dalits, "a small happiness began to sprout" (173). The "public transcript of the powerful," to use James Scott's term, is thus weakened by the resisting strategy applied by the weak. Culturally, it may not be quite polite to write about a subject like lavatory, stench or glorifying the act of dirtying the premises but it is not quite polite either on part of the leaders and officers to deny the people a basic facility. The story is an eye-opener and speaks of the efficacy of peaceful resistance.

The Binding Vine (1993) by Shashi Deshpande is the story of rape but the canvass is vast and there are two sub-plots to the main plot of death. To achieve focus this paper has selected the case of Kalpana's rape because Kalpana's position is peculiarly precarious being a woman and a subaltern. She is doubly deprived of her rights.

Viewing rape through the feminist angle, we find that it is a significant issue for feminists because it denies the right to one's body. In fact, Kalpana's story is just a sub-plot but the novel is so preoccupied with her sad fate that it runs parallel to the main plot and becomes a burning issue. A triangle is formed in which Urmi, the protagonist stands at one end with her mother-in-law (Mira) forming the other end and Kalpana forming the third. Urmi's story becomes the story of all women and the question of women's human rights assumes many shades – should Urmi expect to get equality for Kalpana and her mother; is Urmi free to publish Mira's diary; did Mira have right to her body; did Kalpana have the right to self-assertion? These questions loom large as the reader tries to make sense out of the entangled situation.

The story is told in stream of consciousness technique and the narrative flows back and forth with Urmi's consciousness providing it the required mainstay. The story is simple if narrated in a linear manner – Urmi has lost her little daughter, Anu. She has come to stay with her mother while her husband Kishore has gone to the ship being in the Navy. Urmi's name is Urmila. As Urmi broods over her loss and feels depressed, she interacts with the other members of the family: her mother, her (step) mother-in-law Akka, her sister-in-law Vaana, friends, neighbours and others. One day, Akka brings a trunk full of papers for her perusal and Urmi discovers a treasure. These are Mira's diaries, letters and verses. A vast vista is opened before Urmi who reads the poems between her job, household chores, and her social service activities. During the course of her readings she recreates the life of her dead mother-in-law, Kishore's real mother, Mira (Akka is his stepmother). Mira's poems reveal her anguish; it lies in her inability to have right to her body. She has to succumb to her husband's demands every night.

As Urmi is coping with her grief, a young woman, Kalpana belonging to the working class is raped. Urmi gets interested in the case and fights to get justice for the victim. Deshpande shows the immutable and impenetrable social structure through her art of story telling. The society is not ready to think of Kalpana as the victim of man's lust. There seems no possibility of getting justice under the circumstances because the society lays the blame of Kalpana and paints her almost as a "professional". Another significant point is that even if Kalpana gets justice, she will never be its beneficiary as she is lying in a coma and is struggling with life. But, Urmi and the implied author believe that it would be inhuman were she denied justice. She cannot be deprived of her human rights.

The reaction of the society is either lukewarm or predictably callous. Urmi is almost alone in her fight. Her mother, friends and Vanaa try to dissuade her from getting involved in "such" a matter. By "such a" they mean of a fallen woman. The attitude of the authorities, both police and medical, is not complementary either. They are all eager to hush up the matter. They, indeed, would have filed the entire episode as an accident and steered clear of responsibility to investigate further had Urmi not taken a hard stand. The victim's mother does not want the story to be reported. "No, no, no. Tell him, tai, it's not true, don't tell anyone. I'll never be able to hold my head again, who'll marry the girl, we're decent people. Doctor" ..., "don't tell the police" (58). The doctors and the police inspector find it easier to report that it was a case of accident. Dr Bhaskar comes out with the usual male theory that possibly Kalpana was a "professional". The police officer argues "why make it case of rape, he asked? She's going to die anyway, so what difference does it make whether, on paper, she dies the victim of an accident or a rape? We don't like rape cases, the man said. They are messy and troublesome, never straightforward" (88).

For these people, the important thing is not the woman's misery but what the police officer likes or dislikes. Unfortunately, even Vanaa is not free from prejudice. After the report is published she asks Urmi, "Does it help the girl to be exposed like this?" To this Urmi's acerbic reply is, "What do you mean exposed? ... You talk as if she's the one who's done wrong." This is the crux of the matter. All those who learn of the case, including Shakutai throw the blame on Kalpana. Shakutai and Sulu think Kalpana invited trouble due to her modern living, with lipstick and gaudy clothes and her uninhibited ways, and also for not paying heed to sane advise coming from them both. The worst has been done and who pays the price? Kalpana. But both Urmi and the author are uncomfortable with the society's verdict of honour and dishonour. They have a volley of questions. Can we really blame Kalpana for having a dream; for refusing to be a mistress and a co-wife; for defending herself when the Sulu's lustful husband tried to molest her; for being lively and vivacious; for asserting herself?

The novel provides us sufficient clues to understand what it means to suffer discrimination and how it has penetrated to the very roots of system. Here it assumes human rights colour. Women are not just the body, nor are they only mothers or wives or other relations. They are individuals who experience the joys and pleasures, sufferings and pains, desires and needs within and outside the home and community. When Kalpana wants to enjoy this freedom she is crushed. Not only does the society indict her, her mother also laments that she failed to live within the limits of a woman's existence. What was Kalpana's fault? That she loved life, she liked to dress well and she loved a boy and refused to marry her aunt Sulu's husband who by implication is her uncle. The CEDAW envisages autonomy and individual rights to women. To recognize women's rights as human rights requires political will and the courage to break the dominant hegemony. This is what Urmi does when she gives the story to the press. Once the media brings out facts and exposes the culprit, the tables turn. The facts get publicity; there are questions in the Assembly and the hospital authorities that had refused to keep Kalpana in that dead-alive condition are now forced to keep her in the hospital. Her mother Shakutai gains public sympathy and through this Shashi Deshpande shows the power of the press and of organized action.

Shakutai and others had seen the rape case as a stigma but Urmi challenged the stigma associated with it, defied the prejudices and the blindness of social, cultural and economic institutions. She made it known that women do not just need fulfilment of basic needs, they are also entitled to live a life of self-esteem, dignity and respect. Granted that Kalpana can probably never enjoy these benefits but at least she has the human right to her dignity even in death. She cannot plead her innocence but that does not mean that she should be remembered in death as guilty.

The two novels analysed in this paper point out the importance of human rights for women as well as for men. Bakha, a downtrodden has the right to be free of fear as Kalpana has. Violence against women, children and the weak is also a Human Rights issue. It involves right to life, freedom from torture, personal security and liberty and the right to equality. Bakha as well as Kalpana are victims of violence. In Kalpana's case, she is vulnerable to physical attack because she is a woman. And because she is a woman, the blame comes to her, it never goes to the man. In Bakha's case, the attack is more in the nature of psychological violence through abusive language. Violence does not mean only physical violence, it denotes mental or verbal torture also. The 1991 Convention on Women and Violence categorically states that violence includes "any act, omission or conduct by means of which physical, sexual or mental suffering is inflicted, directly or indirectly, through deceit, seduction, threat, harassment, coercion, or any other means." Any act directed towards humiliating a person or punishing him or her falls in this category. The human rights recognize a person's right to self-determination, which is denied to both Kalpana and Bakha by the society.

Rape has been defined as a "forcible ravishment of a woman by a man. It is one of the manifestations of her oppression and an expression of male chauvinism," says P.D. Mathew in his book *The Law on Rape*. The Law Commission in its report on rape regarded it as the "ultimate violation of the self". It is a humiliating event in a woman's life, which leads to fear for existence and a sense of powerlessness. In 1993, a judge of the Pune High Court said while sentencing a rapist to life imprisonment that the offence of rape could be aptly described as a criminal and violent attack on the body, mind and the fundamental rights of a woman.

Violence is manifested in two forms: institutional or structural and open and direct violence. Structural violence is present in the political, economic and social systems wherein oppression is maintained against those denied social, political and economic benefits. In the case of both the subaltern and women structural and direct violence are complementary. Violence is crystallized in openly discriminatory laws, reinforcing at the same time social conduct, which implies direct violence. It is tolerated as part of the power game.

Creative writers give vent to their anger against the society by creatively and artistically weaving the lived realities. Mulk Raj Anand's Bakha may be a fictional character but he is real because we see him or the likes of him around us. Anand saw the pain of an outcaste in real life, assimilated the experience in his consciousness and presented it artistically in the novel. Shashi Deshpande recounts in one of her interviews that when she was in Bangalore where her husband was a doctor, she learnt about the rape case of a nurse who was in a coma. She wrote of it for *Femina*. Her account generated a lot of public interest and help came through many sources. The incident stayed with her and she used the incident with appropriate changes and wove the story in her novel. As she tells in her interview with Lakshmi Holmstron:

> The theme came to me suddenly. I was actually working on another novel, and one day, suddenly I realized that this was what I had to write. It started with an incident that happened in a hospital when my husband was working there. We were staying next to the nurses' quarters at the time. There was a particular nurse whom we used to see everyday coming and going. A very pretty, attractive woman, a radiant kind of person. She was raped, she was found unconscious in the basement of one of the hospital buildings and she never recovered consciousness. It is seventeen years now and she is still alive.

> At the time when this happened, I reported it for *Femina*. They had asked me to do so, and I'd spoken to the matron and got all the facts. And it stayed in my mind. I thought it was the most terrible thing that I had come across. (Pathak, 1998: 250)

Literature has often portrayed the realities of social life and given a call for change, and for recognizing the human dignity of individual man, woman or child. The post-independence writers give voice to the oppressed; they protest to show that they are not the helpless victims; they defy if need be. Interestingly, these characters are intelligent and show sense of human dignity and understanding. It is significant to note that authors who are themselves from the upper strata of society portray them. The myth that only a dalit could identify with the problems of their class and caste is exploded to a certain extent.

In *The Great Indian Novel,* the author has given voice to Eklavya. He is no longer the tongue-tied pupil blindly devoted to his Guru. He is defiant and aggressive and has the guts to refuse to comply with the uncharitable demand of his revered teacher. Kamala Markandaya's *Nectar in a Sieve,* a novel of the 1950s, has Rukmani, a landless farmer's wife who is aware enough to accept the scientific spirit of the times. When in the town, she uses her ability to write to earn a living. Another farmer woman, Mulk Raj Anand's Gauri protests against her husband's words and fights tooth and nail to save her honour. In Bhabani Bhattacharya's novels the farmers, the village ironsmiths and others are painted as individuals, they are not just stock characters, they have self-respect and the ability to assert the self. Suruchi, in *Shadow From Ladakh,* views Jhanak (the untouchable woman) as "the spirit of the age", having "courage, the resolve to grasp life between her hands; and the boldness to fight tooth and nail to secure whatever she deeply wanted". Even beggars have been the subject of many stories and poems.

Another section of the society is the domestic servant class. The postcolonial Indian urban society demonstrates, in a way, the continuation of the colonial culture. It is a servant-dependent culture. Authors in almost all the regional language literatures of India have depicted the condition of the domestic servants. How the servant children protest makes an interesting thematic study. Sudha Narvane's Marathi short story 'Suud' (Revenge) portrays the defiance shown by Veenu, a servant boy. Ill-treated by the mistress of the house the young lad takes his revenge on her child. He teaches abusive language to the child and makes him repeat the unutterable in the presence of guests. He runs away after accomplishing his mission. In another Marathi story the beautiful clothes, earrings and other goodies possessed by the daughters of the house who are her age, fascinate their young maidservant. Humiliated by the eldest daughter of the family, the servant girl cuts holes in her new birthday sari and feels satisfied for having avenged herself on her tormentor. Talat Abbasi, a Pakistani writer also focuses on the problems of the servants. In some of her stories we see how children internalize adult discrimination and power politics. One of her stories displays the effect of class conditioning on a six-year-old girl for whom her teenage maidservant is "only a servant woman". The servant is supposed to comply with the child's whims as she unknowingly views herself as the little commander. She is aware of her power over the servant who can be "kicked out" by her parents.

Not all masters are cruel, though. There are those who take a humanitarian approach like the protagonist of *Inside the Haveli.* She is liberal and she ascertains that her servants' children go to school. The child-narrator in *Ice-Candy Man* feels sorry for her Ayah. In Shashi Deshpande's novels, many of the protagonists understand the maids' plight.

One of the significant postmodern trends is subversion of the given myths. Writers subvert an existing myth to correct a given picture. Contemporary Indian literature gives voice to the subaltern to expose the society's attitudes towards poverty, discrimination and power politics. The oppressed are no longer inarticulate. By telling their story, by writing about their conditions and circumstances, the writers are bringing out new postcolonial fiction, one that examines the materiality of the local and the present rather than the cultural legacy of the inherited past, one that poses a new set of questions about social stratification. As Gangadhar Gadgil observes, "The development of modern literature in Indian languages is closely associated with the social transformation that has been taking place in the country for a century." These portraits of the oppressed, the downtrodden and the subaltern enable the reader to view them as humans, not just faceless, helpless victims but men and women with their specific individuality, their human rights and human dignity.

References

Anand, Mulk Raj. *Untouchable*. Bombay: Kutub Books, 1935.

Bahadur, Sanjay. *The Sound of Water*. New Delhi: IndiaInk/Roli Books, 2008.

Berry, Margaret. *Mulk Raj Anand: The Man and the Novelist*. Amsterdam: Oriental Press, 1971.

Deshpande, Shashi. *The Binding Vine*. New Delhi: Penguin, 1993.

Forster, E.M. "Preface." Mulk Raj Anand's *Untouchable*. Bombay: Kutub Books, 1935, vi.

Idayaventhan, Vizhi Pa. "Nandanar Street." Trans. Meena Kandasamy. *No Alphabet in Sight: New Dalit Writing from South India*. New Delhi: Penguin, 2011, 169–173.

Kirpal, Viney, ed. *Postmodern Indian Fiction in English*. Bombay: Allied Publishers, 1996.

Mukherjee, Meenakshi. *The Twice Born Fiction*. New Delhi: Arnold-Heinemann, 1971.

Pathak, R.S. *The Fiction of Shashi Deshpande*. New Delhi: Creative, 1998.

Report of the Chief Ministers Conference on Human Rights. September, 1992.

Scott, James C. *Weapons of the Weak: Everyday Forms of Peasant Resistance*. New Delhi: Oxford University Press, 1985.

Spivak, Gayatri Chakravorty. "A Literary Representation of the Subaltern: Mahasweta Devi's 'Stanadayini'." *Subaltern Studies*, V, 91–133.

10 Can We Exonerate Balram Halwai?

Arvind Adiga's debut novel *The White Tiger* (2008) entered the world of literature with the Man Booker Prize in its bag and, as was expected, it promptly received brick-bats and bouquets. While the Booker Committee called it an eye-opener and praised it as a singular voice, and the western reviewers were tickled by the "chatty" murderer protagonist's exposé of "the underbelly of India's tiger economy;" the Indian reviewers were not as amused by its portrayal of contemporary Indian reality. Many questioned Adiga's credentials – he is seen as an insider-outsider – to write about India. For some the novel is "inauthentic", for others just "tedious and unfunny slog". Son of a doctor, and having lived and studied primarily in the USA, England and Australia his knowledge about "real India" seems to be limited to media coverage, contend his critics. But, to be fair to Adiga, let us say that whatever be the merits and demerits of *The White Tiger*, it cannot be denied that it raises some pressing social issues and though we find it hard to sympathize and empathize with the villainous protagonist we cannot but appreciate the caustic humour with which Adiga portrays his protagonist's rise and fall, exposing in the process the ever widening social gaps, the corroding political system and the erosion of values. Nothing is sacred to people like Balram and one wonders at the fate of the country were it to fall in the hands of such criminal "entrepreneurs" and men of "action and change" (4–5), what would be the fate of the country in times to come? "I'm tomorrow," Adiga's protagonist utters with confidence. Will this be the wave of the future – corrupt, unscrupulous and devilish? Many questions arise in our mind to annoy us: Is the famous "idea of India" reduced to this? Is it good to overlook the tremendous progress globalized India has made despite the likes of Balram? Why it is that Adiga has no patience to stop and take look at the other Indian realities that he may have come across the mega cities like Mumbai, Kolkata and Bangalore? These questions have been answered in the course of our discussion.

The novel tells the story of one Balram Halwai, the son of a rickshaw-puller who dreams it big and becomes a successful entrepreneur. But unfortunately, it is not the usual rag to riches tale worth emulating, nor is it the story of Lady Fortune smiling on an underprivileged. It is not even a crime-thriller. It is a grim and angry narrative that seems to be taking the protagonist from "darkness" to "light" to throw him in darkness again, the abysmal darkness of hell within. At the end of the novel Balram Halwai alias Ashok Sharma does not regret his heinous crime, instead he asserts, "I'll never say I made a mistake that night ... when I slit my master's throat. I'll say it was all worthwhile to know, just for a day, just for an hour, just for a minute, what it means not to be a servant" (320–321). In his BBC interview after the Booker, Adiga defended his protagonist on humanitarian grounds, "the people at the bottom have the same aspirations as the middle-class – to make it in life, to become businessmen, to create business empires. They need to be given their legitimate needs – the schooling, the education, the health care – to achieve those dreams. If not, there are only two ways to go up – either through crime or through politics which can be a variant of crime." Despite what Adiga has to say and in spite of Balram's reality, can we as readers corroborate his action? Certainly not! We are left with an uneasy feeling of being with a cold-blooded monster for too long. Is it then the novel's failure? Or is it its success – for having made us angry and aware of our present socio-political set up?

The story is written in the form of letters to the Chinese Premier in the course of seven nights. With his mordant humour, bitter sarcasm and amusing observations Balram reveals his life story from childhood to manhood, from his innocent past to his corrupt present. It is in a way the tale of innocence to experience. He throws one significant question open: who is to be blamed for making him a criminal? Reading on, we put the pieces together and know that his father was an impoverished rickshaw-puller but he had a dream – to educate his son, so that "he should live like a man". Balram goes to school for a couple of years but he cannot pursue his education and becomes a teashop boy. His mother and later his father die, spewing blood in a dirty hospital without medical aid. At some point in this zigzag narrative we feel interested in the boy and want to track how a child who cannot see even a lizard being killed and whose biggest boyhood ideal/idol is the bus conductor, Vijay (with his Khaki uniform and a shining whistle) becomes an inveterate murderer and a grabbing entrepreneur. That is what keeps us glued to the story.

The end is well-nigh predictable because in the beginning of his story Balram has already given a few key points to his readers: first, he is a fugitive murderer; second, the police are after him; and third, he cannot be caught as long as he has the "brown" envelope and there are officials ready to accept it. Another significant pointer pertains to his identity. As a boy he has had no name because his father and mother and aunts did not have "time" to give him a name. Possibly, they did not ever think in terms of giving the child a name as an identity but amazingly, he acquires four identities that come handy to him in his chequered career. We mark his confidence despite his dilemma on the first day of his registration in school. His name is "Munna", he tells the teacher:

> "Munna? That's not a real name."
> He was right: it just means 'boy'.
> "That's all I've got, sir," I said.
> It was true. I'd never been given a name.
> "Didn't your mother name you?"
> "She's very ill, sir. She lies in bed and spews blood. She's got no time to name me."
> "And your father?"
> "He's a rickshaw-puller, sir. He's got no time to name me." (13)

So the teacher picks up Balram as his name. Soon, Balram impresses the school Inspector by his quick answers and gets the nick name "White Tiger" because the Inspector finds him "intelligent, honest, vivacious", a rare species in "*this* jungle" (35). Later, amused by his rustic ways, a fellow driver in Gurgaon calls him "Country-Mouse". Paradoxically, the same Country-Mouse turns White Tiger, devours his master, adopts the deceased master's name – Ashok – and flourishes as Ashok Sharma, the entrepreneur. From Munna to Ashok, from a servant to the master of twenty-six Toyota Qualises and as many employee drivers and from a village boy to "An entrepreneur living in the world's centre of technology and outsourcing Electronic City" Balram's rise is spectacular albeit full of deceit, deviousness and crime. Long back in school the Inspector had gifted him a book entitled *Lessons for Young Boys from the Life of Mahatma Gandhi* which he could never read. Instead he became a regular reader of the *Murder Weekly* handed down by his driver friends; that probably made the walk to crime easy.

The grim murder story becomes palatable with Balram/Arvind Adiga's acute sense of humour. One cannot help smiling when he tells the Chinese Premier that one day India will beat China in progress because China may have drinking water, sewage system, Olympic gold but it does not have democracy. India may not have drinking water, good roads, sewage system, Olympic Gold medals but we have democracy. It is another matter that our democracy is run by beastly musclemen, upstarts like the conductor-turned-politician and the Great Socialist with ninety-three criminal cases pending against him. This Great Socialist has embezzled billions of dollars that are deposited safely in a bank in a small European country with "white people and black money". Everything on earth is possible in India and much more is possible in the State named "Darkness" of which Balram is the denizen. In school children are made to read and regurgitate that they are fortunate to be born in Gaya district which is hallowed by Lord Buddha's enlightenment. Balram's village Laxmangarh in particular is doubly blessed because Buddha walked through it. However, looking at the condition of his village with open drains and filth and the family of pigs strolling along, Balram doubts "if the Buddha walked through Laxmangarh – some people say he did. My own feeling is that he ran through it – as fast as he could – and got to the other side – and never looked back!" (18).

The novelist vents his spite on the local zamindars who are animals in human form. With greatest contempt Adiga has his hero recount the terror the four wicked landlords have spread: the Stork has control over all water sources and every fisherman has to pay him the charges for fishing; the Buffalo is the master of all rickshaws and the poor rickshaw-pullers are obliged to pay one-third of their earnings to him; the Wild Boar owes all the good agricultural land and the farmers are his serfs; the Raven owes the grazing land and the shepherds have to pay him the cut. In fact, so strong is their hold on all the poor of the village that getting out of their clutches is impossible. During his brief visit to his village Balram notices how his brother Kishan has emaciated and Balram observes sadly that in the feudal system the landlords would "scoop him out from inside and leave him weak and helpless" as they had done to their father (86).

At this moment he feels that one requires immense courage to get out of this slavery. "They remain slaves because they can't see what is beautiful in this world" (40) quoting a poet Balram boasts of his ability to see "beauty" because he has managed to opt out of slavery. But ask him what "beauty" he has seen and he will fumble. Ask him what he has achieved after getting his freedom and he will be left bewildered. The irony is that Balram has no vision. He is just angry and his main thrust is to grab money, to imitate the moneyed people whom he has despised all along. His world is not different from the world of the dime-a-dozen rich; corruption, nepotism, shenanigans, everything is rampant in his dealings too. He is the one who has hoodwinked the law; he greases the palms of the concerned officer to save one of his drivers involved in an accident; and once he becomes the boss, he acts as one. Let us not forget how he enjoys lording over the Nepali guard at Dhanbad after he has managed to betray Ram Pershad, driver no.1. Every time he takes a bold step, he thinks he is going away from "Darkness" to "Light". What light can a man like him bring to "Darkness" when he himself becomes the devil?

Balram admits that he has become a devil; he pictures himself as one:

> God says: *I am powerful. I am huge. Become my servant again.*
>
> Devil says: *Ha!*

> When I remember Iqbal's Devil, as I do often, lying here under my chandelier, I think of a little black figure in a wet khaki uniform who is climbing up the entranceway to a black fort … . There he stands now, one foot on the ramparts of the Black Fort, surrounded by a group of amazed monkeys (87).

This khaki-clad man is Balram, the devil, whose shocking bid at freedom has cost him everything, his home, his people, and his peace of mind. But he does not mind it because he may not have peace of mind, he has sackfuls of money and a chandelier overhead, symbol of power and wealth.

In the present scenario, money is power and greed is its bastion. Balram has no education, no culture but he has money and with money in his hand he can do any mischief, very much like the Imp in Leo Tolstoy's story. He is, he says "an original listener"; this quality gives him a fairly good amount of knowledge from the bits and pieces of conversation going on at the back of the car while he is driving. This knowledge comes handy when he plans his moves: from Call Centre business he will shift into real estate and thereafter open a school where the children will not be told about Gandhi, Nehru, Buddha, the Ganges and such like aspects of our culture but will be taught *great lessons* of life. What these "lessons" could be, we can well imagine. If education becomes business run by the likes of Balram Halwai one shudders to think of the state of our education. What will we and our future generation be with an illiterate, unscrupulous murderer at the helm of affairs of an educational institution? Earlier, Mr Ashok observes, in another context, that the fate of this country is in the hands of illiterate opportunists like his chauffeur. "He can read but he doesn't get what he's read. He's half-baked. The country is full of people like him, I'll tell you that. And we entrust our glorious parliamentary democracy … to characters like these. *That's* the whole tragedy of this country" (10). Mr Ashok's observation has substance but being from the exploiter clan of the landlords and been too long in America, he does not know how the "half-baked" fellows are produced.

Balram broods over the problem of children like him who are not given a chance to grow into full human beings. Their education is lopsided and incomplete:

> Open our skulls, look in with a penlight, and you'll find an odd museum of ideas: sentences of history or mathematics remembered from school textbooks ... sentences about politics read in a newspaper while waiting for someone to come to an office, ... bits of All India Radio news bulletins, things that drop into your mind, like lizards from the ceiling, in the half-hour before falling asleep – all these ideas, half formed and half digested and half correct, mix up with other half-cooked ideas in your head, and I guess these half-formed ideas bugger one another, and make more half-formed ideas, and this is what you act on and live with. (10–11)

The Rooster Coop analogy, an acerbic attack on the system, is another potent factor to understand the inability of poor to rebel. The Rooster Coop is a suffocating situation of no-return:

> Hundreds of pale hens and brightly coloured roosters, stuffed tightly into wire-mesh cages, packed as tightly as worms in a belly, pecking each other and shitting on each other, jostling just for breathing space; the whole cage giving off a horrible stench – the stench of terrified, feathered flesh. On the wooden desk above this coop sits a grinning young butcher, showing off the flesh and organs of a recently chopped-up chicken, still oleaginous with a coating of dark blood ... . The roosters know they're next. Yet they do not rebel ... The very same thing is done with human beings in this country. (173–174)

Like the roosters the poor are trapped and are made psychologically unfit to rebel and get out. It is amazing, he says, how "a handful of men in this country have trained the remaining 99.9 per cent – as strong, as talented, as intelligent in every way – to exist in perpetual servitude; a servitude so strong that you can put the key of his emancipation in a man's hand and he will throw it back at you with a curse" (176). The sad truth of the coop is that it is "guarded from inside" (194). Balram has experienced how servants forestall any other servant's move towards innovation or experimentation. Freedom is neither permissible nor possible in this set-up.

As the protagonist of an angry narrative out to show the brutality of the society towards the Rooster Coop people like him, Balram should have moved us to pity but unfortunately he does not.

He emerges through his letters as an opportunist, money grabbing, pitiless swindler who never has had any values to speak of – neither cultural nor personal. Nothing is of value to him – his people are all pawns for him, he speaks of them as one would refer to an inanimate object; he acts heartlessly when he drives past his family without ever looking at their wistful faces; his temper tantrums over the issue of marriage are ungainly; he derides all faiths sparing none and he uses derogatory language for all great men. Making fun of every socio-cultural practice he tells the Chinese Premier, "It is an ancient and venerated custom of people in my country to start a story by praying to a Higher Power. I guess, Your Excellency, that I too should start off by kissing some god's arse" (8). A few sentences later he clarifies with intended disrespect, "That's not to say that I don't respect them, Mr Premier! Don't you ever let that blasphemous idea into your yellow skull. My country is the kind where it pays to play it both ways: the Indian entrepreneur has to be straight and crooked, mocking and believing, sly and sincere, at the same time" (8–9).

Adiga makes efforts to depict the tender side of Balram so that he is not condemned outright as out-an-out a villain. The narrative is interspersed with episodes and experiences to show his "becoming" – as a boy he is a coward, has fear of the "black thing" at the entrance of the Black Fort, and a life-long dread of the lizard; he feels distressed at the animal-like existence of the construction workers in the metropolis living in make-shift tents. However, no one cares for what he feels. People only see what he is – a servant to be exploited. For example, though a driver, he has to wash and press his employer's feet and legs. When he presses too hard, the Stork gives him a sharp blow because the servant-class "expect it from us" and "they respect us for it" (72). Acceptance is the only way to deal with such humiliations. "We are like sponges – we absorb and grow" (71), comments Balram. He is treated worst than their dogs, Cuddles and Puddles. "They're worth more than you are!" he is told. Many a time even the good-natured Mr Ashok amuses his difficult wife, Pinky Madam, using Balram as a scapegoat, like making him repeat the word "Pizza" and then laughing at his pronunciation or testing his general knowledge and deriding him and his ilk. Mr Ashok is by and large considerate to him but he too is deeply dyed in the Zamindari ethos, his American polish notwithstanding. He and Pinky Madam shoo him away like a cur; Mukesh Sir takes full advantage of his position and almost tricks the helpless driver into taking on himself the blame of the accident. The point that goes against Balram, the writer of these seven letters, is that he tells his story with much flourish, in the process he loses credibility and looks too devious to be human and humane. Balram's portrait grows dim. He looks like a hardened criminal. His flippancy turns to his own disadvantage. The intension is to expose the system and to exonerate the victims of this system but somehow his mocking tone does not allow us to see him in any positive light. Ultimately one feels disgusted with Balram and also with Adiga. A journalist and a writer, Amitava Kumar, points out in his article in *The Hindu*, "Halwai's voice sounds like a curious mixture of an American teen and a middle-aged Indian essayist." He calls Adiga's villain "cartoonish" like the characters in a bad Bollywood melodrama (Kumar, 2008).

Slowly, as the narrative advances, Balram emerges as an innate cheat and a shirker. As a teashop boy he gets spanking from the owner for shirking work. While at Dhanbad, he betrays his fellow driver, gets him sacked and grabs the opportunity to drive the Honda to Delhi with Mr Ashok and Pinky Madam. Unconcerned and selfish, he heartlessly thrusts aside family feelings and squanders his salary on wine and women. He exploits everything, every situation to turn it to his advantage – his caste (Halwai) to impress upon his master that he does not drink or eat meat; his religiosity (he bows at temple en route to impress Ashok and Pinky Madam); he betrays Ashok's trust and exploits his weakness. At one place in the story Balram tells M. Jiabao that only a person who can sacrifice his family can ever think of breaking away from the rooster coop. So powerful is his craving to get his freedom and the money in the red bag that he becomes selfish, forgets what may happen to his people. Is he so naïve as to think that the powerful Buffalo and Mongoose will let his family go unhurt after his nefarious deed of murdering Ashok? One more point that goes against Balram – killing the inoffensive Mr Ashok who has been kind to him cannot be rated as an act of vengeance for the wrongs done to the subaltern community by powerful clouts of his village. There is no denying the fact that Balram suffers psychologically after the hideous crime. "I stay up the whole night, Your Excellency," he writes in the beginning of his letter. If he sleeps he has nightmares. He is frightened (not of being caught but of his conscience). Despite these psychological problems, he has no regret. He nonchalantly accepts the inevitable and after performing the last rites of his granny and uncles and cousins, he tells the dead flippantly to leave him in peace. At such moments he appears a veritable "cold-blooded monster".

Now, a look at the question of authenticity! Many Indian readers are critical of Adiga for venturing into explicating India to the west with his insufficient knowledge of present-day India. Many critics like Amitava Kumar are angry with the novel. One may or may not agree with Kumar because his bitterness seems to be personal, he himself being from Bihar. What was happening in Bihar when Adiga was writing this novel – lawlessness, the ever widening gap between the rich and the poor, the caste divide, the savage ways to deal with opponents and much more – is common knowledge and cannot be disclaimed. My point of contention is different: Adiga has garnered knowledge about the rich, the political goons and the musclemen from the media (there is umpteen material available in print and electronic media); he has gleaned information about the rickshaw-pullers and the poor through his interaction with them (as he admits having talked to them) but he has not seen their life from close quarters. He has not entered their psyche, their inner quarters. Arvind Adiga lets his hero Balram call his grandmother "Kusum" by her first name. Is it a done thing, even among the poor classes of India? Adiga refers to the last journey of his mother: her body covered with a saffron silk cloth, and people shouting "Shiva's name is truth." Any Hindu would know that it is "Ram's name is truth." And from where and how do these people who do not have enough to cover their bodies, get silk cloth to cover the dead body? Even the descriptions of locations are inauthentic and they lack emotional touch. Moreover, Adiga and his Balram know only two classes: the stinking rich and the smelly poor; what about the real middle class? From our observation of the people around us we know the Bihari educated class to be hard working and intelligent – good people with moderate habits. They are likeable; not fiendish like Balram. The protagonist tells Mr Wen that in olden days there were one thousand castes and destinies in India. These days there are two castes: "Men with Big Bellies and men with Small Bellies." But doesn't Balram himself become the "Big Belly" soon after getting money? So how can he be absolved?

Adiga's "outsider" position becomes obvious by his lack of attachment to the land – not only Bihar but India too. There are not many descriptive passages in the novel but at two places when he depicts Balram's journey to and from Laxmangarh with his master, he is too distant to appreciate and admire the ambience:

> We drove along a river, and then the tar road came to an end and I took them along a bumpy track, and then through a small market-place with three more or less identical shops, selling more or less identical items of kerosene, incense and rice. Everyone stared at us. Some children began running alongside the car. Mr Ashok waved at them and tried to get Pinky Madam to do the same. (82)

His return journey is also as impersonally described:

> I drove through the greenery, through the bushes and the trees and the water buffaloes lazing in the muddy ponds; past the creepers and the bushes; past the paddy fields; past the coconut palms; past the bananas; past the neems and the banyans; past the wild grass with the faces of the water buffaloes peeping through. A small, half-naked boy was riding a buffalo by the side of the road; when he saw us, he pumped his fists and shouted in joy – and I wanted to shout back at him: *Yes, I feel that way too! I 'm never going back there!* (89)

If we compare and contrast these with V.S. Naipaul's intensity of feelings for the land of his birth we are able to judge the difference. Naipaul was as disillusioned and frustrated with the India he saw in 1964 – decayed, dirty, incompetent and corrupt. But he is moved by the country's human side; he realizes that it is not the country of glossy travel books but a land of delight. Naipaul says "Out of its squalor and human decay, its eruptions of butchery, India produced so many people of grace and beauty" (1964: 256–257). Similarly, Sura P. Rath captures nostalgically the sights, sounds and smells of the countryside of his childhood the "dew-damp mornings", the smell of cow dung, the stone steps of the village pond and the mud walls with complex mythic images "where gods smiled in their cosmic glee" (Rath, 2003: 95–96). It could be argued that Naipaul and Sura P. Rath are looking at the country from the vantage point of their caste and monetary status while Adiga's protagonist is the subaltern and since his experiences are harrowing hence his vision is corroded. But, even the disadvantaged have sentiments for their place of birth.

An early review published in *The Economist* likens *The White Tiger* to Dickens's novels calling Balram the 'Pip' of the Call Centre generation. Another critic, Adrian Turpin, asks if Balram is "just another thug in India's urban jungle or a revolutionary and idealist?" (*The Financial Times,* 2008). Nothing can be far-fetched than these comparisons. Balram is not a revolutionary and he is far less an idealist. "An Indian revolution? No, Sir. It won't happen" (304), he asserts with vehemence. He is witty and psychopathic but he is no 'Pip' nor is Arvind Adiga, Charles Dickens.

These small quarrels apart, let us give Adiga his due. He has the knack of story-telling. He has presented the ruthlessness of power and the survival strategies in unsentimental prose with superb control. As Kevin Rushby points out in his review in *The Guardian,* Balram has a voice which may not be the voice of new India but it is "quick-witted, half-baked, self-mocking and awesomely quick to seize an advantage" (Internet source).

References

Adiga, Arvind. *The White Tiger*. Noida: HarperCollins India, 2008. All references are to this edition.

Consulted for summary reviews: www.complete-reviews.com/reviews/india/ adiga.htm.

Kumar, Amitava. *The Hindu* (Literary Review), November 2, 2008.

Naipaul, V.S. *An Area of Darkness*. London: Andre Deutsch Ltd., 1964.

Rath, Sura P. "Home(s) Abroad: Disporic Identities in Third Spaces." *Theory and Praxis*. Eds. Prafulla C. Kar, Kailash C. Baral and Sura P. Rath. Delhi: Pencraft International, 2003.

11 The Collapse of "Cultural Maps"

Terrorism in Asian Literature

It's all happened before and will happen again,
And we the onlookers
But now I'm in it
It's happened to me
At last history has meaning
When you're the victim
When you're the defeated
The bridges bombed
And you can't cross over.

These lines from a poem by Jean Arasanayagam, entitled "Fusillade 26" eloquently express the trauma of dislocation and displacement of the Tamil community in strife-torn Sri Lanka. But this situation is almost ubiquitous in many Asian and third world countries – Afghanistan, Pakistan, Nepal to name but a few, and in our own land it could be Kashmir or Darjeeling or Assam or Jharkhand where terrorism has raised its ugly head. Kiran Desai's remarks in *The Inheritance of Loss* aptly sum up the unstable situation in Kalimpong with reference to history: "This was how history moved, the slow build, the quick burn, and in an incoherence, the leaping both backward and forward, swallowing the young into old hate. The space between life and death, in the end, too small to measure" (276).

The historical experiences of South Asian countries have been almost similar – colonialism, the freedom movements, the rise of nationalist sentiments, state formations after achieving independence followed by postcolonial struggle to decolonize the mind. In almost all the erstwhile colonies the process of nation building started soon after their independence. In the face of intense historical and political changes, the quest for an identity becomes a major preoccupation. Concerns with ethnic identity, cultural authenticity and political positions often mean recreating continuity with the past by exploring collective images as collective memories play a vital role in reconstructing the identity anew. The issue of ethnic and cultural identity takes on aspects of political identity and gives rise to aggressive sentiments. In many of these countries, ethnic conflicts emerged when the state resorted to suppressive measures to forestall their struggle for cultural, linguistic and political survival, and this resulted in escalating tensions. In India, the problems of ethnic/cultural/language identities and many such issues have given rise to divisive tendencies and the consequent militancy. In Sri Lanka, the declaration of Sinhala as the state language brought in sharp reactions to the hegemony from the Tamils. Whatever the reason behind violence and terrorism, it cannot be denied that the sufferers are the masses and ultimately, the country.

The aim of this paper is to focus on terrorism – not only at socio-political levels but also in the domestic sphere – call it "domestic terrorism" if you may. This paper shall primarily discuss Kiran Desai's *The Inheritance of Loss,* Khaled Hosseini's *A Thousand Splendid Suns* and a short story by Sunethra Rajakarunanayake entitled "SMS". But if need be to substantiate a point or two, some other texts from the subcontinent will be referred to as and when necessary to problematize terrorism and look at its effect on culture and also glance at the new cultures it generates.

Terrorism is not a new phenomenon; what is, indeed, new is its global swoop of late. Terrorism is a politically and emotionally charged word and hence difficult to define. A study conducted by the US army in 1988 discovered more than 100 definitions used in different contexts and different situations. Broadly, "terrorism" denotes nefarious activities undertaken by non-government outfits for achieving some political goal and/or state controlled terrorism undertaken to restore peace and order. The common definitions of terrorism refer to those acts which are intended to create 'fear' or 'terror'. The strategy is to induct fear among the masses and, though these acts are perpetrated for ideological goals, they deliberately target the common people. The sufferers of terrorism whether State-controlled terror-mechanism or the anti-social outfits, are the innocent non-combatant civilian population.

Violence is central to terrorism but terrorism cannot be measured only in terms of violence, nor can it be measured in terms of economic loss; it is by itself an all-encompassing monster of losses – loss of peace, sense of security, belongingness, loss of humanity and above all shattering of faith. When brutality erupts into the private spaces it culminates in the loss of human values. As Jasbir Jain avers, the human culture of sharing, bonding, dependence and of sympathy and empathy collapses and it is replaced by a culture of distrust, betrayals and the resultant hatred. "Among the many casualties of genocidal warfare, ethnic and religious conflicts are a permanent dislocation and disorientation. Violence demands a heavy price: loss of trust and faith and freedom; permanent inhabitation of fear, a continuity and inflaming of the feeling of hatred and revenge bringing about a temporariness in relationships as the areas of refuge go on shrinking" (Jain, 2009: 25). Can human values hold on in this atmosphere? It is this question that this discussion seeks to look into.

Hosseini's *A Thousand Splendid Suns* is set in Kabul and the narrative moves between 1974 and 2003 – a period of three decades spanned by the military rule of President Daoud Khan; the long years of Soviet occupation; the internecine fighting that turned swathes of the country into a war zone and its civilian population into targets for practice; and finally, the emergence of the Taliban in mid-1990s.

Desai's *The Inheritance of Loss* is set in Darjeeling of the recent past/the present with the Gorkha struggle for Statehood, giving rise to GNLF (Gorkha National Liberation Front) violence that seeps slowly into the lives of simple, so far invisible people like the cook, Sai, Noni, Lola and even the Judge and questions their identity. Characters like Father Booty and uncle Potty, who have lived all their lives in Kalimpong suddenly find themselves aliens.

Sunethra Rajakarunanayake's short story "SMS" recounts an experience of travel in the war-torn district of Sri Lanka. The description of desolation amid the beauty of nature and of human tenacity to reconstruct the self, and obliterate the emotional experience of trauma proves to be an enlightening moment for the narrator. Her perception changes when she encounters the Tamil squad of landmines defusing women.

Before we proceed further, let me introduce the authors briefly – Khalid Hosseini was born in Kabul in 1965, the son of a diplomat father and a mother who taught Farsi and History in a high school. With the emergence of the Taliban the family suffered and shifted to the USA where they were given political asylum in 1980. *The Kite Runner* is Hosseini's first novel and it is autobiographical to an extent.

Kiran Desai, born in India in 1971 is Anita Desai's daughter and the author of *Hullabaloo in Guava Orchard*, a hilarious first novel. *The Inheritance of Loss* is her second and is a Booker winner. Kiran stays in the USA.

Sunethra Rajakarunanayake is a Sri Lankan novelist, poet, translator and media consultant. She writes in Sinhala and also in English and is a widely published writer. Her Sinhala novel *Nandithaya* entitled *Chameleon* in English won her several literary awards. Sunethra is particularly known for her columns on developmental issues and travels in India.

The Inheritance of Loss is the story of Jemubhai who has all along terrorized his wife; and his story is interwoven with the story of Kalimpong and Darjeeling areas rived by terrorist activities of the GNLF. Jemubhai, a one-time ICS aspirant and now a retired judge seeks peace in the Himalayan town of Kalimpong. He has at his back the history of having tortured his wife; and the presence of Sai, his granddaughter is a constant reminder to us – readers – of what his draconian acts have done to the third generation. Sai, let us admit, shows a kind of lop-sided development. She brings to our mind Anita Desai's Raka of *Fire On the Mountain,* the great granddaughter of Nanda Kaul known in Kasauli as "the crazy one". Raka is the product of domestic terrorism, this much we infer from the novel. It is an acknowledged fact that children living in the atmosphere of domestic violence suffer and develop imbalanced personalities. Besides *Fire on the Mountain*, we can draw examples from novels like Arundhati Roy's *The God of Small Things*; Shashi Deshpande's *Small Remedies,* and *A Matter of Time.* These works may not have domestic violence as the major theme but they show the corroding effect of the home atmosphere on the children.

Jemubhai's wickedness falls to the lowest abyss when he ducks his wife Bela's head into the toilet just because she squatted on the European seat instead of sitting on it. Isolating her, pouring cold water on her head, kicking and boxing on her stomach when she was pregnant are a few of his abysmal acts that broke the beautiful Bela both mentally and physically.

Bela was young, charming and beautiful. About her beauty, the cook comments, "You could tell from her features which were delicate, her toes, nose, ears, and fingers were all very fine and small, and she was very fair just like milk. Complexion-wise, they said, you could have mistaken her for a foreigner. Her family only married among fifteen families, but an exception was made for your grandfather because he was in the I.C.S." (88). She was a simple girl tucked in the security of her father's house till her marriage and had no inkling of the outside world. What her husband expected from her, we know not but things went wrong on the first night. To assert himself, the judge resorted to the oldest trick of phallocentric intimidation. Bela's tale of humiliation, injustice, abuses, violence, and battered life commenced within those four walls on the day of consummation of marriage.

Terming violence against women as "sexual terrorism" Carole J. Sheffield writes:

> The word terrorism invokes images of furtive organizations of the far right or left, whose members blow up buildings and cars, hijack airplanes, and murder innocent people in some country other than ours. But there is a different kind of terrorism, one that so pervades our culture that we have learned to live with it as though it were the natural order of things. Its targets are females – of all ages, races, and classes. It is the common characteristic of rape, wife battery, incest, pornography, harassment, and all forms of sexual violence. I call it sexual terrorism because it is a system by which males frighten and by frightening, control and dominate females. (1989: 3)

It is often contended that Jemubhai was an aberrant and his actions were not normal. But that should not redeem him nor can this justify his behaviour. In an authorial intrusion, Kiran Desai writes, "He would teach her the same lessons of loneliness and shame he had learned himself. In public, he never spoke to or looked in her direction" (170). Thus uncared for, tortured and reduced to nought, she lost zest for life, neglected herself and finally lost not only her beauty but also her human demeanour. Looking at her ghastly appearance, the judge passed his edict, "Don't show your face outside. People might run from you, screaming" (173). Did the judge have a tinge of regret at what he had done to his wife? Reading between the lines we realize that many years later Jemubhai wondered if he had killed his wife for the sake of false ideals. He had condemned his wife to insanity, dumped his daughter in a convent school and in later years was obliged to bring his granddaughter to live with him in Kalimpong.

Juxtaposed with this kind of terrorism is the present volatile situation in Kalimpong where the Gorkhas shout "Jai Gorkha" and indulge in petty thefts, bigger loots, and even killings. The scene is of mid-1980s. As the story unfolds, insurgency is growing in the region; the Indian Nepalese want their own country or state, a Gorkhaland where they will not be treated as servants. The Gorkha boys roam the mountainside looting houses, collecting ammunition, deriding and humiliating respectable people. Cho Oyu, the judge's residence is a big old house where the judge, the cook, Sai and Mutt (the judge's dog) live. The other characters in the novel are the cook's immigrant son Biju whom he sent to the US to pursue the American dream; the anglophile sisters Noni and Lola; a Swiss national called Father Booty; the drunk uncle Potty and the young Nepali tutor Gyan, an activist towards whom Sai is amorously inclined in her girlish fantasy.

The novel shows how terrorism perverts human psychology, creates chasm among communities and other ethnic groups, brings them to war against each other on the basis of religion, caste and creed and other narrow considerations. Fear psychosis is generated in the society whereby it loses its rationality and logic. Terrorism has far reaching effects on the political situation of a country as it brings political disorder and its associated effects.

To counter the extremist activities the security personnel use their own methods; and between them, these forces of terrorism and anti-terrorism make a bon fire of normal existence – an innocent drunkard is beaten savagely by the police on the assumed charge of having stolen Mutt, the judge's dog; dignified and harmless Lola and Noni are spat on by the Gorkha boys; Sai is beaten by her dubious teacher-lover Gyan; and Father Booty finds himself friendless when he is implicated for having breached security by taking a photograph of a butterfly.

A Thousand Splendid Suns is the story of two women whom fate brings together through Rasheed, their devilish husband. Miriam is married at fifteen to Rasheed a shoe maker, thirty years her senior. The man treats her brutally particularly because she is unable to give him a son; she conceives seven times and every time suffers miscarriage that flares up Rasheed who tortures her in every possible manner. This internal terrorism is soon supplemented by terrorism in Kabul, rocket attacks and bombardments in which thousands of civilians are killed.

At this point, Laila's story joins Miriam's story. Laila, wounded in terrorist attack is brought home by Rasheed. Later, he marries her and ill-treats her. Miriam's heart goes out to the young girl and she who had earlier hated Laila as a rival develops affection for her. There is bonding between the two which ultimately ends in Mariam sacrificing herself to save Laila. She engineers Laila's escape even though she has to kill Rasheed.

These two women represent the condition of Afghan women – ill-treated, terrorized as much by their male counterparts as by the terrorist activities going on the larger canvas. Kabul is rived by bullets; human beings are roasted as they are treated as targets for bullet practice. Kabul, of the thousand splendid suns of the poet Saib-e-Tabrizi, is not a place fit to live in. People escape to Pakistan, to the US, or wherever they can. The lucky ones get political asylum and survive on ration tickets; the unfortunate ones are intercepted by betrayals and are brought back for target practice. Betrayals are common for gains – political or monetary. Ironically, the poet's words "Ah! How beautiful is Kabul" can be replaced by what Amir's father says in *The Kite Runner*, "You cannot trust anyone in Kabul anymore – for a fee or under threat, people told on each other, neighbour on neighbour, child on parent, brother on brother ..." Miriam and Laila's experience is not different. They are betrayed by the man they trusted. And at this moment Tagore's Kabuliwala flashes before us – the Pathan who would never compromise his loyalty.

A similar picture of distrust and hostility is there in *The Inheritance of Loss* when Noni says, "these Neps can't be trusted." What has happened, one wonders? After living together in the same town for years and years, on trust and goodwill of each other why this sudden distrust? When the spirit of belongingness to a place is killed, the people, the place, the very landmarks one loves become alien and hostile overnight. Our view of the place as civilized, cultured and safe is shattered as the characters become outsiders in a town they had been living in for decades. The cook feels disheartened, "this place where he had with utter safety genuinely lost his temper with the deaf tailors, the inept plumber, the tardy baker with the cream horns; this place where he had resided secure in the knowledge that this was basically a civilized place where there was room for them all; where he had existed in what seemed a sweetness of crabbiness – was showing him now that he had been wrong. He wasn't wanted in Kalimpong and he didn't belong" (278).

The sense of not-belonging engulfs the narrator of the Sri Lankan story "SMS" when she encounters the reality. She is a Sinhalese but her heart goes out to the Tamil women toiling to defuse the landmines on paltry salaries. The last line of the story "Did you send Pushpam her shoes" (87) displays her pain and bewilderment at the plight of the women working in dangerous conditions; it is also the triumph of human values in the end. But to arrive at this the narrator has to traverse not only the geographical terrain rived by landmines and wars but also her inner landscape weighed down by ethnic and cultural factors. Earlier, there is a faint suggestion of pride for her Sinhalese identity, for having a Parliamentarian lover and for her position as a writer/media consultant. She seems to assume an air of self-importance for her Sinhala language when over and over again she refers to her inability to read Tamil, a language in which most of the posters or road signs are written. But slowly as the vehicle moves across the country side, the narrator faces the stark reality of her country.

The journey from Killnochchi to Wadamarachchi is also her journey to discover the effects of terrorism. In the beginning, she is more concerned about her personal safety, "I was afraid of sacrificing my leg to a landmine or going back to Colombo in an ambulance" (83), she says as she drops the idea of walking up to the abandoned railway coach. The beauty en route thrills her but the desolation around makes her uneasy. Change in her attitude is discernible when all poetry in her heart dries at the sight of the empty cottages and houses and the sad faces for the troubled travellers to Colombo. She sends an SMS to her lover, "I may not be able to send you poems from here onwards ... but you are my poem." This romanticism too withers away when she gets his juvenile reply and she fails to respond to his amorous note.

She says, "The feeling I had then was not something that I could explain, just a subtle feeling that could be experienced while strolling on a war torn road" (85). There is a kind of transformation from a lovelorn young woman to the mature thinker moved by the ravages of terrorism – the cultural annihilation, the destruction of life, the ongoing struggle to survive and the common citizen's efforts to connect to humanity. She learns much more through the smiling faces of the Tamil women workers.

While the people suffer, culture is annihilated and life goes out of gear, the political game continues – be it Darjeeling or Afghanistan or Sri Lanka. In Afghanistan, after the Soviet withdrawal, the Mujahideen took control; they were bad enough but at least a little less brutal than the Taliban. The Taliban not only killed the people but killed the very soul of Afghan culture – schools were closed, there was no question of women's education, hospitals were segregated for men and women with no facilities for women. It is painful to read how Miriam and Rasheed are shunted from hospital to hospital with Laila in labour pain. And finally they find a hospital which is so filthy and ill-equipped that one is horrified at the very description. The attitude of the Taliban towards women is, as Mariam sums up, "Like a compass needle that points north, a man's accusing finger always finds a woman. Always."

In Kalimpong, the Indian culture of assimilation and co-existence, so far followed unquestioningly, has suddenly vanished. As the GNLF violence increases the Gorkha boys engage in arson, looting and killing. They are ruthless and for them human relationship and ethics hold no sanctity. Father Booty who has always obliged people has a harrowing experience with a police officer and later with a Nepali doctor who offers to buy his property for nought and has the guts to tell Father Booty, "I have arranged it and you have no choice. You are lucky to get what I am giving you. You are residing in this country unlawfully and you must sell or lose everything" (222). Thus in cultural and emotional terms Father Booty, uncle Potty, the two sisters and many others are rendered homeless.

One of the cultural symbols of Afghanistan is the statue of Bamiyan Buddha which, under the draconian religious laws of the Taliban is destroyed systematically. In one of the scenes of the novel Laila's father takes the children out on a day trip to Bamiyan. The 2000 year old Buddha statues are the part of the rich heritage of their land and their father wants them to feel proud of it. The terrorism perpetuated by Taliban destroys this heritage and leaves nothing to be proud of – museums, books, universities – nothing is of relevance to them. Relationship of human beings to their past is of cultural importance and it is this that they would destroy.

Similarly, when Vishaka, the narrator of "SMS" looks at a beautiful small house, now deserted, she describes it as a "dream house" and depicts it with loving touches. But the ethnic strife has devastated the area beyond recognition – the paddy fields had not been sown for more than ten years, there is green grass around but it has "flourished on nutrients from human bodies to gain such a luscious look. The bodies had just turned to manure where they fell dead" (83). Snakes, dead bodies, landmines and barren fields are left by the LTTE struggle. The author-narrator looks at a pond with white lotuses blooming unmindful of human cruelty and in her excitement she wishes to take a photograph of the beautiful scene. Next moment she spots some iron spikes jutting out of the pond and the stark reality dawns on her that the pond too could have landmines or bombs planted in it. Her enthusiasm vanishes at the thought.

Nevertheless, life offers hope and despair, life and death, the urge to struggle to live. Human will to survive proves stronger than the destructive hand of the demolisher. Life is an everlasting search for love, family, home, and acceptance. Despite problems man seeks a healthy society and a promising future. But peace, future, and stability seem to elude the victims as well as the perpetrators of terrorism. Hope is there but it is always belied. In one of the scenes in *A Thousand Splendid Suns,* when Laila makes a relevant observation while watching "Titanic", "Everybody wants Jack to rescue them from disaster. But there is no Jack. Jack is not coming back. Jack is dead." This is what life under the Taliban is. The Soviet rule was replaced by Mujahidden who were more corrupt; the Mujahiddens were replaced by the Talibans who proved worse and now the people are expecting America to relieve them from Taliban. The pattern of hope and despair continues.

In *The Inheritance of Loss,* Biju remembers nostalgically his carefree boyhood days spent at play all day long till they were exhausted; he broods over their naughty games of throwing stones and slippers into trees to bring down *Ber and Jamun*. But these were the days when life was peaceful. Biju could not imagine the condition of strife-torn Darjeeling/Kalimpong from the USA where he had been slogging as an illegal immigrant restaurant waiter. Poor Biju was destined to come back and experience the humiliation of being stripped of his clothes and belongings – a harrowing home-coming for him!

Whether it is Hosseini's novel or Desai's or the short story of Sunethra, the picture is recognizable. It is replete with the intense psychological, emotional, ideological and interpersonal human losses that terrorism brings with it. When survival is at stake, where is the time or inclination to think of culture, even everyday acts of goodwill and fellow feeling turn into nightmares and the difference between friends and foes, good and bad becomes blurred when brutality comes from within as well as without. As the narrator of "SMS" laments "How unfamiliar we are with the Wanni, the pre-war Wanni as well as the Wanni of today."

When terrorism raises its head and the state tries to control it, other problems crop up which give rise to another type of terrorism – the State controlled terrorism. In "SMS" the narrator learns the lesson of humanitarian concerns when she encounters the forty-eight Tamil women clearing landmines off an area about the size of a large play field. The hazardous nature of their job, the smile on their faces and their ability to give meaning to their existence makes the narrator brood over the games that politicians are playing. To her lover, a parliamentarian, she sends an SMS "It is better to wear large shoes and defuse landmines than strapping bombs on their bodies and killing people. But I still feel sorry for them ..." (86). Obviously, her lover sitting smug and secure in the Parliament, away from the scene cannot make "head or tail" of her message. The narrator feels disgusted and writes, "Parliament had no head, it is enough if you wag your tail" and distances herself from him. Significantly, as she and her companions drive past a Bo tree, a wave of compassion surges through the narrator and she realizes the significance of the "peace pact". The reason why the women workers have smile on their faces despite the hard life is not the wages – only ₹ 1,000 but the hope that the peace pact will bring life to normalcy. It is, indeed, difficult to live constantly haunted by an uncertain future and the fear of death as Charles opines.

As we read about the sadness of the Himalayan towns – Darjeeling and Kalimpong, the ravaged tropical beauty of Sri Lanka, and the Kabul of a thousand splendid suns now devoured by the terrorists, we turn to some works that bring peace and serenity with each page. I remember two novels set in the Himalayas – one by Karma Ura depicting the simplicity of the Bhutan society, entitled *The Hero with a Thousand Eyes*; and another Manjushree Thapa's *The Tutor of History* set in Nepal before the insurgency. These are pictures of peaceful societies and one wonders how one lives when terrorism and violence becomes a lived reality in many parts of Asia and how it shatters the fabric of life. The great powers like the US and the Soviet or the State powers in India play political games, create a vicious circle and within it are entrapped the ordinary people. The novels under discussion interrogate the war cultures; establish faith in human goodness and try to reach out to those who live in fear and insecurity on the periphery of society.

In one of his interviews Hosseini asserts that in *A Thousand Splendid Suns* love manifests itself in various shapes and ultimately it is love that draws characters out of their isolation which gives them strength to transcend their own limitations, to expose their vulnerabilities, and to perform devastating acts of self-sacrifice. The title of the novel has been taken from a 17th century Persian poem by Saib-e-Tabrizi that reads, "one could not count the moons that shimmer on her roofs/And the thousand splendid suns that hide behind her walls." Despite the distrust, anger, torture and fear, there is hope that sustains the culture. A similar hope throbs through Sunethra's story "SMS". In the visitors' book handed over by Vani, the narrator writes:

> May the children swim in this lake
> And the farmer grow rice
> May the young women
> Pluck jasmines not bombs
> That is my earnest
> Healing wish for this land. (86)

References

Desai, Kiran. *The Inheritance of Loss*. New Delhi: Penguin, 2006.

Hosseini, Khaled. *A Thousand Splendid Suns*. London: Bloomsbury, 2007.

Jain, Jasbir. *Crossing Borders: Post-1980 Subcontinental Writing in English*. Jaipur: Rawat Publications, 2009.

Rajakarunanayake, Sunethra. "SMS." *Indian Horizons*. Vol. 55, No. 4. October–December, 2008, 83–87.

Sheffield, Carole J. "Sexual Terrorism." *Women: A Feminist Perspective*. Ed. Jo Freeman, California: Mayfield, 1989.

12 Re-visiting Ithaca and Re-casting Manali

Quest Motifs in *Journey to Ithaca* and "Scholar and Gypsy"

> The fact is that I did not really come here to get here, I sort of drifted here to get away from there.
>
> —Gita Mehta

> You, you don't even know it's possible to find Buddha in a Hindu temple. Why, you can find him in a church, a forest, anywhere. Do you think he's as narrow-minded as *you*?
>
> —Anita Desai's Pat

The words cited above, spoken by one of the "instant nirvana" aspirants in Gita Mehta's *Karma Cola* (1979), and in Anita Desai's short story "Scholar and Gypsy" (1978) exemplify the basic problem of the western instant nirvana seekers who come to India, become disillusioned and feel what Homi K. Bhabha calls "unhomed".[1] It generates alienation in some, in others the desire to reclaim the past surfaces and while others feel charmed and revolted simultaneously. Quest is closely associated with journeying and in literature, particularly in diasporic literature this fluid state is called "dual affiliation".[2] Anita Desai's *Journey to Ithaca* was published in 1995 which explores physical and spiritual journeys of Nirvana seekers – Sophie and Matteo a young couple much fascinated by India but disillusioned with India's ground realities. The novelist re-inscribes the psycho-cartography and constructs a space away from the binaries of the centre and the periphery. Earlier in 1978, Desai had written a long short story "Scholar and Gypsy" set in Manali in which almost the same theme was used but with some variation and of course, on a smaller canvass.

But before I draw extensively on Desai, I wish to take a quick critical look at the works in which the quest motif has been taken up with sensitivity. Gita Mehta's *Karma Cola* is a convincing portrayal of the Hippy problem and their travels across India. In *A River Sutra,* though there is no Hippy to talk of, it is the movement of the tribals of Madhya Pradesh and of the river that becomes a symbol of travelling; also the protagonist is a traveller in time and so are the others who populate the novel; the Narmada Guest House is reminiscent of Omar Khayyam's "caravan sarai" where the travellers stay temporarily before embarking on the final voyage. By substituting spiritual quest for the personal dislocation, the author surreptitiously rewrites the loss of the motherland and creates a cultural sense that is both literary and personal.

Ruth Jhabvala in *Heat and Dust* has chid, a nirvana seeker but it is the narrator-protagonist who sets in motion the quest motif with her decision to set out on a journey to India against all odds to retrieve her grandmother's past. She moves from place to place till she decides to stay at a hill station – probably in the Himalayas. Amitav Ghose's fictional narrator in *The Shadow Lines* embarks on his search for his family's diasporic identity and in *In An Antique Land,* the author travels to Egypt to know the story of Bomma.

An inveterate traveller among the expatriate writers is V.S. Naipaul who not only travels across the world but also makes profuse use of the material to draw up from. For example, *The Enigma of Arrival* demonstrates his struggle with his location and its relations with the past. In *Finding the Centre,* Naipaul, the author tries to explain how the displaced writer goes back to locate the "centre" of his knowledge to systematize and synthesize the experiences of his travel with the demands of the fictional world: "A writer after a time carries his world with him, his own burden of experience, human experience and literary experience (one deepening the other); and I do believe … that I would have found equivalent connections with my past wherever I went" (1985: 10). Thus, in contemporary writing, the quest motif becomes a steering metaphor to find meaning in one's location at a particular time in history, to come to terms with the cultural deprivation, and by moving away from the chartered locales to expose the quintessential incompleteness of all reality and inauthenticity of all worldly experience so as to magnify the general human condition.

The relationship between diasporas and homeland, a complex and ambivalent one, is amply reflected in the novel *Journey to Ithaca*, though her short story too explores the same theme of hippy influx in India. As Victor Ramraj points out, "Diasporic writings are invariably concerned with the individual's or community's attachment to the centrifugal homeland. But this attachment is countered by a yearning for a sense of belonging to the current place of abode" (1996: 216). To avoid the tension between diasporas and homeland, and the confusion created by the overlapping of cultures, the authors rewrite their texts as journeys to give fresh meaning to the condition of being uprooted. This feature of diaspora is amply illustrated by Anita Desai's personal situation. When she was writing *Journey to Ithaca* in the early 1990s (the novel was published in 1995) the novelist was living in the USA, giving courses in creative writing and also dividing her time between England (Cambridge) and the USA. She experienced the third "space" which signifies an unsettled hybrid location, as a journey. But when she wrote the short story "Scholar and Gypsy" she was living in India. Though the theme of both the works is identical, the treatment given to each shows the difference of her location.

In *Journey to Ithaca*, Anita Desai makes use of the spiritual quest motif to counter the uncertainty of the diasporic condition. Matteo and Sophie are travellers and remain travellers all through, physically as well as metaphorically. By placing two Western characters – an Italian and a German – in India (Matteo is from Italy, while Sophie is from Germany), Desai seems to have inverted her own diaspora and by drawing from her homeland – India – she has tried to see life as a continuous quest, an unending journey of the diasporic consciousness. In the third world immigration fiction the journey/quest is a recurrent motif and as Viney Kirpal maintains, "it entails the transition from one state of inner experience to the other" (1982: 71). Matteo becomes a seeker after what the "Mother" terms it "honey", "the honey made from spiritual nectar, nectar to nourish your soul" (118), which is the nectar of the spirit. Sophie remains a skeptic till the end. The novel is open-ended, and it is possible if one were to judge from her words that she may join her husband in his spiritual journey. Obviously, for Sophie the journeys are multiple – from Italy to India (physical journey), the probe into the Mother's past (outward journey in quest of a secret), and the decision to follow Matteo (spiritual quest). In the end of the novel is the beginning of the real journey, of a consciousness in search of the spiritual homeland.

In the short story the questers are Americans – David, a sociology scholar comes to India to write his thesis; Pat, his wife has accompanied him and moves with him across cities – Mumbai and Delhi and finally Manali. It is at Manali that the transformation takes place and she decides to remain in Manali while he goes back to Delhi. The beginning of the story portrays Mumbai and its oppressive humidity. Pat is miserable and retorts when her husband, David, chides that she should have known about Indian summer, "Hot, yes," she moaned, "but not *killing*" (108). With Pat wilting and drooping, it was impossible to stay in Mumbai and they move to Delhi, from there they board the plane to Manali and she revives as soon as she spots the river and the mountains "It's cooler," she chirps but he cannot feel anything. The situation that Desai builds up is almost akin to the one in *Journey to Ithaca* – the summer months, the tiring and uncomfortable journeys and the constant grumbling of Sophie Pat.

At the surface, the novel appears to be moving on the familiar plane – the story of spiritual India attracting inquisitive Western questers. It could well be the repetitive documentation of the Beatles, the Hippies and the Rolling Stones wave of the 1960s and 1970s, which brought phony seekers of "nirvana" to India on which thrived an equally phony Gurudom. Critics and reviewers of *Journey to Ithaca* have often felt exasperated at it and wondered why an artist like Anita Desai should have chosen a worn-out theme for her novel set in the 1990s. More than one-third of the narrative takes us through hunger, filth, vermin, utter hopelessness and directionlessness of the Hippy camps and the dubious ashrams. Another sore point is the sudden turn the story takes. As if one quest were not enough, Sophie embarks on another quest – a kind of investigation – to dive into the past of the Mother with the impious intention of shaming her devotees by revealing her inglorious past. This part of the novel has come in for further criticism as weak and distasteful.

On close reading, however, one realizes that Anita Desai's concerns are deeper than mere East-West confrontation or conflict between spiritualism and materialism; moreover, she is not interested in the inscrutability of the East and the gullibility of the West like Gita Mehta in *Karma Cola* or Jhabvala in *A New Dominion*. In *Karma Cola*, the observer-narrator's mock-serious style creates absurd situations to reveal the so-called seekers "in pursuit of the meaningfully meaningless" and their opportunist, fraud Gurus. In *A New Dominion*, Ruth Jhabvala is serious and angry with the mess into which the genuine seekers fall and "break". Anita Desai takes her position somewhere between the two – Matteo's urge is genuine but he is directionless, Sophie's concern is Matteo but she is a hard-headed rationalist. Out of these polarities the author provides a critique on the human condition and exposes modern man's dilemma. Between the epigraph from Cavafy's poem and the end of the novel, there lies a vast territory to be traversed. Desai subtly inverts the spiritual quest theme to comment on the inadequacy of human knowledge to grasp the essence. Spirituality is not a formula to be passed on to the other; nor can it be understood by rationalist-materialist dissection. It is a continuous journey, an odyssey, without an end. That Matteo has had an intrinsic pull towards spirituality is made clear by the author when she focuses on his boyhood.

As a boy, Matteo was different, or rather a failure from the worldly angle: clumsy at games, backward in academics and irritatingly closed in social interactions, indeed a veritable problem child for the doting parents. Herman Hesse's *Journey to the East* sparks off his penchant for spiritual India and after his marriage to Sophie, the couple land in India only to encounter her filth, heat and, dust. There follows a period of disappointment, depression, illness and uncertainty as they span the length and breadth of the country, from dirty dingy hotel rooms to dubious ashrams, from the Ashrams to

Hippy camps in Goa. The description of their wanderings is realistic and repulsive.

It is here that one becomes impatient with the author and doubts her motives for having presented the stereotypical, negative picture of India. She is satirical and her portrayal of India is far from sympathetic. Obviously, it is India for the Western readers. But then, she caricatures the half-baked Western seekers also who think Indian mysticism is for sale. Matteo is weak-willed and his behaviour is often shockingly ridiculous bordering on insanity: dancing in front of a funeral procession, shouting that it was the marriage of a goddess; lying prostrate on the floor at the feet of the drinking customers; almost drowning himself in the sea "insisting that it was the Holy Ganga" (66) and so on. Jasbir Jain categorizes this "ethnic trap" as "exotica", and states that such a plot "encashes on (the) marketability" of the homeland.[3] To Makrand Paranjape the central issue of the novel is a journey undertaken "to discover some lost essence" (1996: 403) but as regards diaspora, Paranjape asserts that the new diaspora of Indian English writers living close to their market, in the comforts of the suburbia of advanced capital and drawing their material from the disorderly and messy homeland does not express a longing for the homeland nor do they harbour any guilt for having left it. What we see in their writing "is a narrative logic of continuous incorporation and appropriation which reinforces the self-validating logic of the new diaspora" (Paranjape, 2001: 10). However, Desai's use of the multiple journey metaphor throughout the novel suggests that she is not moving away from the homeland, nor has she accepted the host country on its terms. She is passing through the difficult terrain of assimilation and rejection to the beyond which itself is difficult to grasp.

Anita Desai is more successful in revealing the cultural shock through Sophie than through Matteo; Pat than through David. Sophie and Pat go through intense diasporic experience – they cannot appreciate anything Indian, they hate the sights they see in India, they are confused by the culture. For Matteo, things become simple: he has found the Mother and he decides to stay on; he has accepted India and her spiritual wisdom; how much he has really grasped is debatable but he is not a skeptic like Sophie and herein lies the end of his journey and the beginning of a new voyage to know the unknown. The journey, however, is complicated for Sophie. India does not capture her. She can at best see it from the eyes of an outsider – the possibility of enjoying as tourists its exotic charm, the death of a child at the end of the pilgrimage, the futility of the Hippy life, the inscrutability of the Mother's hypnotic hold on the psyche of her devotee, and the dubious past of the Mother.

In "Scholar and Gypsy" things take a turn for Pat rather than for David. Let us remember that David is a researcher. His interest is in his work and not in extraneous scenes and activities. Pat is bowled over as much by exotic Manali as spirituality. She is keen on exploring the town, its surroundings, its ambience; he is loathe to go out. She is thrilled by nature's beauty, the apple trees, the cuckoo calling and the mountains, he is just unmoved by these. Now the ground is set for quest – ferns, brooks, deodars, the turfs and other aspects of the landscape. Then, there is spiritual quest when coming out of a temple they feel a "Presence". "They came out in silence and walked away slowly, as though afraid something would jump out at them from it, or from the forest – they were so much a part of each other, that forest and its temple" (123). Although David does not share her enthusiasm for temples and the simple hill-people and their gods, he tolerates her outbursts and remains her companion.

In the novel, Sophie remains Matteo's companion all through his wanderings but she cannot identify with his spiritual craze. She seeks a normal married life and when it does not come her way, she turns acerbic, nags Matteo, quarrels with him and makes things difficult; nevertheless, she sticks on to him, nurses him when he is ill, acts as his moral prop when he is dejected and bears him two children. To guard her children from the corroding effect of their father's way of life, she sends them to the protective, insulated environment of her country and feels secure for their future. Interestingly, Desai does not seem to share Sophie's rationalism. There are subtle suggestions that Matteo's son gets hallucinations even when thousands of miles away from his father; even his daughter shows the effect of the Eastern spell when she kneels down before the statue of the Buddha, shocking her grandmother. Does the author believe in the hereditary nature of spiritual quest?

Sophie turns cynical, and gripped by an uncontrollable desire to dig the Mother's past she embarks on her quest with sadistic zeal whereby her search acquires the tinge of investigative journalism (It may be clarified here that Sophie was a journalist prior to coming to India). With jet speed she moves across continents/countries: Egypt, Paris, Venice, New York and Mumbai, collecting facts about Laila before her metamorphosis as the Mother, so as to fling these on the ashramites, distract and disillusion Matteo and seek his release. The Mother's story satisfies and thrills the mundane mind of Sophie but these facts acquire esoteric dimensions when discussed with the believers. To the question if Laila had sexual relations with Krishna, the reply of the devotee is incomprehensible to Sophie. "Did they marry?" Sophie wants to know. Montu-da's answer is: "we are not speaking of – of ordinary beings, please. We are talking of supramental beings and the union of the divine." When she insists, "Did they live as man and wife ... physically?" Montu-da is perplexed. He mops his face and utters, "As body and soul are one, yes." Desai seems to have adopted a tongue-in-cheek attitude. On the one hand she is deriding the cryptic Indian style of putting things and on the other she is disapproving the Western approach to relationships.

Sophie's quest is dominated by her own passions and desires to flaunt her knowledge and to prove her Western superiority. The novel here changes its course to become a narrative of female quest in which one woman embarks on a journey to find another woman's enigmatic life who too had been a quester. Laila is also an exile, a voyager who had left her homeland long back, reached India with Krishna's dance troupe and stayed on to immerse herself in India. She seems to substantiate Jhabvala's assertion that India always changes people. Laila becomes the Mother, a great motivating force of the ashram and an anchor for seekers. The story of the novel starts with Matteo's spiritual search, turns into Sophie's personal vendetta, becomes a social and intellectual quest and reaches the point of spiritual quest again. The movement is circular physically as well as metaphorically. Physically, Sophie reaches the ashram from whence she had started her investigations and as she stands dazed by the mysterious turn of events, there are clear indications that she is ready to follow Matteo's path.

By juxtaposing Matteo's obsession for spiritual knowledge with Sophie's rationalistic-materialistic position, the novelist shows the inadequacy of both. First, spirituality cannot be administered in a capsule form nor can salvation be granted in herds; the soul has to undertake its journey. Second, it is not given to humans to transcend the limit; that intellectual knowledge cannot substitute spiritual wisdom; and that though the rationality of the world is transparent to the intellect, its mysteriousness cannot be understood by the finite mind. Thus Desai deglamourizes the Western concepts of instant "nirvana" as well as its rationalistic approach.

"Scholar and Gypsy" has charming descriptions of natural beauty of Manali. But where is the intense spiritual quest? In the Deodar forest Pat goes ecstatic over the soft turf, clumps of wild irises in full bloom and fern surrounded rocks looking as if stranded. "Pat fell upon the wild strawberries that grew with a careless luxuriance – small, seed-ridden ones she found sweet" (121). Pat appreciates the local Kullu villagers that pass by quietly, "Such independence ... so self-contained. True mountain people, you know" (121). This alarms David. And when he asks tentatively, "Do you feel one of them yourself?" she laughs an affirmative laugh. This incidence is short but reading between the lines one finds deeper tone to it. David notices her carefree gait though we are not told what he surmises; he seems to be wary and withdrawn. In fact, more than spiritual quest, this story focuses more on the usual relationship tensions – the taciturn and matter-of-fact man, a hypersensitive wife and the incompatibility that we find in *Cry, the Peacock* and other works of Desai. She drifts away from him, becomes fascinated by the Hippy way of life, its lack of restraints and her forays in the dubious "Nirvana on earth" fascination when dazed with bhang. He is clear in his ideas: "Nirvana on earth!" he snorts, "That's a contradiction in terms, you know?" he retorts (131). David, who came with a purpose, was happy in the beginning but by the end of the story, he is just a bored and detached onlooker on life. Pat tries to immerse in the environment, but it is not the local, Indian ethos that she appreciates but the hippy style of life. Ultimately, she decides to stay back; he goes back to Delhi. One significant question arises: Is she really after spiritual knowledge? Probably, Anita Desai gave a twist to the familiar relationship problem by using the Hippy cult that was quite fresh in the 1970s. What does Pat want? Not nirvana, to be sure. She seems to be enjoying her freedom here in Manali. Probably, Desai realized that the treatment she gave to the socio-cultural problem was superficial in this story, and consequently, she tried to give it more space and strength in the novel.

In *Journey to Ithaca* Sophie is diasporic and so is Anita Desai in real life situation; both turn to their homelands for stability and belongingness. Desai draws her fictional material from India but her text does not appear to be nostalgically missing the Indian ethos; at the same time she is not attempting to glorify the West. She wards off her diaspora by showing the indeterminate character of the quest and the journey-period; she looks wistfully towards the positive end of the voyage. Sophie too, like her creator, is a traveller caught in the compelling situation of home and "not-home". When in India she experiences diaspora's typical problem of identity. The question of belongingness vexes her so acutely that she often broaches the subject of leaving India, "When you are well, Matteo, we will leave," (4) she coaxes him. Later in exasperation she snaps at him, "Couldn't we stay in our own country? To die there?" (57). Everything Indian nauseates her. But when in Italy, with her own people, she is unable to belong there. She raps at Paolo when he asks probing questions about India and suggests that they travel together to India and from there to the ashram to give surprise to her husband, "You? You are not fit even to enter his presence. He – he is a god" (155). To her parents' proposal to baptize the children she reacts sharply and rejects the Christian ritual as tribal. Sophie's inability to relate to her home culture shows the complex diasporic condition of being what Sura P. Rath calls "Trishanku", Sophie longs for the accepted pattern of her culture but revolts against it. The diasporic discourse thus marks a continuous shifting, a kind of wandering away from the lost golden past towards the promised future. What is significant is the voyage and this message of the novel is contained in the epigraph. A few relevant lines from the poem are quoted here:

Always keep Ithaca fixed in your mind.
To arrive there is your ultimate goal.
But do not hurry the voyage at all.

Ithaca has given you a beautiful voyage.

And if you have found her poor, Ithaca has not defrauded you.
With such great wisdom you have gained with so much experience
You must surely have understood by then what Ithacas mean.

Desai uses the epigraph to affirm that the most significant and satisfying experience is the journey itself; maybe, it is beset with difficulties, but it is worth the trouble. It gives us experience, wisdom and knowledge; and to get that knowledge one has to travel oneself; it is always the journey of self-discovery. The Mother could transmit the knowledge only to a small extent; beyond that even she has to embark on an expedition of exploration. Each experience is unique in itself, for one never knows what lies at the end of the journey. Desai quotes the poem at length to underscore the significance of diving deep inside oneself to find the riches within. Ithaca cannot give external "riches" to the questers but it can certainly vouchsafe inner direction. The analogy fits India well enough.

Notes

1. See Homi K. Bhabha, *The Location of Culture*. New York: Routledge, 1994. According to Bhabha, to be "unhomed" does not mean to be homeless; "nor can the 'unhomely' be easily accommodated in that familiar division of social life into private and public spheres. The unhomely moment creeps up on you stealthily as your own shadow ..." (9).
2. See C. Vijayasree, "Survival as an Ethic: South Asian Immigrant Women's Writing," in. Makaranda Paranjape ed. *In-Diaspora*. (New Delhi: Indialog Publication, 2001) p. 133. C. Vijayasree uses the phrase "dual affiliation" in connection with the difficulty to balance the old inherited traditions with the requirements of the new culture and the complications the process of relocation generates. She specially refers to the women's diasporic experience.
3. See Jasbir Jain, "The New Parochialism: Homeland in the Writing of the Indian Diaspora," in Makarand Paranjape ed. *In-Diaspora* (New Delhi:

Indialog Publication, 2001). Jain maintains that "the narrative of the diaspora is above all a narrative of the 'self,' for the very act of migration implies a 'bodily' lifting out of the familiar and relocation in the new and the unfamiliar," p. 79.

References

Bhabha, Homi K. *The Location of Culture*. New York: Routledge, 1994.

Desai, Anita. *Journey to Ithaca*. New Delhi: Minerva, 1995.

——. "Scholar and Gypsy," in *Games at Twilight*. New Delhi: Penguin, 1978, pp. 108–138.

Jain, Jasbir. "The New Parochialism: Homeland in the Writing of Indian Diaspora", in Ed. Makarand Paranjape, *In-Diaspora*. New Delhi: Indialog Publication, 2001.

Kirpal, Viney. *The Third World Novel of Expatriation: A Study of Émigré Fiction by Indian, West Indian and Caribbean Writers*. New Delhi: Sterling, 1982.

Naipaul, V.S. 1984; rpt. *Finding the Centre*. Harmondsworth: Penguin, 1985.

Paranjape, Makarand. "Introduction," in *In-Diaspora*, op. cit., 2001.

——. "Journey to Ithaca: A Letter on Recent Indian English Fiction," in Ed. Viney Kirpal, *The Postmodern Indian English Novel*. Bombay: Allied Publishers, 1996.

Ramraj, Victor. "Diasporas and Multiculturalism," in Ed. Bruce King, *New National and Post-Colonial Literatures: An Introduction*. Oxford: The Clarendon Press, 1996.

Vijayasree, C. "Survival as an Ethic: South Asian Immigrant Women's Writing," in *In-Diaspora*, op. cit., 2001.

13 Milk and Honey

Mother-Love in Anita Desai

When Lotte, in Anita Desai's novel *Baumgartner's Bombay* (1988) hugs the bunch of old letters from Hugo's mother as the only legacy of her deceased friend, it does not take a reader long to understand the importance of mother in Hugo's life. Though away from him in time and space, the mother remains a vibrating presence all through and keeps her hold as much on the narrative as on the psyche of her son. Hugo Baumgartner's is not an isolated case, however, wherein mother plays a significant role in a protagonist's life. In Desai's earlier novels also mothers or mother-figures form an important matrix. Mothers may not always be physically present in the action of the story, but they remain just near the surface of the consciousness of the characters to influence their life. Many a time their inner troubles are related to the absence of the mother or her too dominating a presence. This paper seeks to study the role played by mothers and mother-figures in Desai's novels in moulding the protagonists and influencing their behaviour.

The neurotic difficulties of both Maya and Sita in *Cry, the Peacock* (1963) and *Where Shall We Go This Summer*? (1975) respectively, spring from their motherless childhood, apart from other complementary causes. In *Cry, the Peacock* the main triangle is of Gautama, Maya and her father. Father doles out love and Gautama harbours a tolerant and sympathetic attitude; but they fail to give Maya a sense of fulfillment and security. Here, Anita Desai explores an emotional situation that is without redemption. Maya has no conviction to fall back upon; Gautama has no sensibility to comprehend the intricacy of her suppressed physical demands and the resultant emotional state. Life, and a greater reality beyond life – death – ravage her mental world. Mother, it is felt, would have trained her for life in a better manner than her father could. Basing his study on Indian culture, Sudhir Kakkar looks at the psycho-social aspect of mother's absence and observes that for a girl's "emotional preparation" for marriage and subsequent motherhood, a daughter's best counsellor in the bewildering years of adolescence is the mother. He also points out that the unconscious wish for the benevolent presence of the mother is always there and if it is not fulfilled, a person feels left alone and breeds in a tendency to react with fear to the threat of being left alone (1978).

Maya has never consciously spelt out her need for mother, but the gap is there; and to fill it in she turns to her mother-in-law for mother-love. The urgency with which she wants to rush up "those filthy stairs to that dismal flat and ... kiss the mother's hand ..." (52), speaks of her need. Unfortunately, her mother-in-law cannot give her the affection she longs for. Her "absent" smile baffles her, and the matter-of-fact query: "when will your father send me another cheque, Maya?"(47), leaves her distressed. She is pained that for Gautama's social-worker mother Maya is important only insofar as she can provide monetary help for her social work activities. Maya is "not even one of those human beings whose comfort and health she felt responsible for, but merely one of those outsiders who could be used for this purpose and therefore necessary, though not necessarily loved" (48). At such moments the void in her life becomes unbearable and then "with fiercest desire", she thinks of her father.

Sita's problem in *Where Shall We Go This Summer?* is much more intricate. Her mother had deserted them all and gone to Benaras. It cannot be ascertained when exactly did she leave, but since Sita has no "recollection of that dim relation"(79), one presumes that it must be fairly early in Sita's childhood. When Sita herself becomes a mother she carries the void within her and remains bewildered. Sita as a mother cannot nurture her children "baffled as she is by her own predicament as a woman, as a human being" (Krishnaswamy, 1984: 258). This obviously points back to her motherless childhood. Psychologists stress the need of a mother, not for the gratification of daily requirements only but also for granting emotional lease of life. This relationship plays a significant role in a child's life – be it a boy or a girl. Absence of the mother pre-supposes incoherence in the inner image of a reassuring world and shatters the foundation of the "true self". Sita obviously misses this vital link and starves for the intensity and candour of developmental awakening and experiences.

Perhaps Sita was not consciously aware of this deficiency in her life. Somehow she wove a fantasy around her motherless existence and satisfied herself with the idea that she came in this world without a mother. In her scheme of existence there is no place for this relationship, till she sees the pearls and jewels which, Jivan tells her, belonged to their mother. Her tragedy multiplies on hearing that their mother was not dead but had run away to Benaras. She is shocked:

> 'Ran away? And left us?' Sita stood clutching her hair about her ears and feet sinking rapidly into the sand. Then she shook her head and let her hair all come loose and stamped her foot so that one footprint in the silver sand was deeper than all the others, one desperate footprint among the oblivious other. (83)

This resentment is symbolic of any child's rage and confusion at finding the image of mother broken. A mother dead and lost is far easier to accept than a callous and deserter mother. Sita is an adolescent at the time this disclosure is made so blatantly by Jivan. She lands in an anxiety-arousing situation. A deserter mother hammers in the notion of a "bad mother" and no child whether a girl or a boy likes to see the sacred image so sullied.

The concept of "good" and "bad" mother is a world-wide phenomenon. In the Indian socio-cultural context it acquires an added significance. A good mother not only fulfils a child's physical needs but also provides him or her reassurance through her confirming presence. Sudhir Kakkar observes that an Indian child experiences his mother totally as a good mother. She is a "nurturing and fear-dispelling presence" (1978: 83). This is true even in the West. Hugo Baumgartner experiences his mother as a "good" mother. She is the security, the prop when he is scared of the dark, she is there at the school "holding the traditional cone of bonbons, wrapped in gold foil and decorated with rustling silver streamers" (32), to welcome him at the end of the first day; and finally she is ever-present even when he is in India, thousands of miles away from home. Her love sustains him during those harrowing years in the Camp in India.

Returning to the problem of Sita, we see her ill-at-ease since the day she learns the bitter truth about her mother. Her restlessness leads her to a relentless quest for the mother. In the beginning it is a mental search, later she pesters Raman to go to Benaras to find her. After knowing the truth, she feels isolated, "separated from them, the chosen ones, chosen by the ghost of a flashing vision of its jewels although it remained invisible and fleshless itself. She found herself turning into a wanderer, always in search of the ghost. "Who, what was she?" (85). For Sita, it is "a fevered time," "haunted time," without mother Sita fails to internalize womanhood. She loses her sense of identity and her "self".

Sita is left to grow alone and face the baffling physical as well as emotional changes without aid. Psychologists believe that mother is indispensable for girls, particularly during puberty and adolescence. Similarly, friendship with girls of the same age-group is also essential to give them a sense of separate identity. "Friendship with girls is of the greatest importance. Identification with a similar being can strengthen the young girl's consciousness that she is an independent ego" (Deutsch, 1966: 22) Unfortunately, Sita lacks both: mother and girlfriends. There is no reference to any of her friends all through the narrative. In the case of Maya, there is at least the Ayah and a girlfriend to help Maya through her adolescence. In the Das household in *Clear Light of Day* (1980) Mira Masi fills in the gap left by the mother. But, Sita "deprived of a mother, a true elder sister or girl companions struggled along with infirmity as a cripple without crutches ..." (93). During the traumatic transition period, she gets no reassuring exchanges of confidence. Her temper tantrums in later life are a direct outcome of her lost self.

Voices in the City (1968), on the other hand, contains notable mother-figures – the real mother, the foster-mother (Calcutta), and the archetypal mother, Goddess Kali. They influence and shape the unconscious lives of Nirode, Monisha and Amla. In the final chapter of the novel, we see the tremendous control of mother over Nirode's psyche during his neurotic convulsions. Kali, the goddess and demon converges in his mind and becomes his mother. Nirode's difficulties start with "bad" mother experience which shakes his faith in life. His father being "unfair" to him, he clings to his mother for love and security. Their mother, we are told, is "a very beautiful mystery" (209). She remains an enigma to the children. She has a frivolous nature as is clear from their father's observation. Amla recalls during her conversation with Dharma how her father once, looking at a butterfly, had remarked: "Look at that. Study that. Forget yourself in that study. Then you will be fortunate like your mother" (207). Symbolically, the butterfly represents frivolity, gaiety and colour – attributes so very befitting their mother.

Erich Fromm uses the Biblical symbols of "milk and honey" to express the pervasive nature of mother-love. "Milk is the symbol of the first aspect of love, that of care and affirmation. Honey symbolizes the sweetness of life, the love for it and the happiness in being alive" (1976: 46). According to Fromm, while most mothers give "milk", only a few are capable of giving "honey" because for giving honey to the children, a mother herself must be a happy person which most are not. The Ray children in *Voices in the City* could get loving care but their mother could not infuse in them the sweetness for life, the joy of living. Later, the Chadda affair makes the children unhappy. While Amla and Monisha try to understand their mother, despite her inclination towards Major Chadda, Nirode finds it almost impossible to forgive her. The girls have a silent sympathy for the mother, but Nirode has nothing but hate. It is because girls do not idolize mother-figures, while boys do. Adoring her as an idol and placing her on a pedestal is a typical male construct. Girls require mothers to train, guide and protect them. The benign presence of mother is enough for their psychological satisfaction. Bhabani Bhattacharya describes the influence of mother on Sumita in his novel *Shadow Over Ladakh*. Here, Suruchi, Sumita's mother is the safeguarding, supportive presence.

The fundamental benevolence of mother helps a child in developing confidence in self as well as in others. Mothers provide them with a safeguard against the onslaught of a hostile world. However, if the image of a good mother is shattered by some mischance, an individual's fear, dislike and contempt are fierce. These are in proportion to the intensity of his emotions towards the idealized good mother. Eric Neumann, in his study of ancient cultures and myths suggests that the bad maternal image is that of a demanding, destroying and devouring female (1963: 77). In *Voices in the City*, the children have a shattering experience when their mother shows soft-corner for Major Chadda. Amla secretly emulates her mother but Nirode is filled with hate because he is trapped between an idolized image of the mother and the reality of her life.

Even a mother-surrogate like Mira Masi in *Clear Light of Day* can give "milk" and "honey" to the children. Mira Masi is the "tree" who gives shelter to the four Das children. The following line eloquently expresses her role, "She was the tree, she was the soil, she was the earth" (111). The children can rely on her. She brings up Baba; she is often a saviour for Tara when the older two tease her; she is a steady support to Raja and Bim. She is least like their mother. The children can think of their mother only as spending "long hours at a dressing table before a mirror, amongst jars and bottles that smell sweet ... who commanded servants and chastised children and was obeyed like a queen" (111). On the contrary, Mira Masi is nurturing, supportive and docile. She is like the ever-smiling divinity that Erikson calls "the numinous element, the sense of hallowed presence" (1966: 604). She is simple and unassuming; and she feels elated to see the children growing up, "as the leaves and flowers and fruits of the earth. So beautiful, she murmured, touching, watching ... so beautiful and strong and living" (111).

Totally different vignettes of mothers appear in *Fire On the Mountain* (1977) and *In Custody* (1984) than the ones discussed earlier in this paper. Although Anita Desai does not give us elaborate pictures of their plight, we get sufficiently clear view of their helplessness with the few deft touches with which she paints them. Deven's mother in *In Custody* is a disappointed and disgruntled woman who somehow pulls on with a husband not up to her expectations. In *Fire on the Mountain* Raka sees her mother being beaten by her father and Tara, Raka's mother, may have seen her own mother Nanda Kaul slaving for a Vice-chancellor husband who was carrying on with another woman. These are helpless mothers. They can give "milk", i.e., love and care to the children but not "honey".

Anita Desai gives us a kaleidoscopic view of the lives affected by mothers and mother-figures – some positively, some negatively. She seems to believe that mothers are, after all, the central figures in one's life. Her plots do not necessarily have the presence of mothers, but this relation is significant for the physiological as well as psychological growth of a person. Desai appears to agree with Devaki Jain that "everything life-giving is mother" (Jain, 1975: xix).

References

Desai, Anita. *Cry, the Peacock.* New Delhi: Hind Pocketbooks, 1963.

——. *Voices in the City.* New Delhi: Orient Paperbacks, 1965.

——. *Fire on the Mountain.* New Delhi: Allied Publishers, 1977.

——. *Clear Light of Day.* New Delhi: Allied Publishers, 1980.

——. *Where Shall We Go This Summer?* 1975; rpt. New Delhi: Orient Paperbacks, 1982.

——. *In Custody.* London: Heinemann, 1984.

——. *Baumgartner's Bombay.* London: Heinemann, 1988.

Deutsch, Helen. *Psychology of Women: A Psycho-analytic Interpretation.* London: Research Books, 1946.

Erikson, Erik H. "Ontogeny of Ritualization," in *Psychoanalysis: A General Psychology in Honour of Heinz Hartman,* eds. R.M. Lowenstein et al. New York: International Universities Press, 1966.

Fromm, Erich. *The Art of Loving.* 1957; rpt. London: Unwin Paperbacks, 1976.

Jain, Devaki, ed. *Indian Woman.* New Delhi: Publications Division, 1975.

Kakkar, Sudhir. *The Inner World.* New Delhi: Oxford University Press, 1978.

Krishnaswamy, Santha. *The Woman in Indian Fiction in English.* New Delhi: Ashish, 1984.

Neumann, Eric. *The Great Mother: An Analysis of the Archetypes,* 2nd ed. Princeton: Princeton University Press, 1963.

14 Flight from Responsibility or Search for Freedom

A Study of Withdrawal in Fiction

When Henrik Ibsen gave his Nora in *A Doll's House* the courage to say "No" to man's superior authority, its echoes were heard far and wide. Nora could slam the door on a so-called happy marriage and receive approbation from discerning critics for, every "No" to coersion presupposes "Yes" to the self, to individual identity; but could a woman follow Nora's example in real life? That was in 1879. Mary Wollstonecraft's writings had already made a sizeable dent in the male bastion by then, though woman's condition was more or less unchanged.

Closely following Ibsen came Kate Chopin's rebellious call to women towards a "frank, free independent expression, untrammeled by conventions and meek female acceptance of traditional roles" (Stern and Gross, 1992: 199). She gave to literature heroines with strong urge for freedom. Edna Pontellier in *The Awakening* (1899), Mrs Mallard and Athenaise in the short stories entitled "The Story of an Hour" and "Athenaise" respectively, were driven out of their homes by an indefinable awakening. But, unfortunately, their quests ended in death and defeat. The quest motif, however, caught on, and D.H. Lawrence, Margaret Atwood, Anita Desai, R.K. Narayan and even Mulk Raj Anand to an extent (in *Gauri*) used it to show woman's strong reaction when her individual identity is trampled or is in danger of obliteration.

Traditionally, questing is a male domain. The male experiences linear historical time through the quest, while women experience time as stasis. The pattern of life that evolves for women is that of either perpetual repetition, or passive waiting, or eternal return. Thus, when women became the questors, critics questioned its propriety. Fictions dealing with heroines who chose to leave the security of their homes came under a two-fronged attack: first, it was contended that the works were not realistic and second, that such women were "mad". Those who defended woman's quest considered it a journey within oneself leading one to rebirth and transformation. Annis Pratt, for example, in her book *Archetypal Patterns in Women's Fiction* (1981), asserts that the female quest is distinct from a male quest in that the latter is a quest outward, for the holy grail, while the former is a journey into the inner self. Pratt divides the quest further as spiritual and social and avers that the spiritual quest is for self-awareness while the social quest is for social integration. Carol Pearson and Katherine Pope, the authors of *The Female Hero* also assert that female quest has an inward nature and that a woman needs to know herself before she is able to gain real freedom from patriarchal oppressions.

In this paper the author wishes to analyse Anita Desai's *Where Shall We Go This Summer*? (1975) and Kate Chopin's *The Awakening* (1981) to show that these texts are not anti-realists, nor are the protagonists "mad". The paper also examines the validity of the claim that the heroines achieve self-knowledge and transformation as a result of their quests. The attempt of the critics to save the novels' wholeness by proving that by withdrawal the characters resolve their conflicts results in reducing the characters to an illustration of a theme. It can strip the characters of vitality and thus impair the powerful impact of the works. In order to understand the specific demands of the psyche of Sita and Edna, the psychological tenets of Karen Horney as a theoretical base will be used.

Both *Where Shall We Go This Summer?* and *The Awakening* afford an excellent example of the handling of the universal human dilemma through female protagonists. The question these authors seem to ask is: what is bigger: self, family, or society? While the rhetoric draws us toward recognizing the 'self' as bigger, the mimesis weighs in favour of family in *Where Shall We Go This*

Summer? and in favour of "society" in Kate Chopin's novel. The theme of *The Awakening* centres round Edna – young, good-looking and self-absorbed, who discovers at twenty-eight, that her life so far has been a dream. The theme of Anita Desai's novel centres round Sita: middle-aged, mother of four, depressed and angry. In Edna's case, love awakens her "gradually out of a dream, a delicious, grotesque, impossible dream, to feel again the realities pressing into her soul" (219). After that, life never returns to normal. Back home in New Orleans, the usual household chores appear drudgery and social responsibilities become meaningless. Children, home, husband, their friends, all get on her nerves. She is never happy. She is either brooding or sad or angry. Her behaviour puzzles and annoys Mr Pontellier. He thinks she is influenced by the woman's rights movements "concerning the eternal rights of women" (272). Mr Pontellier and Dr Mandelet both are suspicious of the "circle of pseudo-intellectual women," whom Dr Mandelet calls "super-spiritual women". (273). Edna's unhappiness is not so much because of her unfulfilled love, as out of a sense of rejection when Robert leaves for Mexico. His return reenkindles her joie de vivre, but she knows she cannot discard her home and children. She therefore, chooses to walk out on her life, and commits suicide.

Sita's case is not identical. She is not awakened by love, as is Edna; she is rather maturer, and moreover, she is an Indian for whom the value-system is rigidly internalized, conditioning her. But, she certainly has her vision of romantic love, as is substantiated by her views on the Muslim couple in the Hanging Gardens.

> They were like a work of art ... so apart from the rest of us. They were not like us ... they were inhuman, divine. So strange ... that love, that sadness, not like anything I've seen or known. They were so white, so radiant, they made me see my own lifelike a shadow, absolutely flat, uncoloured. (146–147)

Sita demands such an elevating love from her husband, unconsciously and mutely. She, like Edna, remains unhappy, sad and brooding. She irritates her husband and puzzles her children. She, too tries to turn her back on life, withdraws temporarily to Manori but ultimately she accepts life and compromises with it. Anita Desai does not allow her heroine to slam the door. "No, no door is ever slammed – for good. No problems are ever shut out or escaped. Not by anybody" (Ram, 1995: 96–99) says Anita Desai in an interview. In another interview Desai categorically mentions that in order to survive, one has to compromise with life. She transfers this vision to Sita and makes her take a maturer decision. Edna's withdrawal, first psychological and then physical from her home, children and husband, and Sita's withdrawal from her family have both been interpreted by critics as quest for identity. Sita, critics feel goes back home a renewed being, as the time spent away from her usual milieu affords her a chance for introspection. She gains "strength of personality" (Jena, 1990: 34) and "autonomy" after the temporary withdrawal. In Edna's withdrawal a critic sees her existential dilemma and her determination to realize her "self", and reads her suicide as a struggle to free herself from being owned (Bharathi, 1995: 101).

We shall first discuss Edna. The problem created by her awakening is both social and psychological. Socially, she accepts her role as a wife and mother and, forgetting her past "infatuations," she becomes a "devoted wife of a man who worshipped her" and "closes the portals for ever behind her upon the realm of romance and dream"(198). When the novel opens, we see Edna as a passive, contented, dependent and obedient wife. Mr Pontellier, the masterful patriarch, wields the power and she the obedient wife submits to his power. The tone is set in the first few pages of the narrative. It is an ideal family with a doting husband, a dutiful wife, two kids, plenty of money and no worries. But while the narrator tells us all this, she gives a wrong signal. In the last line of chapter III Mrs Pontellier is "forced" to admit that Mr Pontellier is the "best" husband in the world.

Critics take the clue and surmise that Edna's melancholy has much to do with martial discord. To me, however, she appears a torn person with a rift between her inner and outer selves. As stated above, Edna plays the role of a well-adjusted wife. She has no illusions about her marriage which she considers "purely an accident". She does not expect much out of it and quietly slides into the role of a rich man's wife. But then there are chinks in the armour: she has an aversion to "domestic harmony," of the kind enjoyed by Mrs Ratignolle. She rejects it as "colourless existence";

secondly, she secretly resents the picture of herself as a "mother woman". Mother women, she feels, "idolized their children, worshipped their husbands, and esteemed it a holy privilege to efface themselves as individuals and grow wings as ministering angels" (181). To her, children mean "responsibility". This second image cannot fit in the frame of feminine virtues. So long as Edna was not aware of the two separate images: one of a self-effacing, docile wife and mother and the other of a detached wife and uncaring mother, she was not conscious of her conflicts.

Her newly awakened feelings toward Robert jolt her out of her complacence. First, her conflicts tear her when her feminine, compliant trends clash with her expansive and resigned selves. She cannot recognize herself as her subdued feminine self, but then she cannot break the feminine self's boundary line and accept Robert. On the one hand, there are amorous feelings for Robert with a strong urge to break free from Mr Pontellier and join Robert; on the other, there is the sense of duty toward her family.

Edna is ravished by self-hate when her questioning conscience assaults her after a weak moment with Arobin. That she has not only betrayed her husband but has also been infidel to Robert gnaws at her. When self-berating and self-hate become unbearable, she chooses suicide as a solution. Critics consider it the first step forward to self realization. According to my reading, Edna is still her "idealized self," a victim of emotional conflicts as she walks into the sea and hence far away from self-realization.

Turning to Sita, we find that though her case is different, she shows some identical whims. Like Edna, Sita too plays the role of a well adjusted wife for quite some time. She bore her four children, she admits "with pride, with pleasure – sensual, emotional, Freudian, every kind of pleasure" (31). But, a time comes in her life also when children appear as "responsibility". Her anger, melancholy and aggressiveness irritate Raman. He considers her "mad" and lets her have her will. Sita goes to Manori. The reason, she says, is to keep her foetus within her by evoking the magic. A mad wish! The rhetoric built in the first part of the novel sways us and we get prepared to encounter an insane woman.

The narrative soon leads us into Sita's past and as we try to understand her conflicts we see her as human. She had a peculiar childhood which did not give her any sense of belonging or love. After her marriage to Raman she finds in him a saviour who could give her give her security and love. Sita is a compliant person for whom love, security and belongingness are of prime importance. But, Raman, too involved in his work-a-day life does not see her need. Sita counts it as a rejection of her claims and reacts sharply. She tells him, "I thought I could live with and travel alone – mentally, emotionally. But after that day, that wasn't enough. I had to stay whole, I had to" (148).

When her compliant self is rejected by Raman, she becomes rebellious. First, she criticizes the "vegetable existence" of the women relatives of Raman, then she takes to smoking, criticizing, condemning and verbally attacking Raman's friends. He is particularly bewildered and indignant when she refers to his business associates as "animals". This is the period when Sita shows sign of "physic fragmentation". Soon, aggression gives way to resignation. She withdraws from life, denying herself joy, enthusiasm, anger, fear. She just sits, smokes and waits. Her husband and children are as puzzled by her gloominess as they were by her rebelliousness. It is about this time she decides to escape to Manori.

In part III of the novel, entitled "Monsoon 67", we encounter a serene Sita. Here she discovers her potential to "connect". She establishes a contact with the earth as she plays in the mud with Karan with "oblivious joy". She recognizes her latent ability to be happy. In D.H. Lawrence's poem she finds an answer to her problem. Giving birth is a creative act, not an act of violence. Much of her conflict gives way after this. Raman's visit and a long discussion with him reduces her tension further. So far, she had seen Raman as she wanted to see him. Now, she realizes his strength. He is matter of fact and deserves her admirations, she admits. Compared to his taciturn approach to life, her sentimentality appears weak. If life is to be lived, then it should be lived on its own terms. With these thoughts she decides to accompany him home. It is symbolically represented when she walk into his footsteps on the sand.

Sita withdraws both physically and psychologically, rejecting life as it is lived but she comes back to accept life though she knows, "life has no periods, no stretches. It simply swirled around, muddling and confusing, leading nowhere" (155). Interestingly, Sita goes in search of magic and undergoes a magical transformation herself.

Sita has, in fact, managed to change some of her perceptions. Raman's visit to the island to take them back has made her feel wanted. Though he, in his anger, tells her that he has come to fetch Menaka for her admission, she knows that he has come for them all. She feels less isolated and more needed. By accepting to accompany Raman, Sita has changed the external situation for the better and there is possibility that with the evolution of her potentialities, she may march toward self-realization. Surely, Sita has not grown inwardly, nor has her escape transformed her into an autonomous being, only she has been able to change the environment which might vouchsafe better human relations.

Both Sita and Edna withdraw from their milieu and achieve a semblance of peace within. But their detachment is not healthy. Karen Horney (1951: 259–290) suggests that healthy detachment is constructive and is not associated with the need to detach from life's activities. Neurotic withdrawal is practiced as a solution of the intra-psychic conflicts. In it, a neurotic withdraws from the battlefield and becomes an onlooker on life. He or she loses the zest for living and opts for a life of emptiness in which there is no pain of friction because there is no emotional involvement. He shuts himself away from life's realities. Actually, what one has achieved is freedom from, not freedom for. Theoretically, the outcome of this empty living is frustration. A person moves away from himself in centrifugal way losing depth and intensity of his feeling. Edna, finding the onlooker position unbearable, commits suicide. Sita manages to shed her psychic withdrawal when she interacts with her children on the island and finds the connecting link through intense introspection and retrospection.

In a way we can appreciate Sita and Edna both for showing courage to "choose". The real self is an inner force and it is a consciousness of oneself "as being capable of choice," but, as both Horney and Simone be Beauvoir point out, the cultural definition of the ideal feminine self marks the annihilation of the real self because women's existence is choiceless. A woman "is required to attempt constantly and fantastically to achieve the internalized ideal femininity ... the goal is already established; she has only to try to merge with it and judge herself accordingly" (Westkott, 1986: 149). Horney and Beauvoir want woman to reject this choicelessness and affirm her freedom to create herself and her future. Sita and Edna make attempts to affirm their freedom and reject choicelessness. Herein lies their triumph. Whether Edna could have achieved self-definition or not had she not committed suicide, or whether Sita lives happily hereafter as an integrated person or not, are speculative questions. But, certainly in their attempt to rebel and withdraw lies the message that by demystifying the past, by learning not to fear feelings and by experiencing the power of the "self" a woman can hope to achieve her autonomous self.

References

Bharathi, V. "The Existential Dilemma of Edna Pontellier in Kate Chopin's *The Awakening*", in Iqbal Kaur, ed., *Kate Chopin's The Awakening: Critical Essays.* New Delhi: Deep and Deep, 1995.

Chopin, Kate. *The Awakening and Selected Short Stories.* New York: The Modern Library, 1981.

Desai, Anita. *Where Shall We Go This Summer?* New Delhi: Vikas Publishing House, 1975.

Horney, Karen. *Neurosis and Human Growth.* London: Routledge and Kegan Paul, 1951.

Jena, Seema. *Carving a Pattern Out of Chaos.* New Delhi: Ashish, 1990.

Pratt, Annis. *Archetypal Patterns in Women's Fiction.* Bloomington: Indiana University Press, 1981.

Ram, Atma. "An Interview with Anita Desai," in Atma Ram, ed. *Morality in Tess and Other Essays.* New Delhi: Mittal, 1995.

Stern, Milton R. and Seymour L. Gross, eds. *American Literature Survey: Nation and Region 1860–1900.* New Delhi: Light and Life Publishers, 1992.

Westkott, Marica. *The Feminist Legacy of Karen Horney.* New Haven: Yale University Press, 1986.

15 Cactus Country

An Assessment

Manohar Malgonkar's *Cactus Country* is at once a historical novel, a novel focusing on army life and a novel of partition dealing with this fateful event after almost two decades. But what makes the work different is the point-of-view with which the story is recounted. Though it is third person narration, the central consciousness is of Aslam Chisti, a Pakistani army officer. The action is set partly in West Pakistan and mainly in East Pakistan which was soon to be Bangladesh. The vast land-mass, that is India, spread between the two Pakistans, East and West, and the significant role played by her in the liberation of Bangladesh is "watered down". Not to discredit her though; only for the exigency of his story. Soon a reader realizes that the author's preoccupation is not so much with the march of history, as with the fate of the individuals involved in it.

It is necessary, at the outset, to focus on two factual statements with which the book starts: first, its epigraph and second, the Author's Note. The epigraph records Zulfikar Ali Bhutto's statement, "The Hamoodur Rehman Report (on Pakistan's Bengal Campaign) is a story of rape, plunder and loot … a macabre conspiracy!" The author's note clarifies his stand that *Cactus Country* is a work of fiction but the "background is authentic and its account of Pakistan's Bengal campaign straight history. If anything, I have watered down the violence and left out the more gruesome excesses so as to keep within the norms of fiction."

The story opens with a graphic description of Aitchinson's College cricket ground, Lahore where a cricket match is being held for the selection of a test series in England. (Those septuagenarian Indians who studied in Lahore before the partition and have memories of the by-gone days will be thrilled to re-live their youth when the boundaries did not divide the two countries). The hero, Aslam Chisti, establishes himself as an excellent batsman and is tipped for England. The first twenty pages build the tempo so fast that you would think it is going to be a novel on the life of some cricketer. But soon, the 10th Chakwal Rifles, General Tarik Chisti, Mr Bhutto and the reports of "Crush India," published in the papers make is clear that it is going to be a historical novel about the birth of Bangladesh. Aslam Chisti is a lieutenant in the Pakistani army. He is the son of "the No. 2 man in the Junta ... straining every nerve to become the No. 1" (13). As General Tarik Chisti's son, however, Aslam has responsibilities. He cannot go to England to play cricket when trouble is brewing in East Pakistan, and General Tarik is on the brink of making it to the top. It would be damaging if tongues wag and the General is blamed for showing favours to his son. "... every thing is balanced so precariously that the slightest scandal, and the whole thing will blow up in our faces. Asloo, that's why I just cannot afford to be exposed to the charge of showing special favours to you" (41). Aslam is not much convinced by the argument. His selection has been fair, in fact, on the basis of his performance, not on the count of his being General Tarik's son. But, a "good" son as he is, he bows to the wishes of his father, accepts mutely the code of "an officer's obligations, to his country, to his service, to his regiment" (42) and goes to Bengal to join his regiment, to fight for his country (or rather to help his father grab the No. 1 position as President, with Mr Bhutto as the Prime Minister of Western and Mr Mujib as the Prime Minister of Eastern Pakistan?)

Bengal has its share of adventures in store for Chisti. On reporting at the MLA HQ for his duty, Aslam comes in contact with Major Pirzada, a Bengali officer who is beholden to the Chisti family for a favour extended to him. Major Pirzada, his Begum Sahiba and their daughter Wahida react to the arrival of the young Chisti differently. While the Major is officer-like in his dealings, the

Begum is motherly, but Wahida is suspicious. She is fresh from the trauma of a combing out operation with its rape, murder and allied atrocities, carried out in the Dacca university. She is angry and snappy.

Initially, Captain Aslam is given Military Intelligence duties which he carries out efficiently but with resentment. His "Abbu" would not approve of his involvement with the "Spooks". So, Aslam would rather be with his regiment. Since no officer would like to incur the wrath of the powerful man in the Junta, General Chisti, Aslam gets the desired orders to join the 10th Chakwals. After some adventures of minor nature *en route* with the Mukti Bahini guerillas, Aslam reaches camp Kathihari and is stranded there, till he and his people manage to get out only to be killed or be POW's.

As a POW Aslam compromises with Major (now Brigadier Pirzada), lives in comfort and develops emotional ties with Wahida. Finally, with the graciousness of Brigadier Pirzada, Aslam tries to join his unit but by then the Pakistani army is in a deplorable state. Before the final surrender, however the author saves his hero from dishonour or harassment as POW Aslam conveniently escapes into India, finds his maternal uncle Ganga Singh in Jalandhar and feels safe, but entrapped, under the protection of the patronizing kin.

Though the novel concentrates on Pakistan's military action in Bengal, it is saved from being a documentation of army campaigns by the author's constant focus on Aslam Chisti. The military words and terms occur frequently but they are intelligible to a non-army-back-ground-reader. No scenes of battle are actually depicted except a couple of "operations" and skirmishes which leave the reader mildly shaken and the hero greatly upset. For example, after Sheikh Mujib's capture during "Operation Search-light," Aslam feels a stab of pain on seeing his men rejoicing. For Aslam, it is mean to capture "an unarmed man who had been sleeping in his house" (138). He disowns any responsibility in the episode and feels that "this was not an experience ... to recount to one's children with pride and a thump of the chest saying: 'I was there.' Because this was not something a soldier could take pride in" (138).

Throughout the narration, the author seems to be at pains to project his hero as an honourable man, too good to resort to "rape, plunder and loot" with which the Pakistani army was discredited. But unfortunately Aslam fails to impress. He is an able officer and a kind hearted man, no doubt, but he is too young or rather to weak to make his mark. Aslam is a soldier – honest, generous, good-natured, loyal and brave. He is not much different from Malgonkar's Kiran Garud. Both follow the code of conduct of the army with impunity. But, whereas Garud is mature, Aslam is a stripling youth, just twenty-four, much under the awe of his father's name and fame. The novelist denies him the satisfaction of independent thinking. Always concerned with his Abbu's reactions: "What will Abbu say?" "Abbu would not approve" and the like Asloo moves under his father's shadow. He fails to grow. In the end, when he decides to go to India, he seems to have wriggled out of his Abbu's awe but, now, it is his mother's people who hold the rein of his life and decide the course for him. "We will teach you to say prayers," are the words with which the novel ends. Aslam shrinks from the realization that he is not entering a sanctuary, but "a trap" and that, asylum also means "conversion."

The other characters in the novel are meant to further the character of Aslam. Most of them are military officers and have set characteristics. Major Pirzada is an opportunist who changes sides according to the demands of his "personal loyalties". While in the British Indian army, he joins the INA of Netaji Bose for the cause of India's freedom; given a second chance in the Pakistani army, he stabs his people on the back and works for the Mukti, this time for the liberation of his second motherland. Somehow, the author is not angry with Pirzada. He gives him scope to help Chisti and thus exonerates him. Despite his so-called treachery, Pirzada is neither despicable not petty-minded. He cannot, however, escape poetic justice. The Nemesis take revenge. Pirzada suffers the shock of his only daughter's death. Begum Pirzada is an endearing character who comes alive as a soft Bengali woman given to music and art. The other two women characters – Wahida and Bimba – though made only to serve the cause of Aslam's initiation into manhood, are strong, alert and yet soft and living. Despite her miserable condition, Bimba is not a pathetic person and inspite of her fiery personality, Wahida is feminine.

In short, the novel celebrates the army code of conduct. Aslam Chisti too seems to be saying with Colonel Kiran Garud of *Distant Drums*, "To me the army, the profession itself, is a great thing ..." The partition of the country as seen in retrospect is a process of history which Aslam can neither understand nor appreciate. It has divided families but it could not obliterate individual affection. Kiran Garud and Abdul Jamal in *Distant Drums* had an urge to meet because they belonged, not long back, to the same army. Now, after about a quarter of century in 1971, understandably, Aslam does not have the kind of pull for an Indian brother-officer but then, he is human enough to be moved to tears on hearing "Sonar Bangla".

As for reader response, an Indian reader may find the ending satisfactory. What about a Pakistani reader?

16 Gender, Education and Development

Issues in Life and Literature

> The schoolmaster is abroad, and I trust more to him, armed with his primer, than I do to the soldier in full military array, for upholding and extending the liberties of his country.
>
> —Lord Brougham (January 29, 1929)

The above words, though they form part of a speech in the House of Commons and uttered in connection with colonialism, aptly exemplify the impact of education to bring in smooth social and political changes and to work as an optimistic alternative to open confrontation. Transformatory movements and politics have articulated challenges to the hegemonic culture, informed by caste, class, gender, and community. In the modern context, an important site for the articulation of citizenship is education. The mainstream educational system through its institutions, curricula and teaching-learning materials constructs and communicates notions regarding the "ideal" citizen. It has also been recognized that if development goals have to be achieved, the system needs to address the question of women's development first. The successive Planning Commissions' documents have often emphasized that the programmes for alleviation of poverty should thus have a strong focus on development of women.

The aim of this paper is not to give a sociological assessment of women's and girl's education in modern, globalized India but to evaluate it from the angle of literature. The title chosen has feminist overtones; feminism, let us admit, is politics directed at changing existing power relations between the sexes in a given society. These power relations structure all areas of life – family, education, welfare, culture and leisure. Literature holds the power to bring changes in social thinking. This paper will, therefore, focus on life and literature to see how the question of women's education and real life issues created a criss-cross pattern and, how and where we stand today is related in a big way to changes brought in the basic social thinking by various thinkers in the field of education.

The question of women's education has always been linked to the question of power and fear that women may tilt the power balance; the caution that they should not erode and challenge the existing power structure of the society. That's why we see that the story of what is to be taught to women begins long before the story of literacy or formal education. The whole body of knowledge is transmitted to girls warily to ensure that they contribute to the maintenance of systems of power. Younger women are educated by older women who teach them the roles that those in power expect; they transmit those values that maintain the status quo. The aim has always been to perpetuate the gender system. For the hegemonic system, any attempt at empowerment means erosion of power and any reference to gender and education automatically points towards empowerment.

Essentially, empowerment means decentralization of authority and power. It aims at ensuring participation of the deprived section of people in the decision-making process. In other words, it signifies giving voice to the voiceless. From another angle, empowerment means giving equal status to women and providing opportunities and freedom to develop themselves. The goal of empowerment depends on three things: change people's heart; create a change in their lives; change the social structure. Many women have long recognized the gap between the distorted beliefs about their capabilities for education and work and the actual experiences they have had as women who labour and learn. Women are attempting to increase their knowledge, through their work and through education, for they see such processes as important to transform their lives. But they have to counter the ingrained biases and attitudes.

Attitudes are potent determinants of one's behavioural patterns – actions, reactions, and responses. Our behaviour towards others is influenced by our perception of that person's worth and social status. In other words our attitude depends on our judgement. If we judge a person as competent and accomplished we treat him/her with respect and if we perceive him/her as ineffective or incompetent we become a little brash or disdainful. In brief, our behaviour is guided by our image of that person, so to say. Taking a page out of literature let us see how attitudes impose rules and regulations on women. Githa Hariharan's novel *The Thousand Faces of Night* portrays some telling situations when the husband reiterates the rules his wife is supposed to follow instinctively; he need not lay down the rules afresh; rules for familial and social behaviour are already there and he expects her to know them. Any deviation is met with stern replies and decisive silences. Here are a few situations:

> "I want to learn Sanskrit," I said.
> "Why?" Mahesh asked.
> "So I can understand Baba's quotations better," I said.
> "Don't be foolish," he said, "The English translations are good enough. And what will you do with all this highbrow knowledge?" (Hariharan, 51–52)

Or, let us take another example equally arrogant:

> "I must look for a job, I have so little to do," I said.
> "What can you do?" Mahesh asked like a ruthless interviewer stripping away the inessential. (52)

If this is what Devi, a highly educated, US returned urban woman of the last decades of 20th century faces, one can imagine the lot of her less fortunate sisters.

Another eloquent example comes from Shashi Deshpande's *The Binding Vine.* Mira, a budding poetess shows her poems to a renowned poet Venu who visits their college. His immediate reaction was, "Why do you need to write poetry? It is enough for young women like you to give birth to children. That is your poetry. Leave the other poetry to us men" (127).

Unfortunately, that has been the general attitude towards women – educated or illiterate. Society saw them as good enough to breed and nurture children and liked to keep them bound to that image. Education, the society knew would give them the tool to prove themselves and so care was taken to keep them where they were. Today, we are passing through a phase when a lot of talk is going on about the status of women. It is being felt that they have remained exploited and kept as 'underdog' for too long. And now there is emphasis on the empowerment of women, improving their lot and bringing their status at par with men. In order to being about this change it is necessary to change the perception about women so that suitable modification comes in the behavioural pattern of men. The main point is to build their self-esteem and education is a field which can do this.

To speak of girls' education today may appear an anomaly because we are well into globalization, the millennium goals are set and the focus is on development. All along the ideal situation in education was this: "education is the basic human right and all girls must get their entitlement." Today, we no longer debate the issue whether women should be educated or not; but we do take cognizance of how education is to be made effective. Girls' education does not mean opening schools and making the parents send their daughters to school. Education of girls/women has a whole gamut of socio-cultural aspects strung to it. How would one send the girl to school without change in mind-set? How would a poor family afford to spare one earning hand to go to school when there is the question of making both ends meet? These and several such searing questions need to be addressed at every level.

At the UN level, the Millennium Developments Goals (MDGs) set out powerful agenda for a global partnership to achieve a shared vision of a better world. MDGs pertain to (1) eradication of poverty and hunger, (2) achieving universal primary education, (3) promoting gender equality and empowering women, (4) reducing child mortality, (5) improving maternal health, (6) combating HIV/AIDS and other diseases, malaria, (7) ensuring environmental sustainability, and (8) developing global partnership for development. Each of these goals is as much for men as for women and significantly points towards the betterment of women's lot which can only happen through education.

Each clause is somehow related to girls' education because it is felt that without gender equality women's empowerment cannot be achieved and without empowerment none of the MDGs can be accomplished. Women's education cannot be studied in isolation of the larger context of gender justice. It has a whole socio-cultural matrix behind it: a given society's traditions, ways of thinking and reacting to change. Closely intermingled with women's education are issues like violence, health and child care, environmental sustainability, combating diseases like HIV/AIDS, alleviation of hunger and poverty and above all gender justice. Change is slow to come in a traditional culture like ours, yet over a century and a half we have achieved considerable success. A review of imaginative/creative literature provides us an interesting picture of how the stranglehold of culture slowly loosened its grip.

In the 19th century, considerable work in the field of women's education was undertaken by various missionaries. Advancement of women was considered a prerequisite for advancement of nation. Rev E. Storrow, a missionary who came to India in 1848 opined that in historically powerful countries much of the strength and courage and virtue of the race was due to the position of women. Sir Herbert Risley pointed out that a society which accepts intellectual and moral stagnation as the natural condition of its womankind cannot hope to develop the higher qualities of courage, devotion and self-sacrifice which go to the making of a nation. Goaded by such ideas the Indian elite class was filled with an enthusiasm to reinterpret the traditional institutions. But the idea gave rise to a complex amalgam of juxtaposing the traditional and the modern which agreed that women should be educated but also did not want them to be modern in the sense of imitating the western woman. Literature coming out in the 19th century provides an excellent picture of this dichotomy.

> Taking all matters into consideration, the poor woman of this country should be an object of compassion rather than of our contempt. The stimulus given to India by British example, and capital employed for the education of Indian females, is not

> among the least of her beneficial operations. The time will come when their worth shall be duly appreciated by the daughters of India; and then, should this work chance to be perused by them, they will sigh at the follies of their ancestors, smile at their own good fortune. (Willard, 1834/1962: 76)

This picture of women "perfectly ignorant of all knowledge" may be too sympathetic and too self-righteous but such ideas gave impetus to women's education albeit with a grain of salt and with efforts to give a model education to women based on the concepts of the culture as envisaged for the "bhadramahila" in Bengal and as per the ideas prevalent elsewhere. The emphasis was on cultivating genteel norms and domestic virtues.

Talking about the paradox of Indian woman's situation, Partha Chatterjee shows the reception Indian woman's education got which he calls "reproach mixed with envy" (122). He records some writings of 19th century Bengal where English education was made fun of:

"Take, for example, a character called 'Mister Dharma Pakrashi', whose educated wife constantly calls him a 'fool' and a 'rascal' (in English) and wants to become a 'lady novelist' like Mary Correlli. This is how their daughter, Phulkumari, makes her entrance:

Phulkumari: Papa! Papa! I want to go to the races, please take me with you.

Dhurandhar: Finished with your tennis?

Phulkumari: Yes, now I want to go to the races. And you have to get me a new bicycle. I won't ride the one you got me last year. And my football is torn; you have to get me another one. And Papa, please buy me a self-driving car. And also a nice pony. And please fix an electric lamp in my drawing room; I can't see very well in the gaslight.

Dhurandhar: Nothing else? How about asking the Banerjee Company to rebuild you this house upside down, ceiling at the bottom and floor on top?

Phulkumari: How can that be, papa? You can't give me an education and then expect me to have low tastes?" (122).

This denotes the pervasive anger against and fear of westernization of Indian woman. This fear was not restricted to the 19th century, it seems to have travelled and remained in the psyche of the society even in the early parts of the 20th century. In Mulk Raj Anand's novel *Gauri*, when the heroine Gauri returns to her village home, people are horrified to see her using soap and a towel, items of luxury considered vulgar for a woman. Partha Chatterjee also observes that the idea of a Bengali woman trying to emulate or even remotely resemble the Western woman in her dress or use of western jewellery or cosmetics was the butt of ridicule, "raucous laughter and moral condemnation." Thus education does not mean only literacy or refinement, it has all the gamut of other allied personality and behavioural problems attach to it – dress, mannerism, language, self-confidence. The change was immediately resented by patriarchy.

Julie Stephens in her article "Feminist Fiction: A Critique of the Category 'Non-Western Woman' in Feminist Writings on India" studies at length the cultural ideals of Indian womanhood from the feminist angle and traces how "erasing the West" has been the prerequisite for subjecthood of Indian woman during the nationalist movement. "Western woman" and "Western feminism" have always been derogatory terms Julie asserts.

In 1878, the first Oriya short story by Fakir Mohan Senapati, had a female protagonist, Rebati, who displays the forbidden desire for learning and thereby seems to invite misfortune upon herself and her community. In Fakri Mohan's hands Rebati becomes an icon; her story an allegory of female education and emancipation. The narrative marks the beginning of a new tradition and heralds a new breed of women who learned to read and write and created a literature of their own. Rebati's agonizing quest in the story becomes a beacon light for real-life women. Approximately by the same time Hari Narayan Apte in Marathi wrote his revolutionary novel "Pan Laakshat kon ghetto" (*But who Bothers?*) in which the protagonist tries to educate herself stealthily late at night. Her husband gives her full co-operation but unfortunately, the husband dies suddenly and the in-laws who had an inkling of her aspirations for education blame her squarely for the misfortune. For them, she invited widowhood by treading the forbidden territory. Thus education becomes the nemesis of many a heroine in literature. What happens in fiction also happens in life and vice versa. We know stories of women like Pandita Ramabai and Kashi Bai Kanitkar from Maharashtra, Kaveri Bai from Karnataka, Ras Sundari Devi from Bengal who had to struggle to be educated.

For educating themselves the women then had to move away from Hinduism and convert to Christianity. Reverend Tilak and his wife Ramabai in Maharashtra, the Dutt family in Bengal, Krupabai Sathianandhan from Madras, all found the door open when they embraced Christianity, educated their women and helped them to write. Those who did not take this extreme step, but who found the path smoothened by Brahmo Samaj or Arya Samaj too got education. In Rabindranath Tagore's novel *The Wreck* (Nauka Doobi) the Brahmo father educates his daughter and gives her tremendous self-confidence. If there was Brahmo Samaj in Bengal, there was Arya Samaj in the North taking up the cause of women's education. In Manju Kapur's novel *Difficult Daughters* the heroine Lajwanti is given full scope by her Arya Samajist father to go to school and college in Lahore and Amritsar while her mother opposes it.

The 19th century was a period of great awakening; the renaissance was making its presence felt and the question of women's education became a hotly debated issue. There were three blocks: (1) in favour of women's education; (2) those opposed to education for women; and (3) those who opined that women should not be given western education because that will infuse western ideas of non-traditional woman into their heads. The last lot was afraid of its effect and so they immediately produced books which were conduct manuals for women. Education should make them "good housewives". Accordingly, many primers were composed for them and in one of the *Gruha Laxmi* issues the writer said:

> Be a well deserved Aryan woman by performing the right action, and get worshipped in the world. Nothing will be achieved only by the reading of books ... women who have the noble task of bringing forth children into life must acquire the right kind of knowledge. It is not enough for them to pass only BA or MA. The knowledge that will make them the ideal wife, mother, daughter

> and the Laxmi of the house is what must be cherished. So after duly elevating the woman to spiritual heights of goddess Laxmi, hold out an appropriate warning. The fear was that after getting education the wife will not enter the kitchen: to relax in bed and read novels is not the duty of the wife. Alas, the modern educated wife, a veritable terror at home, has begun to hate cooking. Cooking is the most important duty among all activities. For, without cooking what shall we eat? And without food how shall we survive.

In Bengal the concept of "Bhadra Mahila" became prominent, in Maharashtra it was the "Sambhrant Stree" and in other parts of the country too there were ideals that the society wanted to hold on to through keeping their women ignorant. Literature imposing norms for educated women came up. Stories were written deriding an educated daughter. She was made to look like an Amazon woman. She was caricatured. This residue of the mind-set could be seen even in the cinema as late as the 1950s. The ultimate of a good wife or a daughter was the semi-literate type heroine who could be cooed and wooed while the more assertive, educated was often the dancing girl with some non-descript name like Ruby, Rosie, Daisy. The short stories particularly by women writers of the early 20th century took up the issue of education for women. In one Marathi short story I remember the self-confidence of the heroine after she gets education and learns to stand on her feet. It is a simple story, the like of which we may encounter in literatures in India. A boy studying in Bombay for his BA gets married. His semi-educated wife nauseates him and he spurns her on the nuptial night with bitter remarks. He goes away and she stays in the in-laws house. The boy's *bua* (father's sister) comes to know of the unfortunate incident. She and the in-laws give the girl full support. She studies, does her Master's degree and from a docile and meek, tongued tied woman she becomes a self-confident one who participates in freedom struggle, wears immaculate khadi saris. Her husband happens to see her giving a lecture on the Independence Day. He is dazzled because he could never imagine the change. The lecture is a grand success. She is honoured. After the lecture she hurriedly leaves in the car for some other engagement without as much throwing a glance at him. The crest-fallen young husband stands looking aghast but he lacks courage to speak to her. There are many stories in the Bhasha literature of the time situating women in conditions where the importance of education is shown.

The leaders of our freedom movement realized the importance of girls' education and had put it as a prime agenda for national development. However, when India attained independence it was a formidable challenge that the new government had to face. The national female literacy rate was an alarmingly low 8.9 per cent, Gross Enrolment Ratio (GER) for girls was 24.8 per cent at primary level and 4.6 per cent at the upper primary level (in the 11–14 years age group). Social and cultural barriers to education of women and lack of access to organized schooling had to be addressed immediately. Things have changed considerably now. Some of our states have achieved cent per cent literacy. Special measures have been taken to help girls join the schools. These include setting up of girls toilets and providing separate girls' schools at upper primary level to counter community resistance to girls' studying in co-educational schools. Some schools are residential ones – the recent addition to residential schools being the Kasturba Gandhi Balika Vidyalayas that target the most disadvantaged girls at the upper primary stage. A new thrust was provided to girls' education in the National Policy on Education 1986 (as modified in 1992) which provided a holistic vision for the education of women and girls and recognized the cross cutting issues that inhibited the realization of this goal. It aims at using Education as an agent of basic change in the status of women in society.

The development of women has been the central focus in development planning since independence. Empowerment of women implies process by which women's power of self-organization is promoted and reinforced. They develop the capacity for self-reliance by out-crossing the relationship of subordination on account of gender, social and economic status and the role of family and society. Empowerment gives them self-esteem. As Benjamin Franklin once observed, "Being ignorant is not so much a shame as being unwilling to learn to do things the right way."

Let us admit that the concept of education has changed today in several ways. It does not mean opening schools and sending girls to these. Instead it takes cognizance of the various allied factors. But when the question of education for girls started to take shape with the institution of British education in India, things were pretty bleak. And literature reflected these issues. The stronghold of traditions was tight and to think of educating women was blasphemous; nothing short of sacrilege.

References

Chatterjee, Partha. *The Nation and its Fragments: Colonial and Postcolonial Histories*. New Delhi: Oxford University Press, 1994.

Stephens, Julie. "Feminist Fictions: A Critique of the Category 'Non-Western Woman' in Feminist Writings on India." *Subaltern Studies, VI, 92–125.*

Willard, N. Augustus, *A Treatise of the Music of India*, 1834; rpt. in William Jones and N.A. Willard. *Music of India*. Calcutta: Sushil Gupta, 1962.

17 Human Values and Dr Radhakrishnan's Concepts of Education

Education is for Life, not for Livelihood.

—Satya Sai Baba

The type of education we give to our youth, depends on the fact that what kind of teachers we get.

—Dr S. Radhakrishnan

The concepts of human values and Dr Radhakrishnan's philosophy of education are so inextricably linked that it is well neigh impossible to segregate one from the other. Human values are basic to human beings as a species. These sustaining values of love, truth, peace and righteousness proclaim man as a superior self-actualizing being, always aiming at the final realization of the "self". Some Western psychologists term them B-values, i.e., Being-values, which are conducive to healthy development. Indian philosophical thought acknowledges human strivings for these higher values that are common to all human beings irrespective of clime or culture. Dr Radhakrishnan, an idealist and a universalist as he was, saw immense potential in education to produce the spiritual man who would be a universal man. His vision of education was based on his visualization of man as a moral and spiritual entity aiming for higher goals. He had profound faith in world unity and he knew that the right type of education could be a harbinger of oneness of all humanity. In one of his speeches delivered in Paris in 1946, he asserted,

> The world has become a physical unity in our time but not a psychological unity. World Unity can only be founded on a sense of world community and this sense can only develop from interchange of the treasures of the mind and imagination between people, and a true understanding of the values of the different cultural and artistic tradition.

The attainment of the highest goal cannot be sudden and immediate; for this, individuals have to proceed step-by-step. Inculcating values in the students so that they are able to look beyond the divisive tendencies and work in the true spirit of world citizens will be the first step in this direction. A perfect education, according to Aldous Huxley, is "one which trains up every human being to fit into the place he or she is to occupy in the social hierarchy, but without, in the process, destroying his or her individuality." This quotation envisages two important aspects of education: individual and social. The purpose of education is thus, not only to provide knowledge but also to inculcate values, train the instincts, foster right attitudes and habits so that an individual becomes a useful member of the society. This can be termed as the first stage of character formation. As the sage Yajnavalkya opines, only that education which gives a sterling character to an individual and renders him useful for the world is real education. Dr Radhakrishnan calls character the "fate of the nation". A country, he says, "whose people have low character can never become great. When we want to build a great nation, we should educate more and more young men and women in such a way that they may have strength of character." He places great premium on inculcating discipline, devotion and dedication in the students. With these qualities an individual would be able to acquire knowledge and information, which is the basic requirement, though he agrees "the end of education is not the acquisition of information or technical skills only". Education should give an outlook that makes him/her a person of steadfast wisdom. Dr Radhakrishnan's view of a man of steadfast wisdom is commensurate with the picture given in the Gita. He is pained to see the deterioration of values at individual and social levels and often during his lectures he advocates the need for "self-restraint". Obviously, restraint has to come from within because there lies an inner moral and ethical source within human beings and no outside agency can enforce check effectively.

The ideal man that Dr Radhakrishnan envisages is the spiritual man with faith in his "self" and faith in the divine aspect within him. The man with the faith in the "self" is the man with faith in life and in God. If he loses faith in the self, he loses himself. The divine aspect is responsible for all creativity and freedom that man enjoys in the world. Man has made immense progress not because of the force of events but because he has within him the spirit, which makes him look forward, and helps him see the light. But, Dr Radhakrishnan knows that man has yet to master the self and strive to reach divinity; to achieve this he must direct all his efforts and endeavours towards self-understanding. The seminal advice is "*Atmanam Vidhih,*" know thyself.

Although Dr Radhakrishnan envisions an ideal picture of man, he does not absolve him of his social duties and responsibilities. His approach to social evils is that of a humanist. He sees education as a great instrument of social change, and he enjoins upon the teachers and the students to act as harbinger of social change. "Educational system must find its guiding principle in the aims of the social order for which it prepares, and in the nature of the civilization it hopes to build." It may be noted that Dr Radhakrishnan was writing and lecturing at a time when Indian democracy was in its infant stage. As a veteran teacher, Dr Radhakrishnan knew the needs of the country and he placed his faith in the teachers and in the education system. In many of his speeches delivered at various educational institutions, he gave a clarion call to the students to help ameliorate the condition of the society. Democracy cannot be preserved or strengthened so long as there is poverty, disease, hunger, illiteracy in our country, he often said. He wanted to preserve the spirit of equality, liberty and brotherhood regardless of religion, sex, caste, or creed. He knew that any intellectual progress would demand a spirit of free inquiry and he wanted education to foster that spirit by being liberal. Man he maintained is "not a detached spectator of progress immanent in human history, but an active agent in remolding the world nearer to his ideals."

Dr Radhakrishnan's approach to education is integrated and he supports the cause of every discipline whether it is the discipline of science and technology or literature or social sciences. He advocates the study and mastery of all skills as per the child's/student's aptitude. Existence is of three types: natural, social and spiritual. Since these faculties are inter-related, he sees the efficacy of teaching the different disciplines – Science and technology is concerned with nature, Social Sciences are related to society and Literature and the Arts, including philosophy are concerned with our values and the spirit; they are thus part of the whole and a study of these various disciplines is vital for the all-round development of man.

As a teacher himself, Dr Radhakrishnan, has great faith in the power of the teacher to mould the raw material that is in their hands. He places great responsibility on them and displays confidence in them. What he expects of ideal teachers is devotion besides knowledge and scholarship. Of the personal qualities, he visualizes a high sense of duty, immaculate personal behaviour, moral uprightness and self-control as the sterling qualities of a teacher. For him, "The teachers have a special place in the formation of the mind and heart of our youth." As the Chairman of the University Education Commission he insisted upon recruiting suitable teachers on various levels of education. In this world, which he terms *Samsara Vish vrikhsha* (the poisonous tree) the few glimpses of the eternity and beatitude is afforded by the able teacher.

Dr Radhakrishnan, with his philosopher's vision and educationist's zeal has provided us with sound psychological and sociological foundations of education. In his philosophy of education he considers all aspects of human personality and sees the existence of the human values of compassion, love, peace and righteousness as the mark of an integrated human personality. Transformation of man into a higher, self-actualized being is, according to Radhakrishnan, the real aim of education. Culture and civilization, he often asserts, is not outward progress but inner development; that education is true education, which helps us reshape our inner environment along with our outer atmosphere. If education gives us the spirit of service and renunciation its aim *sarvashastra prayojanam atma darshanam*, i.e., an insight into the inner Reality is the end of all kinds of disciplines, is fulfilled.

Note: This paper was read on 5 September 2001 at the Indian Instt. of Advanced Study during a Seminar on Dr Radhakrishnan's concept of education. Hence no documentation has been given (Author).

18 Rethinking Indian Culture with Dr Radhakrishnan

The need for philosophy arises when faith in tradition is shaken.

—Dr Radhakrishnan[1]

We are living in troubled times – times of trial and tribulations when religious fundamentalism is threatening the very structure of the nation; the impact of the dazzling Western materialism and consumerism is overpowering the minds of the youth; and the rich traditional values are losing their appeal. One might well ask what is happening to the noble concepts of Indian culture that has always prided itself for its assimilative nature and the capacity to synthesize. It is at such a juncture that one tends to re-create its history and retrieve its heritage. It is the shared past from which emanate the honour and the pride of the nation; and it is this pride in the great national heritage that crystallizes itself into the remembrance of the great personalities of the country. Precisely at this time some rethinking on Dr Radhakrishnan's contribution to Indian culture seems relevant.

Dr Sarvepalli Radhakrishnan was indeed a versatile genius. As a teacher, he commanded high respect; as a philosopher, he was an exponent of the Indian philosophical tradition; as a writer and speaker, he was spontaneous and eloquent; as an administrator and diplomat, he displayed judgement and acumen; and above all as an individual, he was simplicity incarnate. On his passing away on 17 April, 1975, the *Daily Telegraph* paid him a rich tribute: "No living head of the state could approach the intellectual distinction of Dr Sarvepalli Radhakrishnan ... he was a world famous philosopher and a pioneer in interpreting Eastern thought to the West" (Murty and Vohra, 1989: 194). George P. Conger considers his contribution to various fields of knowledge as exemplary:

> Among the philosophers of our time, no one has achieved so much in so many fields as Sarvepalli Radhakrishnan of India. William James was influential in religion, and John Dewey has been a force in politics. One or two American philosophers have been legislatives. Jacques Maritain has been an ambassador. Dr Radhakrishnan in a little more than thirty years of work has done all these things and more ... . Never in the history of philosophy has there been quite such a world figure. With his unique appointment at Banaras and Oxford, like a weaver's shuttle, he has gone to and fro between the East and the West, carrying a thread of understanding, weaving it into the fabric of civilization.[2]

These remarks have been given here at some length because they draw attention to two significant aspects: first, Dr Radhakrishnan was well-versed in both Eastern and Western philosophical thought, and second, he expounded Indian thought to the West; he created a bridge of understanding between the East and the West and clarified many of the doubts and misconceptions about Indian philosophy. Dr Radhakrishnan was highly influenced by Swami Vivekananda's exposition of Hinduism to the West and wanted to follow suit; moreover, as he often said, his education in Madras Christian College whetted his interest in Indian philosophy and he decided to counter the negative picture of Hinduism presented by the missionaries. He contested Albert Schweitzer's dictum that Indian thought suffered from "world-and life-negation". Without subscribing to any 'ism' he showed the essential spirit of Indian culture which is basically Vedantic with "the notion of the divinity of man and the humanity of God' (Mukherjee, 1959: 377).

Ancient Indian culture has been deeply spiritual, religious and philosophical, but in the 20th century scenario of social dynamics and rapid internationalism, it could not be followed in its entirety. No tradition however great can be continued without appropriate modifications and wise adaptations. Dr Radhakrishnan was aware of these factors and though he lay emphasize on the spiritual basis of Indian culture, he gave it socio-empirical signification in accordance with the exigent principles of spirituality, unity in diversity, morality and ethics, and the contemporary concepts of science and technology, education and politics. Thus, he envisioned a new cultural ethos in which there will be a synthesis of the past and the present with tenability for the future.

Culture has been variously defined by Western and Indian thinkers. The English word "culture" is derived from the Latin word "cultura" meaning to cultivate; but the Sanskrit equivalent of "culture" is *Sanskriti* which stands for something ornamental, beautiful and refined – essentially the inner qualities of man, both acquired and inherited. The *Oxford Dictionary of Philosophy* defines culture as "The way of life of a people, including their attitudes, values, beliefs, arts, sciences, modes of perception and habits of thought and activity." Alfred Weber, the German sociologist however, focuses on transcendence in his definition when he says, "Not subject to analysis in terms of causal law, culture derives from man's immanent transcendence." According to E.B. Taylor, culture is a complex whole, which "includes knowledge, belief, art, morals, law, custom and any other capabilities and habits acquired by man as a member of society" (1958: 1). Joseph Pieper, in his book *Leisure: The Basis of Culture* presents a Christian theosophical view of culture when he brackets it with all that is morally and naturally good. It is the "quintessence of all the natural goods of the world and of those gifts and qualities which, while belonging to man, lie beyond the immediate sphere of his needs and wants" (1963: 17). Kluckhohn sees culture from the point of view of a behavioural scientist and calls it the product of action and the effect of conditioning upon further action. The essential "core of culture consists of tradition, ideas and specially their attached values" (1962: 73).

From these and various other definitions it transpires that the Western concept of culture is social, material and objective, whereas the Indian idea of culture is integral, spiritual and moral. Culture is not "loud" says Pandit Nehru, "it is quiet, it is restrained, it is tolerant" (Chatterjee, 1987: 62). Dr Radhakrishnan's conception of culture is predominantly Indian, enriched by the contemporary Western thought. For him culture is a living entity with *moksha* or self-realization as its goal. To achieve this objective one has to have a strong spiritual base. All his writings and speeches are pointers towards this purpose. In fact, culture is a coherent and cohesive set of values, beliefs and practices and is more or less an internal property that can be a vehicle for self-realization and self-affirmation. Mahatma Gandhi considered "culture" as true "civilization". "Civilization", he said, "is the mode of conduct which points out to man the path of duty." According to Weber, civilization is an outside agency and is a continuous process.

C.E.M. Joad in his *The Story of Civilization* graphically and convincingly elaborates his views on what being civilized means. Using civilization and culture interchangeably, he opines that utilizing the inventions of science like riding in a bus or boarding an aeroplane, eating good food or wearing good clothes is not civilization. Being civilized ought to bring us some credit, he says, something to be proud of. Great art, sculpture, literature, music, scientific inventions can be counted as being cultured. But to create these things human beings require security, free thinking, and freedom from fear. This is exactly what Dr Radhakrishnan elaborated in his writings and speeches. He was not averse to science; in fact he recognized the merits of science. He always maintained that the scientific inventions like radio, telephone and aeroplane were important for the world but this did not suggest the omnipotence of matter. He considered literature, art, and music as essential elements of culture. "Through poetry and drama," he said, "man reveals himself." Further, speaking on literature at the Sahitya Akademi Award ceremony he once remarked, "literature is the channel between spiritual vision and human beings." Poets he considered the "priests" of the invisible world. He averred that the binding principle of democratic societies is spontaneous conformity not enforced obedience. He made it clear while explaining the traditional Indian concept of an ideal state in his speech in Peking (now Beijing) in 1957. Talking about the significance of freedom to human growth, he said:

> It is only in freedom that man can discover what he really is. It is the individual who feels pain and joy, who bears responsibility, does good or evil. If we overlook this side of human nature, we turn the subject into an object. The objectification is at once the necessary condition of freedom and a perpetual threat to it. Man

> must limit the objectification to what is essential for his freedom. As his fellowmen should be equally free, each individual has to submit to certain limitations. The submission is not servitude, as it is accepted in the freedom of spirit.

Freedom of spirit is indeed, the basis of Indian culture. The fountainhead of culture is the human soul and the objective of culture is to realize it. But self-realization is an integral phenomenon and needs all-round development of human faculties – spiritual, moral, ethical, physical, and aesthetic.

Thus, he presented Indian philosophy in an attractive and elegant manner to bring out the basics of Indian culture, though he did not give any separate treatise on culture as such. So effective was he with his words that Aldous Huxley called him "the master of words," and so clear was he in his thought-presentation that after his Hibbert Lecture in London in 1930 the Vice-Chancellor of London University remarked, "It is true that in these days people are full of doubts and fears, but you have shown how these can be done away with. You have filled us with courage and hope for the future" (Radhakrishnan, 1956: 24). This hope and courage he found in our past that upholds the spiritual qualities of freedom and the concept of *Vasudhaiva Kutumbakam.*

The basis of our philosophical postulates is the divine and transcendental Justice, Truth, and Law which uphold the universe, mind, and people.[3] Dharma defines and regulates both the functions of social life and the goals of the individual and is interpreted across the centuries as the unbounded extension of social relations, as the liberation derived from interdependence and solidarity. Dharma is that which sustains – *dharyate iti darmah*. It is the science of harmony and supreme order. The four pillars of Dharma are Truth, Righteouness, Peace, and Love (*Satya, Dharma, Shanti, Prem)*. Experience of the infinite and the practice of Dharma has always moved us to reach the deeper foundations of life and spread its fragrance around. Comparing Indian culture to an invisible stream and extolling its elevating effect, C.P. Ramaswami Aiyar maintains in his book *Phases of Religion and Culture*, "Indian culture in the past has been analogous to a subterranean spring that has been fertilizing many countries which have not always acknowledged that fertilization, but the subterranean river has its unseen but formative influence not only on the mental landscape but also the outer phenomena" (1949: 3). A strong and abiding culture must realize the deeper fountains of strength without neglecting the worldly realities. Indian philosophical thought is essentially founded on the concept of the gradual evolution of the outer existence as well as the inner being.

Dr Radhakrishnan categorically stated that the present crisis emanates from our lack of faith and inability to draw from our rich past, from the rich sources of truth, righteousness, peace, and love. We prospered when these qualities moved us; we declined when doubt and fear blinded our vision. The root cause of the atmosphere of hatred and violence in which we are living today is suspicion, fear and greed. Humanity has become possessive, power hungry and callous. In his Independence Day speech in 1965, Dr Radhakrishnan remarked, "All forms of violence are symbols of human failure." Peace and non-violence are the pillars of Dharma and these must be a part of our personal and social behaviour. Even the socio-political structures should be based on peace and non-violence so that the culture retains its vibrant qualities of mutual respect, understanding and well-being, inherent in the concept of *Sarve Bhavantu Sukhinah.*

In the same lecture, he further elaborated, "If we believe in peaceful co-existence and not power politics, we should not look upon our enemy with disdain and we should not assume that we are always right and our enemy is always wrong. We must achieve a world of law and free choice, banishing from it violence and coercion" (Radhakrishnan, 1969). In Frankfurt, during the International PEN[4] conference, he talked of nationalistic egoism and said, "No nation is immoral … . If it is wrong for the individual to put his self-interest above national good, it is wrong for the nation to put its interests above those of humanity." He further spoke on the dangers of fanatic love of virtue as harmful for peace, harmony, and brotherhood. In fact, in his view no culture is perfect because perfection leads to stagnation and no culture can afford to be stagnant. No culture has reached its destination and each culture in its different capacity is striving towards perfection. The perfection and preservation of our culture does not mean we disrespect or scorn other cultures. A culture can be great and abiding if it has the capacity to absorb and assimilate, to respect other cultures and to let them grow in their own stride. Radhakrishnan did not exclude culture from politics. "Through mutual education the government and the people get near each other till the interests of rulers and the ruled coincide as in *Ramrajya,* the ideal state of the Indian conception," said he in one of his speeches during his tour of South East Asia, in September 1957.

Dr Radhakrishnan recognized the power of science, but he also understood that under the influence of science and technology, religion was being changed into materialism. With faith diminishing, man was groping in the dark. Today, when we have entered the 21st century, and are encountering globalization, consumerism and materialism and are watching with awe the rapid advances in information-technology, we realize the efficacy of the message of great thinkers like Dr Radhakrishnan who upheld ethical, moral and religious values for the inner advancement of man. "Religion is not irrelevant to life," he said in *The Present Crisis of Faith* (114). It is a form of discipline; it is above shallow nationalism and callow materialism. He further asserted that only a "moral and spiritual revolution in the name of human dignity can place man above the idols of economic production, technological organization and racial discrimination and national egotism" (*The Present Crisis of Faith,* 14).

What Dr Radhakrishnan says can well be substantiated by the psychological tenets of theorists like Eric Fromm, Abraham Maslow, and others. Fromm is critical of modern man's "having" orientation, which makes him a machine, and in the process he loses his "being" orientation. In his book *To Have and To Be,* he cites examples of great men like Buddha and Master Eckhart for whom "being" mode was associated with life, flowing out and productivity. Maslow's "peak experience" also shows the power of the spirit. What the psychologists are explaining today has long since been recognized by our spiritual tradition in many subtle ways. As Radhakrishnan asserted ... "the mechanism of the world is a problem of science, but not its mystery, which is the subject of religion." As a crusader in the cause of the recovery of faith, he often drew the attention of his audience to the supremacy of spirit over things. He wanted faith to assert its authority and find "significance in a world in which science and organization seem to have lost their relationship to traditional values."

It would be viable to quote Mahatma Gandhi's concept of culture when he asserted that culture shows in the smallest detail of one's conduct. "Culture is the foundation, the primary thing. It would show in the smallest detail of your conduct and personal behavior ... Inner culture must be reflected in your speech, the way in which you treat visitors and guests, and behave towards one another and your teachers and elders" (*Harijan,* May 5, 1946). The essence of what Gandhi said and what Radhakrishnan corroborated is that the inner and the outer cultures, the spiritual and the worldly must stimulate us to make our culture a progressive life-sustaining power. The scenario at present is rather bleak; loss of traditional values has made us rootless, fumbling for our identity.

Not science but the wrong approach to science is harmful, he often maintained.[5] Science should not end in war, religion should not end in dogmatism. In his address at the Centenary Convocation of the Madras University in 1957, he eloquently brought out the true purpose and meaning of science and religion. The purpose of religion is not merely to change the opinions of men but to change the lives of men. Religion is needed to civilize our nature and science is needed to usher in a new world where spirituality and science would supplement each other. The forces of science, its method of inquiry and investigation along with the faith and deep urges of religion together can bring about the new world. Science reveals to us the inexhaustible richness of the world, its unexpectedness and wonder. But science does not profess to solve all problems.

As a philosopher, Dr Radhakrishnan's endeavour was to give an interpretation of Indian thought to establish universal peace and harmony through an awareness of the presence of the same divine spirit in all human beings. He conveyed to the West the nuances of Hindu thought and Indian philosophy in the idiom of the Western philosophy that they understood. The purpose of his efforts was to establish the ethical character of Hindu religion, and to prove that philosophy in India is not an abstract study remote from life of man and that spiritual values are realized through love – family love, love and friendship, and loyalty.

Although Dr Radhakrishnan persistently expounded Indian ethos through its religious tenets, he did not ignore the other aspects that bear upon the cultural integrity. As a teacher, his ambition was to educate his pupils to "a belief in spiritual and ethical universe," but as an orator, he advocated the inculcation of those values essential for day-to-day life. He was a votary of democracy and considered poverty and economic backwardness as impediments to democratic ideals. He advocated strongly the cause of education so as to make a solid foundation for our new democracy to stand on. It may be remembered here that Dr Radhakrishnan's span of writing and lecturing covers an important period of Indian history. Prior to the Independence, he had to counter the British view of Indian culture, after the Independence, he was aware of the task before the nation, and so his speeches and writings were directed towards nation building.

Education is the most potent instrument of social change. To initiate a new culture with strong Indian foundation with the benefits of the current scientific and technological advancement we must have a new concept of education suitable to the main structure. As the Chairman of the University Education Commission, he tried to formulate a sound education policy, which would commensurate with our culture yet which would not negate the changes brought in by modern scientific temperament and development. He envisaged education for self-development. Criticizing the present system as inadequate he said, "Our education has not freed us from intellectual bondage. It stimulates the mind without satisfying it" (quoted in Sharma, 2000: 395). He emphasized on the character-building role of education, "We cannot build our country with bricks and mortar," he would say, "It has to grow silently in the minds of and hearts of our youth." He further asserted that the fate of a nation "depends upon character. A country whose people have low character can never become great. When we want to build a great nation, we should educate more and more young men and women in such a way that they have strength of character" (Speeches, Vol. II, p. 267). Here one may refer to E.W. Emerson's famous lines, "Not gold but only men can make/A country great and strong." Radhakrishnan rightly considered education as training of emotions, feelings and behaviour.

For self-renewal he emphasized on good textbooks and a sound system of education to give "the diversity of our country a unity of purpose" (Radhakrishnan, 1970: 115). But, he did not absolve the teachers of their responsibilities. The teacher should have a devotion to teaching if they wish to earn the highest respect as it was in ancient India. "The teachers have a special place in the formation of the mind and heart of the youth," he categorically stated (Radhakrishnan, *Speeches and Writings*, 202). He called upon youth to show a sense of exhilaration and buoyancy of spirit so that a new India, free from disease, poverty and discrimination could be built. In his scheme of things women were not neglected and he advocated the establishment of a woman's university. He wanted them to enjoy equality, but he was not a votary of the Western model for Indian women. The aim of education according to Radhakrishnan was the transformation of the inner and the outer man. It was commensurate with his idea and ideal of Indian culture, which seeks to reform both our consciousness and behaviour. A combination of inner virtues, human values and social and national goals of the welfare of all makes his concept of education universal.

Combining scholarship and statesmanship, philosophy and patriotism, Dr Radhakrishnan expounded the Indian cultural ethos and shook his countrymen from their stupor to awaken them to the beauty of Indian's great heritage. "Civilization is a thing of the spirit," he used to say. "It is not something external, solid and mechanical. It is the dream in the people's soul. It is ... the perception of the mystery of existence" (Dutt, 1966: 31–32). Dr Radhakrishnan's approach to Indian culture was multi-dimensional. He minutely observed the recurrent patterns in the development of the culture and the value structure and understood the underlying continuity of its accumulated traditions and institutions. He tried to make comprehensible the power of the spirit and the meaning of Indian culture. Hiren Mukherjee's remarks would be relevant here: "As head of the state, he symbolized powerfully the spirit of India and the golden words that flowed like a felicitous torrent from his lips when he spoke at world gatherings left most foreign dignitaries somewhat dazed and spell-bound" (1983: 232).

Dr Radhakrishnan's contribution to Indian culture can be summed up in his concepts of ethical religion, spiritual politics, humanitarian science, and value-oriented education. In brief, his paradigm of culture was all pervasive: he saw assimilation and respect for other cultures as its true nature; self-realization and spirituality as its significant aspect, and a combination of the ancient and the modern as its virtue. Dr Radhakrishnan did not confine philosophy to the realization of truth alone but applied it to the real problems of the real world. It may be an idealist's view of Indian culture but it is fundamentally a blending of spiritual experience, material exigency and earthly motivations. His precepts envision a progressive and dynamic life power named Indian culture.

Notes

1. Dr Radhakrishnan records in "Fragments of a Confession," and *My Search for Truth* the reasons why he turned to philosophy. He recounts that in Madras Christian College he felt hurt at his teachers' criticism of Indian thought, religion and tradition. "The challenge of Christian critics impelled me to make a study of Hinduism and find out what is living and what is dead in it. The spirit of the times, in which India, so to say, was turning in its sleep, strengthened this resolve." (*My Search for Truth*, p. 9).
2. Dr Radhakrishnan was, in a way the cultural ambassador of India. While in Peking (now Beijing) in 1957, explaining the traditional Indian concept of ideal state he said, "The binding principle of democratic societies is spontaneous conformity, not enforced obedience. The people's will should prevail. We cannot crush their wishes, cannot trample on their dreams."
3. Gandhi believed, like Radhakrishnan, that the main spring of culture is heart and soul. In *Harijan*, he wrote, "A nation's culture resides in hearts and in the souls of the people" (January 28, 1939). Radhakrishnan averred that cultural synthesis is the natural keynote of history in a land characterized by a variety of races, languages, traditions, and beliefs.
4. International PEN is an association of Poets, Essayists and Novelists, formed in 1921.
5. In one of his lectures in Germany he said, "There is nothing wrong about technology. Signs of decadence do not originate from the machines. They are to be sought in the human soul. It is there that a change of direction is needed. We seem to have lost, at any rate when we work as members belonging to groups, national groups especially, a sense of values, a sense of the sacred."

References

Aiyar, C.P. Ramaswami. *Phases of Religion and Culture.* Bombay: Hind Kitabs, 1949.

Chatterjee, N.N. *Nehru's Thoughts on National Topics*. New Delhi: Publications Division, 1987.

Dutt, K. Iswara, ed. *Sarvepalli Radhakrishnan: A Study of the President of India.* New Delhi: Popular Book Service, 1966.

Kluckhohn, Clyde. *Culture and Behavior*. New York: A Free Press Paperback, The Macmillan Company, 1962.

Mukherjee, Hiren. "Reminiscences of Radhakrishnan," in *Recalling India's Struggle for Freedom*. Delhi: Seema Publications, 1983.

Mukherjee, Radhakamal. *The Culture and Art of India*. London: George Allen and Unwin, 1959.

Murty, K. Satchidananda and Ashok Vohra. *Radhakrishnan: His Life and Ideas.* New Delhi: Ajanta Publications, 1989.

Pieper, Joseph. *Leisure: The Basis of Culture*. New York: The New American Library, Mentor Omega Books, 1963.

Radhakrishnan, S. *Kalki or The Future of Civilization*. Bombay: Hind Kitabs Ltd., 1931.

——. *The Heart of Hindusthan*. Madras: G.A. Natsen, 1948.

——. "The Religion of the Spirit and the World's Need: Fragments of a Confession," in P.A. Schilpp, ed. *The Philosophy of Sarvepalli Radhakrishnan*. New York: Tudor Publishing Company, 1952.

——. *My Search for Truth.* Agra: Shiva Lal Agarwala, 1956.

——. *Fellowship of the Spirit*. Harvard: The Center for the Study of World Religions, 1961.

——. *Speeches and Writings*, second series. May 1964–May 1967. Delhi: Publications Division, 1969.

——. *The Present Crisis of Faith.* New Delhi: Orient Paperbacks, 1970.

Schilpp, P.A. *The Philosophy of Sarvepalli Radhakrishnan*. New York: Tudor Publishing Company, 1952.

Sharma, Ramnath. *A Textbook of Educational Philosophy.* New Delhi: Kanishaka Publishers, 2000.

Taylor, E.B. *The Origin of Culture.* New York: Harper & Row, 1958.

19 Gandhian Ideals and Nehruvian Vision

Notes on the Idea of India in Bollywood Cinema

The Idea of India and the Contribution of Hindi Films

Pandit Jawaharlal Nehru's *The Discovery of India*, written on the threshold of Indian independence, propounded his vision of a shared history and multiculturalism. The three key terms that he tried to reconcile were: industrialization, Indianization and "unity in diversity". Even before the country became independent, the focus of the society was on secularism, national integration, and rural reconstruction. In fact, almost all political parties and leaders upheld visions of a unified, secular, democratic India. It was the time of the great Indian dream when we were visualizing a forward-looking India. No doubt then that literature, art, culture, and the Bollywood cinema were motivated by the ideals to build a strong nation.

Many of the films produced in the mid-1940s through 1950s carried forward the dream that was to become the bedrock of the new democracy. This was substantiated by Mr Yash Chopra, the renowned film-maker when he said, "Nehru and his policies were always part of our consciousness. He used to say that big dams and industries were the temples of modern India. We had internalized his words." Films on children and their travails, the construction of big dams and roads, the spirit of camaraderie and goodwill, the naive poor (often portrayed by Raj Kapoor), and inter-religious and inter-caste goodwill were some of the themes that made it big during this period.

B.R. Chopra's *Naya Daur* (1957), for example, portrays the construction of a dam that encounters numerous difficulties. The song "Saathi haath badhana ..." is one of the sonorous numbers transmitting a message of cooperation and companionship. The dramatic climax is reached when all the villagers join hands to construction work and the benevolent father-figure of the village hopes that a humanist attitude will soon obliterate class divisions. The film starring Dilip Kumar and Vaijayantimala in the lead roles was the hit of the time.

As issues of rural upliftment were many pronged and the government was making umpteen efforts to introduce welfare measures in villages, literature and films looked at the matter from their several angles. Mulk Raj Anand's novels take a look at the plight of the workers, the struggle of the farmers and the pain of the downtrodden. His ideas were Gandhian coupled with Marxian. Kamala Markandaya shows the nuisance that industrialization was creating in villages and also the predicament of the youth migrating to cities. Almost identical issues were dealt with by the films. Bimal Roy's *Do Bigha Zameen* is about a small farmer, the perpetual debt of the merciless zamindaar, the farmer's (Balraj Sahni's) efforts to repay it and his failure to eke out enough to collect the sum and the eventual death, loss of land and the coming up of the factory on his land. Such concerns gave the movie a "realist" touch by putting before the people the conditions of the farmers. Likewise, *Rahi,* based on Mulk Raj Anand's novel *Two Leaves and a Bud* is set in the tea garden in Assam of pre-independence era, and deals with the problems of the impoverished and exploited workers and colonial high-handedness.

Since in the early decades of our independence the inclination of the nation was towards Soviet Russia, understandably many movies showed obvious Russian influence, like adopting Maxim Gorky's classics as in film *Neecha Nagar*, adapted from his *The Lower Depths*. The naïve poor for whom the audience sympathy is generated is often a good-old boy in rags, a homeless wretch, singing jolly good songs and falling in love with the heroine is another image. The eternal tussle between the good and the evil exists perpetually in which the bad man is the rich zamindar or Sahukar of the village who has to eat a humble pie in the end. Despite these stereotyping, the Raj Kapoor's films almost always received encouraging acceptance from the audience.

Another popular theme with the message to rise above the communal sentiments is loud and clear in movies like *Dhool ka Phool* and *Dharmaputra*, both directed by Yash Chopra. In the former, a Muslim adopts an illegitimate Hindu boy while in the latter it is a Hindu family that adopts a Muslim boy. Songs such as *"Tu hindu banega no Musalman banega, insaan ki aulad hai tu insaan banega* make a powerful plea for a secular approach. Meaningful movies like *Lakhrani* (1945), *Gopinath* (1948), *Sujata* (1959) took up the caste issue and shook the society to its roots. *Girls' School* focused on female education and there were umpteen movies on the evils of dowry. Children of the lesser gods too had their share in movies like *Boot Polish, Jagriti, Dosti,* and many others. The situation in these is often romanticized at the cost of realism but they were able to touch the emotions of the audience.

It cannot be denied that apart from these themes, the mythologicals, historical dramas, the fantastic, fairy tales, and the ghost stories were made in large numbers. These appealed to the popular sentiments and were favourites of the public. But since the films with messages were not didactic, they too attracted the movie buffs.

The Hindi cinema took the ideals of the new born nation to the masses. They made the display of man-woman relationship acceptable to the people. Films like *Nau Do Gyara* or *Shri 420* which showed the picaresque hero or heroine made mobility acceptable to the nation's psyche. The young – men and women – are shown moving across the country, there is cultural exchange, and the idea of India is expanded. At a time when people were not mobile, travel and tourism had not become the watchword, and there were limited means at the disposal of the common man, these films provided the masses the idea of one, unified, democratic India.

Today, we still have the same type of problems – a girl leaves her home resenting the proposed marriage, meets her prince charming and Kapoor all is well that ends well (Shahid Kapoor and

Kareena Kapoor starrer *Jab We Met*), but things have changed since and so has the presentation. Then there still are the slum children – *Slum Dog Millionaire* – but the tally has altered from *Boot Polish or Jagriti* days. There are the disabled – *Black* – as in Dilip Kumar's *Deedar* or many such films but the treatment is certainly different.

The nation has progressed and so has the film industry – technically, thematically and acting-wise there is perfection. But, at a time when Indian independence was new, Bombay films and film-makers transmitted the visions of our leaders to the masses. If despite the myriad problems we are standing as a strong democracy today, a part of the credit goes to the popular media of the times.

Rural Realities in Post-Independence Cinema

In the 1957 blockbuster *Mother India* there is a scene when farmers form a chorus outlining the map of India and give a boost to the image of rural India as Mother India. In the same year *Naya Daur* took up the issue of rural reconstruction and the song "Saathi haath badhana, Saathi re" symbolized collectivization for progress; in V. Shantaram's *Do Ankein Barah Haath*, again a 1957 hit, the song "Ay malik tere bande hum" idealized the good versus bad situation. Thus comes rural India into focus in post-independence period with the travails of the peasants, the sacrifices of women, bad-rich versus good-poor themes. The questions of nation building, Nehru's dream projects, road and dams, factories and industrialization come into play and the tempo is built with songs and dialogues that are meant to represent progressive India.

Mehboob Khan's *Mother India* is a beautiful but brutally realistic rendering of rural society and the tribulations of a woman's life who can be loving, tolerant and sacrificing and when time demands an incarnation of Kali. Nargis symbolizes Mother India from a bubbling young woman to the old mother weighed down by the worries of life and indeed, she has carried herself superbly. Married to a farmer, she has a hard but happy life; then life takes a sudden turn; her husband loses his arms in an accident and helpless and disgusted he walks out on his family leaving them all in the village; she is left to manage everything from the field to cooking, from bringing up her sons to warding off the advances of the lecherous zamindar. The heart-rending finale comes when she prefers to kill her rebellious son than to allow him to indulge in his nefarious acts. The film is a tribute to the peasant women of India. That reminds us of Kamala Markandaya's portrayal of her protagonist Rukhmani, a farmer woman as strong and undaunted. She too is addressed by critics as Mother India.

Earlier, in 1953 *Do Bigha Zameen* too picturized farmer's plight. This Balraj Sahni-starrer is the heart-rending story of drought and debt, shattered dreams and lives gone astray. The protagonist goes to Calcutta, becomes a rickshaw-puller but ultimately loses his land and life. The film earned great reputation for its neo-realistic representation. The opening song of the film celebrating the rainfall after two seasons of drought is an expression of every farmer's joy at the prospect of a good harvest. But debt, loans, droughts and poverty seem to be the synonyms for a peasant's life. Recently *Peepli Live*, deals with the problem in tonguc-in-the-cheek manner and indicts the society for not moving any forward despite all the din about development and world-class economic growth. The march from 1950s to 2010 though spectacular has its skeleton in the cupboard.

Honour killings attracted the attention of Ajay Sinha. His film "Khap – A Story of Honour Killing" tackles the recent incidents of same *gotra* marriage and the consequent murders of the couples in villages in Haryana, Punjab, and UP. This may be an unusual theme for a movie but the issue is contemporary and needs focus. Om Puri is the *sarpanch* who believes in the traditional concept of the Khap panchayats. But later when he comes to realize its implications and the loss of innocent lives, he fights to eradicate the system.

The portrayal of villages in two contemporary movies *Lagaan* and *Swades* is typical of the view held by the modern urban elite. Village life is full of poverty, ignorance, illiteracy, superstition, and poor socio-economic conditions but the villagers are romanticized as innocent and uncorrupted by urban influence and modernity. *Lagaan* has for its setting colonial times while *Swades* draws our attention to the disparities existing in contemporary India between rural India and India of the cities. In the end, however, there is change of heart as an erstwhile self-centred NRI takes up the much needed upliftment work in the village Charanpur.

The treatment given to the village themes has differed from decade to decade as per the exigencies of the plot. Manoj Kumar's *Upkaar*, Nitin Bose's *Ganga Jamuna*, Basu Bhattacharya's *Teesri Kasam* are all related to the villages though the issues are handled with dextrous ingenuity and innovative skills. Shyam Benegal's approach in *Welcome to Sajjanpur* and *Well Done Abba* is subtly humourous while Satyajit Ray's *Apu* trilogy was matter-of-fact though he often admitted that being a city-bred he was not too well-equipped to portray the rural realism.

In fact, rural India provides a magnificent backdrop to portray and understand India. Villages are not god-forsaken static and isolated places, nor are villagers the innocent savages as many city-dwellers think. Our cities are not paradises, they have their problems like water shortage, commuting inconveniences, health hazards and crime and frequent political unrests. It is time we look to our villages – not as imaginary Shangri-la's but as idyllic places in a practical sense without gloss.

20 "The Contact Zone"

Translation and Transmission of Folklore

This chapter takes its cue from Mary Louise Pratt's term the "contact zone"[1] used for writing and translation as practices of creation, and Gayatri Spivak's concept of culture as "bonded spaces"[2], to study and analyse the folk narratives from Himachal Pradesh and Maharashtra as translation and transmission and to show the basic solidarity of Indian culture.

Around the 1990s, to counter the threat of divisive forces, a catchy slogan on buses and public places said, "From Kashmir to Kanya Kumari India is one." Incidentally, around the same time V.S. Naipaul's *India: A Million Mutinies Now* (1990) was released visualizing a strong and unified India despite her million mutinies threatening her existence. The mutinies, Naipaul said, are a process of integration and restoration and are not to be wished away. "These were a part of a new beginning of a new way for millions, part of India's growth, part of its restoration" (518). Although it is alleged that by reconstructing and reiterating India's strength as a unitary whole, Naipaul is seeking to compensate his loss of identity generated by his diasporic condition, it cannot be denied that a central will, a central intellect and a national idea has always prevailed underneath Indian culture lending cultural wholeness to the country. What with the efforts of authors to reiterate the unity and integrity of India through the adulation of the Ganga as the symbol of our culture or the eulogy of Narmada as an integrating force (Gita Mehta's *A River Sutra*), the cultural transmission from one region to the other seems to have required no motivation. It took place unobtrusively over the centuries translating the psycho-socio-cultural ambience of one part/region of the country to the other.

Considering the geographical situation of Himachal Pradesh and Maharashtra (the distance from one nearest point to the other could well be over 1,500 kms), and the near non-existence of an effective communication system in centuries past, it is rather surprising that the folklore should have identical strands to an extent. The translation process – not only linguistic translation but also thematic – may have taken place effectively at a certain stage. These transactions have contributed greatly to inter-cultural relations between the ethnic groups living far away from each other. This is, in fact, the "contact zone," the place where cultures come together and establish relationship which binds the members of a national community as a coherent group. The cohabitation of the purity of codes and languages along with the ethnic identity and the constituent difference make India a mosaic of cultures, an immense contact zone.

"Rali" from Himachal Pradesh and "Bahuli" from Maharashtra are two folk games played by young adolescent girls (in fact, these are festivities rather than games but are usually termed as games or play because these are played with the gusto of games. The age-group is between 7–15 years). The religious sanctity of both has now taken the shape of social convention and group entertainment though the basic religious and ritualistic structure remains intact. Both Rali and Bahuli are forms of goddess Parvati, the consort of Shiva and by worshipping Shiv-Parvati the girls are supposed to get the blessings of the divine couple for a happy married life. Rali is celebrated in the month of Chaitra, the first month of the Hindu calendar, roughly March-April; and Bahuli takes place in the month of Bhadrapada after Ganesh Pooja in Maharashtra, roughly August-September. Looking at the seasonal significance of the spacing of the two festivals, we discover that Rali falls in spring and Bahuli after the rains. In the lower regions of the Pradesh where the festival is predominantly popular (in the districts of Kangra, Una, Mandi, Kullu, and Hamirpur) April is an invigorating month with mild but warm sun and the cheer of spring in the air. Bhadrapada in Maharashtra is also a pleasant month; after the rains the sun is mild and the greenery is soothing.

The modes of celebrations are different yet alike. The preparations for Rali start in the last week of Phagun. All the girls of the village (or specific localities if it is a bigger town) gather together to decide the place where Rali will be established and worshipped. Usually, one of the girls comes out with the offer of her home and the group reaches her house to clean and sanctify the earmarked place with cow-dung paste. Let it be clarified here that it is with the prior consent of the mother that the place is offered. This room or the courtyard is going to be the altar for Rali and the drama-stage for the girls for a month now. One day prior to Chaitra, the girls assemble at some appointed spot early in the morning and go, singing in unison, in search of some pure spot where they can get clay-soil. Since the idols are of gods and goddesses – Rali, Vastu, and Shankar – the clay should be from an uncontaminated spot. Now starts another song, a prayer to the Earth to yield good soil so that the idols do not crack and the worship is accomplished without any impediment. Before digging the earth they bury a cowrie shell as a token of payment. Seen from the ecological angle, this is a healthy practice which forbids mindless harm to ecology.

Then start the processes of sifting the clay, wetting it, kneading and making dough to fashion idols, drying, colouring and decorating them. Each activity is undertaken by different groups in which the girls are divided as per their inclination and ability. While one group collects cow dung, the other plasters the floor, another makes the square called "chaukdu" where Rali will be worshiped; one group collects flowers and makes garlands, another decorates the altar. After these initial preparations the idols are installed on the first day of Chaitra by a priest with usual rituals and religious fervour. For a month thereafter it is the girls' domain – performing morning and evening pooja, conducting entertainment programmes, singing bhajans and folk songs, and dancing. Men, women and children all partake in the enjoyment aspect but at the management and conduct levels of the show are the girls. The ritual continues for one month. On the last day, the idols are taken out in a procession and immersed in a nearby river or stream amid singing, dancing and chanting of mantras. The atmosphere is emotionally charged and one may see women in tears as they bid farewell to Rali, Shankar, and Vastu.

Now, a look at Bahuli of Maharashtra! Here too, the girls choose a place to establish Gauri or Bahuli which remains the centre of activities for a fortnight. The idols are fashioned by girls with clay brought from a clean spot and are coloured and decorated as per the custom and in traditional costumes.[3] After the ritual of worship, every afternoon games and entertainment meant exclusively for the females are staged. Unlike Rali, men are not associated with these. One of the popular activities is the guessing game. Each girl in turn invites her playmates to her home, prepares some dish and keeps part of it in a container with closed lid. One has to guess the eatable item that is the day's speciality. A correct guess is rewarded with double serving. For fifteen days the girls thus enjoy tasty preparations and exchange recipes. On the last day, the idols are immersed in water amid much emotion. Songs and chanting of mantras are also part of the ceremony as in Rali.

Both these festivals have many things in common including Parvati pooja for getting a good husband. The fashioning and moulding clay idols, decorating the area, stringing flowers in garland are artistic activities which not only satisfy the inner human urge for creativity and beauty but also train the girls culturally. In a way, we can call them play-schools of yore. While making clay idols the girls get in touch with the earth and though not consciously realizing its impact they develop a cosmic awareness which, psychologists say, denotes a unifying sense of oneness with the Elements. Decorations of floor with Rangoli patterns in Maharashtra and Likhnu in Himachal Pradesh have symbolic significance. These patterns contain swastikas, dots, circles, and lines denoting oneness of all, movement of the sun from east to west, supremacy of Brahma, and cycle of seasons and life.

The songs sung for the occasions have aesthetic significance. For example, while stringing flowers for Rali the songs tell how flowers need to be arranged in a pleasantly colourful array – red and then white embellished with green leaves which enhances the girls' sense of colour combination. Later in the song, the girls complain that the naughty wind is blowing off the petals to which the mother's rejoinder is, "never mind the wind, daughter we will make petals of silver, petals of gold for your Maharaj" (Lord Shiva). By implication, it means for her groom. In Bahuli songs too, while decorating the idol the girls sing of various ornaments of gold and silver – heavy Nath (nose ornament) of pearls set in gold, pearl bangles (todey), heavy gold bangles (patlya), anklets of silver and so on. In fact, the performances of both Bahuli and Rali are lyrical; every occasion has a song, sung in unison, from plastering the floor with dung to decorating the altar and onwards.

Most of the songs have ecological significance too. The Rali girls going out to pluck wild flowers name various flowers available in the season – gulab, gainda, basuti. But plucking is not meant to be an unmindful act of destruction. It is an act of consideration for nature. For example, the song entreats the plant to yield its bounty:

> Gadua dala, gadua dala, gadue tere charde
> Das kusumbe barde bara bara patriyan
> raliye maye diyan sisa.

The last line assures the plant of being blessed by Rali maa. The girls not only become conversant with various flowers but also learn to look at nature with reverence. The Vedic ritual of praying to plants and trees before touching them is reflected in the local idiom. The Bahuli songs while decorating Parvati sing of blue bird and the black bird sitting on the babul tree. The animism in both the rituals is typically Indian and speak well of inter-cultural transactions.

Evening entertainment programmes of Rali performances have cultural and aesthetic colour. The lighter vein of the dialogues generates mirth, while the Bhajans have religious fervour. Apart from entertainment, these festivals provide freedom to the girls to sing and dance and be themselves who otherwise have cloistered in existence. In the Bahuli, the guessing game is meant to perfect their culinary skills on which hinges much of their future happiness. Socially, these festivals are a reminder to the girls that marriage is the ultimate goal of their life. Songs and dances and other games like Kikali (called phugadi in Marathi) are vigorous, full of mirth, and muscular exercise.

Although so far we have concentrated on similarity of Rali and Bahuli, we cannot disregard the local colour that gives them difference and a distinct identity. The Rali story from Himachal

Pradesh is associated with Rali, the daughter of a Brahmin who marries her off to a child groom. Rali does not know that her husband is a boy of twelve till the wedding ritual is over. On their way to the groom's house, she asks the palanquin bearers to stop near a river. She gets out and jumps into the turbulent current. Before ending her life, however, she tells her brother that she is committing suicide because she cannot think of being a child-groom's wife and ekes out a promise from him that he will start Rali Pooja in his village in her memory. This was meant to be a reminder to the parents that no girl should be sacrificed on the marriage altar henceforth. Her example would be a warning to the parents not to be unjust.

No such incident is associated with the Maharashtra performance of Bahuli. Bahuli or Bhulabai means a doll. In a way this is the favourite doll game of girls. But the doll here is Parvati and the usual game has got the tinge of religious festivities coupled with entertainment.

Some folk-narratives from Maharashtra and Himachal Pradesh also make interesting reading. There are two identical stories about old couples. Both in the Marathi story and the Himachali story the couples are poor. One day the wives discover that they have wheat flour enough to make five rotis only. The five rotis create ground for argument. Now comes the difference. In the Marathi story the husband asserts his claim to eat three because he has to earn a living, go out to the bazaar to get things and do so many chores, while the wife remains at home doing nothing. But the wife has her own argument to offer about her importance – cooking and washing and so on. In the Himachali story both husband and wife argue offering the other a bigger share – the wife wants the husband to eat three while she would be satisfied with two and vice versa. Ultimately, in both cases they decide to go out for a walk on the condition that whosoever breaks the silence will be the loser. For miles they keep on walking. Nobody speaks. In the Marathi story the woman ultimately cannot keep quiet. She sees a field with red chillies looking enticing on the green plant. She asks, "Tell me, darling, what is this red-red thing?" The man takes the opportunity to tease her for her folly, laughs and utters, "So my Mynah, you have spoken first." He is happy at the prospect of three rotis. In the

Himachali story also the woman loses the bet but here it is to her advantage because she has to eat three now. The stories are hilarious and are significant pointer towards the social aspect. In the Marathi story, the woman is given a voice. She recounts her chores and feels important. She shows assertiveness as she puts forward her claim. In the Himachali story, the couple is more caring and ready to sacrifice for the other.

There are two allegories – stories of the crow and the sparrow – which though not identical speak of the transmission of culture across the regions. The Marathi story of "Cau-Chiu" (the crow and the sparrow) is popular all over Maharashtra. Almost every child is told this story. Rather this is the first story told to a child. A crow has a house made of dung and the sparrow, made of wax. One day a ferocious storm accompanied by rain and hail breaks out and destroys the crow's house. Wet and shivering, the crow rushes to the sparrow for shelter. The sparrow, however takes her time to open the door. Every knock of the crow is answered by an account of the work she is busy in. The conversation is like this:

> "Sister sparrow, sister sparrow, open the door."
> "Wait a bit, brother, I'm busy bathing my little one."
> "Sister sparrow, sister sparrow, open the door."
> "Wait a bit, brother, I'm busy feeding my little one."

And so it goes on till finally she opens the door. The sparrow has a spacious house well stocked with sacks full of rice, sugar and coconut kernel. She gives the crow a choice to select the perch for the night. The crow chooses the sack of coconut. He has evil designs. At night he does not sleep a wink, eats all the stock of coconut and dirties the area. In the morning, the horrified sparrow sees the mess and resolves to punish the crow but the clever crow, sensing danger has already vanished. A.K. Ramanujan mentions same story popular in Karnataka.

The story from Himachal Pradesh is also about the crow and the sparrow but the idea is different. Once a crow spots the beautiful, healthy young ones of the sparrow but instead of attacking them on the sly, he openly challenges her, saying, "Sister Sparrow, I want to eat your little ones. They are healthy and will make a sumptuous meal for me." The sparrow says, "Welcome brother, but your beak is dirty. First go and wash it." The crow flies to the river and explaining the reason for his hurry, he requests the river to give him some water. The river tells him to get a pitcher for water. He flies to the potter; the potter wants clay to make a pitcher, he sends him to get clay. The crow flies to the clay, the clay tells him to get an implement to dig. The crow flies to the antilope and entreats him to give him one of his anteliers. The antelope suggests, "Get a dog to chase me through the thick woods. My antelier will get caught in trees and will break. You can have it then." The dog agrees to do his bit but he wants milk; the crow goes to the buffalo for milk who needs grass; for cutting grass the crow needs a sickle; for sickle he flies to the iron-smith. Thus he is made to go from pillar to post. The iron-smith, on hearing his story understands his evil design, refuses to help him and shoos him away.

The story loses much of its rhythm and humour in recounting in prose in English but in the local version, every activity is sung in verse and generates mirth. Besides, both the stories above have allegorical allusions – the crow standing for wickedness and selfish motives, the sparrow denoting credulity and weakness. Recently, women writer have explored rich feminist implications in the stories. Particularly, the Marathi story has been used meaningfully in their narratives by writers like Gauri Deshpande, Shashi Deshpande, Sanya and many others. In one of her stories, Gauri Deshpande raises a tirade against the society for distortion of facts. In the story, the Chieu has a beautiful house. OK. But in reality do women really have a house of their own? And if at all they have it, the male (crow/Cau) encroaches upon it, spoils it, leaves everything in a mess and abandons it.[4] The sparrow (female) can ward off trouble temporarily, but real help must come from the society as in the Himachali story where the iron-smith refuses to help the crow.

Another pair of folk stories that can be studied here are: the honest lamb from Himachal Pradesh and the clever old woman from Maharashtra. In the Marathi story, an old woman is going to her daughter's house to help her with delivery. En route she meets following animals in succession: a jackal, a hyena, a wolf and a tiger. Each one says, "old woman, I want to eat you." To each one her reply is, "Look, I am so bony. There is no flesh on me. I am going to my daughter's house. There I shall be looked after. You may eat me on my return journey." "Don't try to be clever with us," they exhort. She stays with her daughter for a month and when the time for return comes she hollows a big pumpkin, sits in and asks her son-in-law to kick it down the slope. As the pumpkin rolls down, she meets now, the tiger, wolf, hyena and jackal. Each one asks, "Oh rolling pumpkin, have you seen an old woman on your way?" The old woman says from inside, "No old woman is there. Come on my pumpkin, roll on." Others take her for her words but the jackal senses trick. He runs after the pumpkin but the old woman reaches home and shuts the door.

In Himachali story, a lamb is sent on an errand by his master. He too meets animals on the prowl who want to eat it. He assures them that they may eat him after he accomplishes the master's task. He will come to offer himself as per his promise. And after accomplishing the job he tells his master that he has to honour his promise and goes out to be eaten by the animals who are waiting for him. Touched by his honesty, the master accompanies him and seeing the man, the animals run away and he is saved. In both these stories there is reflection of culture, animal imagery and the inherent characters of the various predatory animals. In the Himachali story honesty is upheld and in the Marathi story a clever woman is depicted.

The two games and the stories recounted here are the most structured and socially oriented form of folklore to portray the social dynamics of the two areas. These folklores are not literally translated but they do rise out of the natural contours of the land and reject the unnatural man-made geographical boundaries. Folklore is oral literature but how it has got transmitted and translated across the regions is a multi-dimensional question. As Redfield, a scholar of culture and society points out in his book *Peasant Society and Culture*, traditions, culture and folklore seep slowly into the communities and get translated according to local dialogic process:

> In a civilization there is a great tradition of the reflective few and there is a little tradition of the largely unreflective many. The great tradition is cultivated in schools and temples, the little tradition

> works itself out and keeps itself going in the lives of the unlettered in their village communities. (1973: 42–43)

Oral traditions produce texts of their own cultural performance of every kind, for example, plays, rituals, games are texts by themselves. In the context of Indian heritage where the interplay between the national versus regional plays an important role and local culture is a vital factor, the transmission of folk texts is an interacting continuum. Written and oral creative expressions are distinct from each other but they are not incompatible with each other. Rather they are complementary in many a way. Scholars in these fields recognize the obvious differences in the process of creation and transmission, speak of a two-way traffic operating between what are termed as written and oral literatures. What is important for interpretation of an oral text or of an oral folklore is its context. As Dundes points out, "The context of an item of folklore is the specific social situation in which that particular item is employed (1978: 27). These stories and games represent wider sociological contexts and have different contexts for different shades of meaning and implication but the nature of performance and the response of the audience depend on the native's understanding of the text. That's why Malinowski's assertion holds good when he says that "native setting" is important to interpret and understand the text and the context and the meaning (Malinowski quoted in Bascom, 1981: 42–43). Translation and transmission of folklore is not only a linguistic process; it is a challenge to the negotiation of a complex cultural conception and to its plurality.

Notes

1. According to Mary Louise Pratt writing and translation are practices of creation and they meet at some point which can aptly be called "contact zone". This is the place where cultures, previously apart, come together and establish an ongoing relation (see Pratt *Imperial Eyes: Travel Writing and Transculturation*. London and New York: Routledge, 1992, p. 6).
2. Spivak refers to "bonded spaces" in her discussion of Mahasweta Devi's "Daulati" and observes that cultures are bonded spaces charac-

terized by a plurity of codes and languages. (See *Nationalism and Sexualities,* p. 100).

3. It may be mentioned here that now-a-days readymade idols are available in the market and these have become popular in both Himachal Pradesh and Maharashtra. It is probably because girls are going to schools and have no spare time to indulge in elaborate preparations.
4. See Chapter entitled "Of Parrots and Mynahs – Reconstructing Gender Through Folklore" where a feminist interpretation of parrot and mynah lores has been worked out.

References

Bascom, W.R. *Contributions to Folkloristics*. Meerut: Archana Publications, 1981.

Dundes, Alan, *Essays in Folkloristics*. Meerut: Folklore Institute, 1978.

Naipaul, V.S. *India: A Million Mutinies Now*. New Delhi: Penguin, 1990.

Pratt, Mary Louise. *Imperial Eyes: Travel Writing and Transculturation*. London and New York: Routledge, 1992.

Redfield, Robert, *Peasant Society and Culture.* Chicago: Chicago University Press, 1973.

Spivak, Gayatri. "Woman in Difference: Mahasweta Devi's 'Daulati' the Bountiful", in *Nationalism and Sexualities*. Eds. Andrew Parker et al., New York and London: Routledge, 1992.

Index

A River Sutra
a novel by Gita Mehta, 32
A Thousand Splendid Suns
by Khaled Hosseini, 127, 128
"Absolution"
a story by Dina Mehta, 65
Adiga, Arvind, 114
Aiyar, C.P. Ramaswami, 190–91
Anand, Mulk Raj and Krishna Hathee Singh, 87
Anand, Mulk Raj, 84, 95, 97
Apte, Mahadev L., 56
Asian literature
terrorism in, 127, 128–38

Bahadur, Sanjay, 102
Bala, Suman, 69
Bande, Usha and Him Chatterjee, 41
Bascom, W.R., 213
Beauvoir, Simone de, 87
Berry, Margaret, 98
Bhabha, Homi K., 139
Bharathi, V., 161
bird folktales, 16
bird metaphor/analogy
use of in women writings, 16
borrowed beauty, 48
Brewster, Earl, and Achsah Brewster, 82
B-values, 182

Cactus Country
by Manohar Malgaonkar, 166
Call Centre generation, 125
CEDAW, 96, 108
Chatterjee, N.N., 188
Cheung, King-Kok, 22
Chitrangada
a dance-drama by Rabindranath Tagore, 39
Choma's Drum (1919)
by Karanth, 96
Chopin, Kate, 159

civilization, 189, 195
civilized means, 189
Cixous, Helene, 22
colonialism, 29, 72
  cultural implications of, 29
contact zone, 204
Cowasjee, Saros, 89
culture
  definitions of, 188
  Dr Radhakrishnan's conception of, 188–89
  Gandhian concept of, 193
  Indian concept of, 188
  Western concept of, 188

de-colonization
  process of, 37
Desai, Anita, 139, 159
Deshpande, Gauri, 24
Deshpande, Shashi, 97
de-toxification, 95
Deutsch, Helen, 154
Dharma, 190
  pillars of, 190
diasporic writings, 141
double-voiced discourse, 22
Du Bois, William E.B., 22
dual affiliation, 139
Dundes, Alan, 213
Dutt, K. Iswara, 195

education
  Dr Radhakrishnan vision of, 182, 194–95
empowerment, 172
Erikson, Erik H., 156

Fanon, Franz, 72
female hero
  concept of, 45, 159
female laughter, 62
female quest, 159
feminine mystique
  concept of, 84, 87
feminine power, 39
  in the folklore of Himalayan region, 40
  Tagore's views/depiction of, 39, 42–53
feminism, 51, 172
feminist discourse(s)
  role of folktales in examining, 16–17
feminist, 51
fictional narratives, 30
  as vehicles of culture, 30–36
folk songs, 56
folktales/folklore
  modes of, 25
  role of, in examining feminist discourse(s), 16–17
  transmission of, 205
  use of revisionist technique in, 25
Forster, E.M., 98
framed narrative, 32
Fromm, Erich, 155
Frye, Northrop, 78, 82

Gauri (1960)
by Mulk Raj Anand, 84, 177; use of myth in, 85
Gray, Frances, 62

Hariharan, Githa, 21
Henley, Nancy M, Mykol Hamilton and Barrie Throne, 20, 61
Hindi cinema
in post-independence period, rural realities in, 201–3
Horney, Karen, 164
human rights, 96, 101
in Indian fiction/literature, 95–112; of contemporary time, 112
human values, 182
humour, 55, 60
as a tool of resistance, 61
in literature, 55–56
in Punjab's Gidda, 57–58
in women, 55, 56, 61

Ibsen, Henrik, 92
ideal man
of Dr Radhakrishnan, 184
India
idea of, and the contribution of Hindi cinema, 198–201
Indian culture, 186, 190, 204
Dr Radhakrishnan's contribution to, 186, 190–96
Indian culture/tradition, 36
mytholization of rivers, 36–37
Indian fiction
human rights in, 95–112
Indian narrative tradition
role of *sutradhar* in, 32
Indian writing/literature in English, 63, 74
mapping Indianness of, 64–65
Indianness, 63
in Indian literature in English, 63–65; depiction of, 65–73
Iyengar, K.R.S., 44, 64

Jacobson, Mary, 19
Jain, Devaki, 157
Jain, Jasbir, 10, 30, 49, 52, 128, 144
Jena, Seema, 161
Jha, Gauri Shankar, 46
Joshi, Arun, 30
Journey to Ithaca (1995)
by Anita Desai, 139; quest motif in, 141–44

Kakkar, Sudhir, 152, 153
"Karma"
a story by Khushwant Singh, 72
Kashyap, Padamchandra, 42
katha
Indian narrational technique of, 32
Kaushik, R.K., 92
Kirpal Viney, 95, 141–42
Kishwar, Madhu and Ruth Vanitha, 17
Klien, Violka, 90

Kluckhohn, Clyde, 188
Krishnaswamy, Santha, 152
Kumar, Amitava, 122

laughter, 56
  phenomenon of, 62
life-death-reincarnation
  Indian concept of, 32
literature, 95, 98, 172
  aim of, 98
  human rights in, 95, 111
  women's education in, 175–81

Mahila
  concept of, 179
Mehta, Gita, 139
Millennium Development Goals (MDGs), 174
Moers, Ellen, 16
Moi, Toril, 19
mother-love
  in Anita Desai's novels, 151–57
Mukherjee, Hiren, 195
Mukherjee, Meenakshi, 30, 64, 86, 99
Mukherjee, Radhakamal, 187
Murty, K. Satchidananda and Ashok Vohra, 197
mutinies, 204
myth, 78
  in story-telling, 78

Naik, M.K., 77
Naipaul, V.S., 73, 124, 140, 205
Narasimhaiah, C.D., 64
Neumann, Eric, 156
"Night of the Scorpion"
  a poem by Nissim Ezekiel, 76, 78

Paranjape, Makarand, 144
participation mystique, 78
Pathak, R.S., 111
Pieper, Joseph, 188
Pinto, Vivian de Sola, 76
Pratt, Annis, 159
Pratt, Mary Louise, 204
postcolonialism, 30

quest motif, 140
  in literature, 140–41
quest, 159

Radhakrishnan, S., 186, 187, 190, 191, 194, 195
Ram, Atma, 161
Ramanujan, A.K., 17
Ramraj, Victor, 141
rape, 109
Rath, Sura P., 125
reconstructing gender
  through Folklore, 17–26
Redfield, Robert, 212–13
reinscription
  process of, 29–30
re-mapping culture
  through literature, 30–36
revision
  method/technique of, 25

revisionist mythmaking, 15, 25
Rich, Adrienne, 15, 25
Riemenschneider, Dieter, 89
rivers
  in Indian culture, place of, 36; mythologization of, 36–37
Russ, Joanna, 91

Sagar, Keith, 76
Sangari, Kumkum, 25
Scavenger's Son (1919)
  by T. Shiv Shankar Pillai, 96
"Scholar and Gypsy" (1978)
  a short story by Anita Desai, 139, quest motif in, 145–47
Sen Gupta, S.C., 52
sexual terrorism, 130
Sharma, Kavita, 51
Sharma, Ramnath, 194
Shaw, Harry, 40
Sheffield, Carole J., 130
single parents
  concept of, 42
"SMS"
  a short story by Sunethra Raja Karunanayake, 127, 129
"Snake"
  a poem by D.H. Lawrence, 76, 77
Som, Reba, 53
South Asia, 126
  historical experiences of, 126–27
speaking subject, 57
Spivak, Gayatri Chakravorty, 98, 204
Stern, Milton R. and Seymour L. Gross, 158

Tagore, Rabindranath, 42
  news of, about women, 44
Taylor, E.B., 188
terrorism
  phenomenon of, 127–28, 130
Thapar, Romila, 84
The Awakening (1981)
  by Kate Chopin, 159, 160
The Binding Vine (1993)
  by Shashi Deshpande, 106, 173
The City and the River (1990)
  by Arun Joshi, 31
"The Faltering Pendulum"
  a story by Bhabani Bhattacharya, 70
The Inheritance of Loss
  by Kiran Desai, 127, 128
The Last Labyrinth (1981)
  by Arun Joshi, 30
The Sound of Water (2008)
  by Sanjay Bahadur, 102
The Thousand Faces of Night
  by Githa Hariharan, 173
"The Treatment of Bibi Halder"
  a story by Jhumpa Lahiri, 88
The White Tiger (2008)
  by Arvind Adiga, 114
Tiwana, Dalip Kaur, 18

unhomed, 139
Universal Declaration of Human Rights (1948), 95, 96
Untouchable (1935)
  by Mulk Raj Anand, 95

Vasudev, Uma, 88
Vasudhaiva Kutumbakam
  concept of, 190
Verghese, Paul C., 91
violence against women, 130
violence, 109, 128
  forms of, 110; institutional/structural, 110; open/direct, 110
Visweswaran, Kamala, 57

Walker, Nancy, 61
Walsh, William, 79
Westkott, Marcia, 45, 165
Where Shall We Go This Summer (1975)
  by Anita Desai, 159
Willard, N. Augustus, 176
Wiseman, Christopher, 77
women
  as questors, 159
women's education, 172, 174
  in literature, 173–81
  in the 19th century, 178
women's empowerment, 172
women's status/position
  in Indian society, 84, 87
women's writing, 22, 56
  humour in, 56